COMANCHE

IMBRIFEX
BOOKS

Also by Brett Riley

The Subtle Dance of Impulse and Light

COMANCHE

BRETT RILEY

IMBRIFEX BOOKS

IMBRIFEX BOOKS
8275 S. Eastern Avenue, Suite 200
Las Vegas, NV 89123
Imbrifex.com

IMBRIFEX.
BOOKS

IMBRIFEX® is registered trademark of Flattop Productions, Inc.
ISBN: 9781945501364

Library of Congress Cataloging-in-Publication Data

Names: Riley, Brett, 1970- author.
Title: Comanche / Brett Riley.
Description: First edition. | Las Vegas, NV : Imbrifex Books, 2020. | Summary: "In 1887 near
    the tiny Texas town of Comanche, a posse finally ends the murderous career of The Piney
    Woods Kid in a hail of bullets. Still in the grip of blood-lust, the vigilantes hack the Kid's
    corpse to bits in the dead house behind the train depot. The people of Comanche rejoice.
    Justice has been done. A long bloody chapter in the town's history is over. The year is now
    2016. Comanche police are stymied by a double murder at the train depot. Witnesses swear
    the killer was dressed like an old-time gunslinger. Rumors fly that it's the ghost of The Piney
    Woods Kid, back to wreak revenge on the descendants of the vigilantes who killed him.
    Help arrives in the form of a team of investigators from New Orleans. Shunned by the local
    community and haunted by their own pasts, they're nonetheless determined to unravel the
    mystery. They follow the evidence and soon find themselves in the crosshairs of the killer"--
    Provided by publisher.
Identifiers: LCCN 2019036660 (print) | LCCN 2019036661 (ebook) | ISBN 9781945501364
    (hardcover) | ISBN 9781945501371 (epub)
Subjects: GSAFD: Mystery fiction. | Western stories.
Classification: LCC PS3618.I532724 C66 2020 (print) | LCC PS3618.I532724 (ebook) | DDC
    813/.6--dc23
LC record available at https://lccn.loc.gov/2019036660
LC ebook record available at https://lccn.loc.gov/2019036661
Jacket designed by Jason Heuer
Book Designed by Sue Campbell Book Design
Author photo: Benjamin Hager
Typeset in ITCBerkley Oldstyle

Printed in the United States of America

Distributed by Publishers Group West
First Edition: September, 2020

*This book is for Kalene, Shauna, John, Brendan,
Maya, Nova, and all our fur babies.
Thanks for putting up with me.*

*And to Pedro, who always made a trip to
Comanche interesting.*

Disclaimer

Comanche, Texas, is a real place. The streets and many landmarks in this book are real. There is an actual Comanche Depot building. It has been renovated and now serves as the chamber of commerce. Because it would be devastating to his story, the author has ignored that fact. He has also ignored the near impossibility of getting a cellphone signal in the town of Comanche.

The people and events depicted in this book are entirely fictional. The author has also significantly altered the geography of and around the depot grounds for dramatic expediency. He wanted to make that known in case any local readers thought he was trying to represent the exact layout of town and spectacularly failing.

CHAPTER ONE

July 23, 1887—Comanche, Texas

P.D. Thornapple did not own a watch, but he believed it was roughly 2 a.m. when he saw the Piney Woods Kid lurking near the Comanche Depot. That sight would have alarmed P.D. any time. The Kid had earned his reputation as one of the bloodiest outlaws in central Texas by gunning down two sheriffs, a U.S. Marshal, a Texas Ranger, and enough private citizens to fill a boneyard. When you saw the Kid coming, you ducked behind the nearest building, and if you could not run—if, say, he showed up where you worked, where you stood the best chance of getting a little respect and enough cash for whores and whiskey—you kept your eyes on the floor and your mouth shut, and you prayed he would leave. But now P.D. Thornapple almost fainted because, in the early morning of July 23, the Piney Woods Kid had been dead for a week.

On the fifteenth, P.D. had been thinking about the way shit rolled downhill and how he always seemed to be standing at the bottom, stuck with the most sickening, degrading duties—sweeping up after the cattlemen with cow shit stuck to their boots, washing out vomit when drunks staggered over from the Half Dollar Saloon and mistook the depot for a privy, mopping up their piss after they passed out and soiled themselves, sometimes right on the platform. When randy young couples tried to do their business behind the dead house, P.D. chased them off. And when the Piney Woods Kid and Sheriff Demetrius McCorkle fought across the depot grounds two years ago, who had to scrub away all the blood from the woman the Kid took hostage, from the deputy he gut-shot, from the three men he executed at close range, from the Kid himself? Who had picked up a misshapen mass of tissue that turned out to be the end of McCorkle's nose? P.D. wanted to quit, but begging his asshole brother for a job seemed worse than dealing with blood and shit.

So P.D. endured everything, even the dead house itself. A squat building ten yards from the depot, it looked new and downright inviting in the daylight, but at night it turned the color of old bones bleaching in the desert, its very presence pricking the base of his spine. Why didn't the railroad just paint the goddam thing or burn it down?

But a raw eyesore worked just fine for the bosses, and the corpses did not care one way or the other. P.D. had been forced to load bodies into the dead house, to transport them onto waiting trains, to guard the building as if it held treasure instead of cold, stiff flesh. He checked the lock on its door twice every shift. Constant exposure should have rendered the place familiar, even banal, yet he had never shaken the feeling that something was inherently wrong with the whole idea of a dead house: a way station for cadavers, a hotel for stiffs. If only one of the day-shift men would quit or die so he could take their spot and never have to look at that building in the dark again.

P.D. had never been that lucky, though. He sat in the depot just after dark on the fifteenth when McCorkle's runner, Deputy Rudy Johnstone, brought news that their posse had killed the Kid. It was the biggest event in Comanche County history, even bigger than when that son of a bitch John Wesley Hardin murdered Charles Webb back in '74. Sheriff McCorkle and his riders trapped the Kid and his old Comanche *companero* in an empty cabin beside Broken Bow Creek late that afternoon. The outlaws and the posse shot at each other for fifteen minutes or so, until McCorkle got sick of waiting and set fire to the place. The Kid and the Indian escaped out the back, making it a hundred yards up the creek before McCorkle's men rode them down. According to Johnstone, the outlaw's torso looked like an old woman's pincushion, and the Indian's face had been shot clean away.

They could have let the Kid rot where he fell. They could have planted him by the creek. But no.

Sheriff wants to haul the carcass through town, Johnstone said. Maybe that way folks will finally stop talkin about how the Kid shot off his nose.

Of course. Revenge for the carnage and misery the Kid had wrought. Besides, the undertaker was out of town, so what was the hurry?

No one spoke of the Comanche's corpse. Likely the white men had left it to the elements and scavengers, one more slaughtered and nameless dark skin among the thousands blanketing the land, some buried and some abandoned, their final resting places unmarked as if they were ants or scorpions crushed under pedestrian feet.

After Johnstone delivered his news, P.D. sat on the bench outside the depot and waited for the posse.

The insects thrummed around him like locomotive engines until, from town proper, came whoops and cheers and gunfire and, soon enough, the muted clop of hooves on dirt. P.D. looked at the moon—likely close to 10 p.m. McCorkle must have stopped at every shack and tent so folks could sing hosannas. Torches glowing in the distance grew closer. Individual men and horses coalesced from the shadows, McCorkle riding his gray at their head. A dozen mounted men followed, most hidden in the gloom, but there came Charlie Garner's spotted roan, the one that looked like it was caught in its own snowstorm, and Shoehorn Wayne's black mare. Roy Harveston's chocolate gelding with the white star on its forehead. The half-wild pure-white horse Beeve Roark called Ghost. Rudy Johnstone walked in leading a mule on which a figure lay crossways, tied like a roll of carpet. Someone had thrown a saddle blanket over the body, but dusty, cracked, bloodstained boots hung uncovered off one side, pallid hands off the other. Without thinking, P.D. took off his hat. Beeve Roark glared at him and spat a thick stream of tobacco juice near his feet as the procession headed for the dead house.

Each of these men had stuffed a hatchet into his belt, except for Johnstone, who carried a hacksaw.

P.D. shivered. He dashed inside and grabbed his keys and a lantern. As he trotted back out, the keys jingled like a tambourine. The lantern cast pendulous, cavorting shadows across the grounds and the tracks. The posse had dismounted by the time he reached them. Most fell back into the shadows, faceless and ephemeral. McCorkle, Roark, Garner, Wayne, and Harveston flanked the door as some of the others untied the body. P.D. hung his lantern on a hook and unlocked the door. When they hauled the Kid into the dead house, P.D. caught a glimpse of the outlaw's pallid face splashed with blood, eyes wide open and glazed.

Once the men and the corpse disappeared into the dead house's dark maw, Garner and Harveston and Wayne and Johnstone followed. McCorkle nodded at Roark, took P.D.'s lantern off the hook, and walked inside. P.D. started to follow, but Roark pushed him back.

Well, P.D. croaked, I reckon you boys don't need none of my help.

Roark spat in the dust and wiped his mouth on his shirtsleeve. I reckon not.

The faceless riders exited the building, saddled up, and rode away, murmuring among themselves. Then Roark stepped inside and closed the door.

P.D. lingered a moment, unsure of what to do or say. *Reckon I better get back to my post.* He walked away but managed only a few steps before a steady *thuk thuk thuk* emanated from the dead house. Such an everyday sound, like someone chopping wood two houses over, might have been comforting during the day, but there, then, it sounded awful, the sound of an emaciated, hollow-eyed man with corkscrew hair standing over a coffin in an open grave, hacking up a body and tossing chunks into a bag.

Goddam magazines, with their stories about grave robbers and folks gettin buried alive and such—enough to drive a grown man crazy.

Back inside the depot, under the lanterns' warm glow, P.D. dropped the keys into their drawer. He went to the doorway and leaned against the jamb, watching the dead house. The lantern light flickered inside, shadows gamboling against the curtained windows. Soon P.D. returned to his desk and did not look outside again.

They wanted to prepare the corpse their own damn selves, so let em.

McCorkle and the rest left just before dawn. P.D. stood on the platform and watched them ride away. No one acknowledged him. They carried old flour sacks tied at the necks. P.D. believed he knew what those sacks held.

Two days later, P.D. passed the undertaker on the street and asked about the Kid's funeral arrangements.

The old man looked puzzled. Funeral? he said, scratching his cheek with dirty fingernails. Hell, I ain't even seen the body. Rudy Johnstone's been braggin they butchered the Kid and threw the pieces in three or four different cricks. But hell, you know how Johnstone likes to hear himself talk. It's probably bullshit.

Now, at 2 a.m. on the twenty-third, most everyone in Comanche could be found in one of two places: home in bed or at the Half Dollar, listening to Johnstone tell about the Kid's last stand, as he would likely keep doing as long as some sodbuster or cowpoke fresh off the trail offered to buy the drinks. Even free whiskey had not prompted Johnstone to reveal what the posse had done with the Kid's body, though. Given what P.D. had seen a week ago, the undertaker's story seemed credible. In any case, those fellas had taken the corpse off P.D. Thornapple's hands, which suited him just fine. He lay on his cot behind the main office, pulling on a bottle of tequila and singing to himself, planning to do little else for the rest of his shift.

Then he sat up. A while back, Mr. Sutcliffe from the rail company telegraphed about an upcoming inspection of the personnel and facilities.

Hellfire. When did that old coot say he was comin?

P.D. went to the front desk and dug through the top drawer, where they kept all the important correspondence. He found Sutcliffe's telegram three sheets from the top and scanned it.

In part, it read, WILL ARRIVE ON 23RD STOP.

Shit, P.D. said.

As the night man, it was his job to air out the dead house when fewer people wandered by to smell it, and he had not done it since that cursed night. The goddam place probably stunk to high heaven. If Mr. Sutcliffe smelled anything like Shot-to-Hell Outlaw or saw any stray drops of dried blood on the floor, that would be the last the depot would see of P.D. Thornapple, who would have to move back to the family ranch with his hulking, sharp-tongued brother and the asshole's shrew wife and five runny-nosed brats. And, echoing the plight of mistreated younger brothers all the way back to Abel, P.D. would have to sleep in the barn because they were already stacking kids in the main house like cordwood. He took two long swigs of tequila—probably the last of the night, though he took the bottle, just in case—and grabbed his keys, grumbling.

P.D. walked out of the depot and turned left.

Someone stood in front of the dead house.

He dropped the tequila and the keys. The bottle hit the platform and rolled to the edge, where it teetered, the liquor gurgling out. P.D. ran and grabbed the bottle, saving about half the alcohol, and celebrated by taking another long gulp, Sutcliffe be damned. The liquor burned going down.

When he turned back to the dead house, the figure was gone.

P.D. tittered. *You damn fool. Nearly jumpin outta your skin thataway. Probably just some cowboy from the Half Dollar with a head full of Johnstone's tale and a bladder full of hot piss. Walked right by the outhouses in the dark, like folks sometimes do.*

Go piss in the privy like civilized folks! P.D. shouted.

Lanterns hung from iron hooks on either side of the depot's doors.

He retrieved the keys and took one of the lanterns and held it high, swinging it back and forth. No further sign of the visitor. P.D. started across the lot.

Upon reaching the dead house, he unlocked the door and pulled it open. Sure enough, the place smelled—dank, like old leaves and damp earth, with undertones of meat gone bad. Grimacing, he pulled his shirt over his nose and found the block of wood the depot workers kept for propping open the door. After setting the block in place and putting the lantern on the floor, P.D. went inside and pulled back the curtains—dark ones made of some thick, rough-spun cloth that kept people from seeing the coffins the workers lay on the floor or, when too many people dropped dead, stacked on top of each other like packing crates—and opened the windows. Walking back outside, he let his shirt drop and breathed in fresh air. He hoped the stink would clear out by morning.

When he thought he could stand it again, he went in. The floor looked terrible. Once raw and unpainted but sanded smooth, the center of it now bore evidence of those hatchets and that hacksaw, small chunks gouged from the wood here and there, the marks of serrated teeth having dragged across the boards, as if demented children had broken in with their fathers' tools and vandalized the place.

Well, I ain't no goddam carpenter. I just hope a stray dog or a wolf don't wander in and shit everywhere.

Against the far wall sat a pair of sprung, dusty boots with an empty gun belt coiled around them. They were covered in dark stains—water damage or dried blood or Lord only knew what. Next to them, a pile of clothes—filthy denim jeans, a pair of rancid socks, a wadded-up cotton shirt shot full of holes and stiff and stained dark, the frayed remains of a leather vest, a weather-beaten cowboy hat.

Hellfire, P.D. said.

He walked to the discarded clothes and picked everything up, struggling to keep hold of the lantern. He kept dropping items—a boot, the crusty shirt—and picking them up again until, cursing, he set the boots and gun belt on one of the supply shelves built onto the back wall. Just his luck, this shit would take more than one trip. On the way back, he would probably trip over a skunk and land on a cactus.

Carrying his burdens, P.D. wondered how to dispose of the clothes. Burn them? Bury them? Throw them in the street? Go down to the Half Dollar, and tell people they probably belonged to the Piney Woods Kid, and see who would buy him a drink for his story?

He walked outside.

The Piney Woods Kid stood ten feet away, between him and the depot, staring with gray and vacant eyes.

P.D. stumbled backward and swore.

The Kid could not be here. McCorkle had killed the shit out of him. The town—hell, half of Texas—had scorned and laughed at and dismissed the Kid, all those outlaw exploits already corrupted in people's memories as little more than the sting of a particularly loathsome horsefly. Yet there the man stood, covered in dried muck that might have been mud or might have been blood. He wore the same clothes P.D. carried. An impossibility, but even beyond that, something seemed off. The Kid looked *bleached*, like a garment rotting in the desert sun. Stringy, oily hair framed his pallid face. His arms hung slack, his guns holstered.

Calm down. This ain't the fella to spook.

P.D. tried to spit, but his mouth had gone dry.

The Kid stood silent, staring.

McCorkle must have killed the wrong man and claimed it was

the Kid. No wonder the posse drove P.D. away from the dead house
that night. How had the deputy managed to fool everybody at the
Half Dollar? Somebody should have noticed. Maybe Johnstone's mania
scared them all shitless.

Damn McCorkle and Johnstone. Damn my luck.

Still, P.D. Thornapple did not intend to stand out here all night
with some murderous asshole who was supposed to be worm food.

Jesus God, Kid, you scared the shit outta me, he said, his laugh rising in pitch until it disappeared. You better get on before old Noseless
sees you.

Actually, if McCorkle had come along, that would have been just
fine. Whatever got P.D. away from this maniac and back to his nice,
safe cot. But you had to handle these gunfighter types a certain way,
mainly by kissing their asses until they left.

The Kid said nothing. His eyes were the color of clouds on a moon-
less night.

In town, someone fired two shots in the air and whooped. P.D.
jumped.

The Kid did not move.

Tiny slivers of spit and phlegm stuck in P.D.'s throat. He wiped his
sleeve across his forehead, its fabric coarse on his damp skin.

Word has it you're killed, he said, but I guess Johnstone's tellin tall
tales. That sumbitch always had a mouth on him.

Maybe an unkind word about the local law would afford P.D. some
favor. The Kid had been standing there a full minute, maybe two, and
had not even blinked.

That was some damn good shootin here, that day you took
McCorkle's nose. Them laws thought they had you, but you blasted
right through 'em. Never seen nothin like it.

The Kid stared. He might have been someone's displaced scarecrow.

P.D. shivered, even as sweat dripped down his forehead and coated his back.

Say somethin, he whispered. Don't just stare at me thataway. Talk to me. Please.

The Kid seemed not to have heard.

Someone fired another shot near the main thoroughfare. Then they whooped again. Who was it, and what were they up to? If only P.D. were there, or anywhere else. The middle of the ocean would have been fine. The Kid had always been a motormouthed lunatic but seemed even worse now that he had turned mute. If only somebody, anybody, would come along. They could piss, shit, vomit, or squirt all over the depot floor for all P.D. cared.

But no one came.

When P.D. looked back, the Kid stood two inches away. And his eyes were the gray, empty sockets of a skull.

P.D. cried out and stumbled again, falling onto his ass this time, feet over his head. The lantern flew out of his hand and landed near the dead house, where it shattered and burst into flame. P.D. crawfished backward through the dust. The Kid moved with him, arms slack.

P.D. screamed, clutching the reeking clothes like a shield.

The Kid stared straight ahead. He might have been looking into hell.

The broken lantern's fire flickered and ebbed. Shadows stretched across the grounds and onto the platform, where they danced up the depot walls like the furtive movements of desert creatures. A wedge of light spilled from the main building's door. But the Kid cast no shadow. His feet hovered an inch above the dust.

P.D. Thornapple opened his mouth to scream again. And then the Kid slapped leather, drawing both pistols and firing.

Slugs drove into P.D.'s belly. He flopped backward through the dust, the garments flying from his hands and landing in the fire behind him. The moon, a waxing crescent, grinned at him. His guts burned. He groaned and tried to sit up, but he had no strength. He coughed and spat a mouthful of bright blood into the dust. With arms made of lead, he searched his abdomen for bullet holes.

He found nothing.

The Kid floated closer, watching P.D. with those empty holes where his eyes should have been.

Pain blotted out all conscious thought. Darkness closed in. When he tried to speak, blood erupted from his mouth, some pattering onto his face, the rest raining around him. He turned his head and spat.

What'd you do that for? he whispered. I didn't kill you.

But the Kid had vanished. The fire began to die out, and the rest of P.D.'s strength went with it. His head fell back to the earth, and he lay staring at the glimmering stars. They were cold and far away, like the eyes of dead gods.

CHAPTER TWO

February 14, 2013—New Orleans, Louisiana

The headache was a dagger in Raymond Turner's brain. His stomach spasmed, and he rolled over and vomited into the grass. Then he straightened, wincing against the sunlight. The ground felt frigid, the dead grass like dull needles. His Kia Optima's grille sat only inches from the front steps of his little one-story house. Above, the bare branches of an oak thrust toward the sky.

His partner, Darrell LeBlanc, leaned against the tree trunk, trimming his fingernails with a pocketknife.

Raymond hocked and spat. His mouth tasted like something slimy had died in it. His leg ached.

What'd you do? he asked, rubbing it. Kick me?

LeBlanc glanced at him. Yep.

Well, what the hell did you do that for?

You looked like you needed kickin.

Raymond struggled to his feet, his stomach flip-flopping. An empty whiskey bottle lay on the ground near the Optima's driver's-side door.

Shit. I guess I drove myself home last night.

I reckon so, LeBlanc said. Almost parked in the middle of the den, too.

Just about. When Raymond bent to retrieve the bottle, the world swam out of focus. LeBlanc grabbed him. Thanks, he said. I feel like the Saints used me for a tacklin dummy.

Let's get you inside, LeBlanc said.

Raymond sat at his kitchen table. Morning sunlight winked in through the blinds. Had LeBlanc parted the teal curtains, or had Marie left them that way months ago? The aroma of eggs and frying bacon and coffee made Raymond's mouth water and his stomach gurgle as LeBlanc stood at the stove, spatula in hand.

I don't know how much of that I can eat, Raymond said, rubbing his temples. His pants were grass stained and dirty.

It ain't for you. LeBlanc took the bacon out of the skillet and dropped it on a paper towel–covered plate.

What are you doin here this early, anyway?

Early, hell. I've been up since two, lookin for you. Billy Jackson over at the River Ridge called. Said you could barely stand up. He tried to take your keys. You threatened to shoot off his pecker. I half expected to find you in the goddam river.

Well, you didn't.

Yep. You made it. And for all you know, you killed somebody's wife on the way.

Raymond recoiled as if LeBlanc had slapped him. For a moment, he said nothing as the blood drained from his face. Then the anger came.

Maybe you better get the hell outta my house before we do somethin we'll regret.

LeBlanc pulled the paper towels from under the bacon. Then he dumped eggs beside the strips, set the skillet back on the stove, turned off the gas, and poured himself a cup of black coffee. Plate and cup in hand, he joined Raymond and ate three forkfuls of eggs and sipped coffee.

Raymond sat there, fists clenched, watching.

Finally, LeBlanc looked at him. This has gotta stop.

What? You eatin me outta house and home?

Marie died eleven months ago, and you've been drunk damn near every night since.

I'm grievin.

No. You're wallowin. And I've been carryin the agency alone.

I miss my dead wife. I'm sorry it's inconvenienced you.

You're killin yourself. And if you keep drinkin and drivin, you're gonna take somebody with you. Last night, a mother of three got T-boned at an intersection. The other driver was drunk as hell. He walked away. She didn't. That fella could have been you. Then you'd be no better than the piece of shit that killed Marie.

Raymond's guts churned. His head thundered. Don't say that. Just don't.

Or you'll what? Puke on my shoes?

Get outta my house, Raymond whispered. Get out, or I'll kill you.

LeBlanc ate his bacon and drank his coffee. His expression did not change. The Gradney case, he said. You remember that one? We took it right after Marie's funeral. Missin teenager, just run off from home one night. I got stumped, and you had already crawled inside a bottle of Jack Daniel's.

When did you become such a goddam mother hen?

With the family breathin down my neck and you AWOL, I got desperate and called a psychic. Local woman, name of McDowell. She talked to the parents. Seemed to calm 'em down. Then she went in the boy's room and felt—I don't know—somethin. She said he was safe, near water, someplace with stairs and a fishin boat. Wasn't much. I got me a guide and hit the bayous and swamps in a fan boat. Found the kid holed up in an old stilt house, eatin campfire-charred fish and workin his way through a keg of beer he stole from somewhere. Got no idea how he toted it all the way out yonder. Anyway, McDowell. I've used her on two cases since then. She's good.

Why do I give a fuck? Raymond said. The coffee smelled glorious, but damned if he would ask LeBlanc to fetch him a cup.

Well, for one thing, she's helpin keep our business above water, LeBlanc said. For another, you met her. In the office, three weeks back. I reckon you were too drunk to remember.

What's your point, Darrell? My head hurts.

LeBlanc pushed the empty plate away and drained his cup. Your life's passin by. You're tryin to follow Marie, but you ain't got the sack to shoot yourself. Well, I've had enough. If you're gonna pussy out, you ain't takin the agency with you.

Raymond gestured toward the door. If you've had enough, get gone. I don't see an anchor tied to your ass.

I'm your friend. If I just walked away, I couldn't live with myself. Not until I try one last thing.

Nope, Raymond said. I'm sick of your tryin. And since you don't seem to remember where the door is, let me help you out.

He stood up, circled the table, and grabbed LeBlanc by the shirt.

LeBlanc let Raymond pull him to his feet. Then he grasped both of Raymond's wrists and headbutted him across the bridge of his nose.

Raymond awoke in bed, his nose throbbing in time with his head. He sat up, groaning, and rubbed his eyes. His mouth tasted like blood and spoiled meat. He hocked and spat, not caring where it landed. LeBlanc sat on a kitchen chair against the far wall.

Jesus, Raymond said. You didn't have to do that.

LeBlanc shrugged. Seems like I did.

I need a drink.

You've just about drunk yourself outta your own agency and probably half pickled your liver. It ends here. I can't watch you do this anymore.

The room was in shambles. Soiled clothes piled in the corners, smelling of old sweat and desperation. Empty bottles poking out from under the bed. Sheets rumpled and sweat stained. The rest of the house was no better, some parts even worse. When had Raymond last cleaned his bathrooms, or even opened a window? Eventually, if he kept living this way, the neighbors would call the police, complaining of a terrible stench. The cops would find him in bed, maybe on the floor, rotting away with dried vomit clogging his throat, another empty bottle nearby. If he went out like that, what would Marie say when he saw her again?

LeBlanc sat silent, watchful.

Raymond licked his dry lips. Help me, he said.

LeBlanc exhaled. He looked relieved, but there was steel in his eyes. Okay, he said. Let's get started.

CHAPTER THREE

June 16, 2014—Comanche, Texas

Within Comanche's city limits, Highway 16, running north to De Leon and south to Goldthwaite, was called Austin Street. Interstate 67, leading west to Brownwood and east all the way to the Fort Worth Mixmaster, was known as Central Avenue. When these two roads intersected only yards from the county courthouse, they formed one corner of the town square. Turning south onto Austin from Central, any traveler looking east would see Comanche First National Bank and its parking lot and, when passing Oak Avenue, a feed-and-seed store.

One block south, the old Comanche Depot sat within shouting distance of a feed mill. Steel silos jutted against the sky. A small, widely spaced copse of live oak trees grew to the north between Mill Road and the Central Texas Railroad tracks, which ran only feet from the depot's rear walls. The old rails snaked through this part of town like a dry riverbed, the prosperity and health and cattle drives of olden times long gone. South of the building, buffalo grass grew all the way to Fleming avenue, beyond which Austin Street wound past a brand-new apartment complex.

For nearly 130 years, the elements had worked their will on the depot's paint and wood. Bored teenagers and tweakers had vandalized the place with sticks and sharp rocks and knives and spray paint. Its yard was overgrown, the calcium carbonate of the undersoil poking through in spots.

Mayor C.W. Roark stood in front of the depot at dusk, the sun blood-red in an orange sky lined with strips of gray clouds. He was six feet, two inches and weighed 220 pounds—fit and solid for a fiftyish politician. His black hair had salted at the temples and was slicked straight back from a tanned face adorned with a bushy mustache. Despite the heat, he wore black slacks, black cowboy boots, a black coat, and a dark gray tie as he considered the yard's bare spots.

Goddam caliche. May have to resod. Time for that later, if we get the land.

He had submitted his final bid on Friday. Today, a Monday, had come and gone with no word. If the city refused to sell him the lot and buildings, the county historical society would secure its newest landmark. What a waste.

This part of the lot would be perfect for a concrete parking area. They could lay a three-foot-wide walk leading to the front steps. Rennie, Roark's wife, insisted on keeping as much of the grass as possible. She liked the green, and C.W. had been married long enough to know which battles to pick. Besides, he could hardly refuse her the grass when he had already decided to keep the live oaks. They could add more parking later, if business required it, but for now, he liked the place's isolated feeling—trees behind, grass before, a ditch to the west, and a fence to the east.

Morlon Redheart's rattletrap Ford pickup turned onto Austin and parked behind Roark's white Chevy extended cab. Redheart got out, shut his door, and jumped the ditch. Perspiration glistened on his dark skin. His braided black hair descended to the small of his back, swaying in the sporadic breeze. He was *mestizo*, half Comanche and half Mexican.

When Redheart approached, Roark stuck out his hand. Morlon. How do?

Redheart shook with him. Can't complain, and even if I did, nobody would care. What's the word?

The town council's leanin toward the historical society. They think Comanche needs more landmarks for the tourists.

Redheart spat. Tourists. They come once a year for the Pow Wow. We're offerin steady commerce.

It's hard to sell 'em on a restaurant. Too unstable, they say.

They ain't tasted my cookin.

Maybe they should.

Roark and Redheart listened to the traffic on Central, the crickets, the last birdsongs as the sun edged over the horizon. In the dusky light, the mayor studied the outbuilding ten yards from the depot proper. It was half as big as the main structure—one door, dusty and spider-webbed or broken windows, the wood's paint flaked away in places, faded to no color in others.

So what now? Redheart asked.

The mayor ran one hand over his face and flung away the sweat. I'll handle the council, like I always do. Fred Deese wouldn't wipe his ass unless I handed him the White Cloud. Bill McAllister owes me a few favors. And Mary Jones will vote my way if I promise to find her dumbass nephew a city job. You and Silky just get ready to cook. Hire eight or ten folks at minimum wage, less for the servers.

Rich white people. Y'all hang onto your money like it's your liver and kidneys.

The mayor grinned. That's how we stay rich. Don't worry. You'll get plenty of paleface cash.

Redheart sneered. You've seen too many John Wayne movies.

Maybe. But I keep my word.

Where's your wife? She didn't want to look at the grand empire you're buildin?

Rennie was at home, on the phone with her drunkard brother's partner. C.W. Roark had once loved Raymond Turner like a real brother, but the man had carved too many worry lines around Rennie's eyes. Now he could crawl into a Jack Daniel's bottle and stay there, for all Roark cared.

She's seen it before, he said.

You want me to handle supplies?

Roark clapped him on the back. Yep. My accountant will call you with the budget specifics. But first, get a crew on that there shed.

Morlon glanced at it. Tear it down?

Hell, no. Get it in usable shape. That's our storage overflow.

Redheart crossed his arms, his expression cold. Storage, he said. You're gonna leave that abomination standin. Worse, you want me and my wife to go in and outta there a dozen times a day.

Didn't take you for a superstitious man.

It's a bad place. You know what happened there.

I'm countin on it. People love Old West stories. The bloodier, the better.

It ain't gonna make your family look good.

Or yours. That Comanche runnin with the Piney Woods Kid was a Redheart.

My ancestor was an outlaw, but he wasn't no blasphemer like yours.

Roark laughed. Back then it wasn't called blasphemy. They called it *frontier justice*. Red Thornapple's gonna write an article about it for the *Warrior-Tribune*. We'll hang a copy on our wall. Make it part of the place's ambience.

Redheart shook his head. Ambience. Well, it's your money. But me and Silky ain't goin in that shed.

After Redheart left, Roark turned back to the depot. He closed his eyes and breathed deeply. *It'll be nice to have a place of our own where we can eat a bite and drink coffee with our friends after we retire. Maybe Rennie and me can talk Will into workin here on weekends. Get his hands dirty before college.* Who knew? The boy might even want to run the place one day.

C.W. started toward his truck as the wind kicked up, blowing grit from the yard.

Near the old storage building, the air shimmered for a moment, like heat wafting off a summer highway. Then the shimmer faded, and everything lay in shadow. Somewhere nearby, the first cricket chirped.

CHAPTER FOUR

October 7, 2014—New Orleans, Louisiana

Rennie Roark sobbed. The sound seemed to imbue Darrell LeBlanc's Samsung with physical weight. He had just told her that Raymond had refused professional help again. It had been about eighteen months since her brother had admitted his drinking problem, but in that time, he had fallen off the wagon twice. Whenever LeBlanc found Raymond unconscious under the tree or face down on the floor or slumped over the toilet, the agency had to close while they played cards or checkers or watched television cooking competitions. Raymond shook and trembled and groaned and sometimes upset the board or threw the remote at LeBlanc's head and dashed for his car, intending to find the nearest liquor store and drink himself into a stupor. LeBlanc tackled him, fought him hand to hand, and sat on his chest until the fit passed. Today Raymond slept in his easy chair, an old episode of *Gilligan's Island* on TV, as LeBlanc gave Rennie the details. She wept and offered to fly out and beat Raymond's ass like their momma should have done. LeBlanc told her it would be all right.

When they hung up, Raymond still slept, his brow furrowed, his nails digging in to the armrests. He was coming to the worst of it again. LeBlanc might be forced to restrain him, which could technically be called kidnapping. That, or try to have him committed.

No. Underneath his grief, he's still strong. I hope.

LeBlanc sat on the couch, the springs creaking under his six-foot-three, 260-pound defensive end's muscular frame, and changed the channel to ESPN. Soon a game of some sort would come on, and for as long as Raymond slept, he would watch a lower-stakes contest play out according to a set of defined rules and a clear time limit, a moment in which everyone would know it was over and who had won.

In the easy chair, Raymond twitched and groaned, his unkempt dark hair sweaty and plastered to his forehead. He was probably six inches shorter than LeBlanc but only thirty pounds lighter. The booze had gone to his belly, which distended over his belt. A graying, three-day, patchy beard covered his sallow cheeks and chin. Hard living made you old. Nightmares did not help either.

The dream never changed. Raymond tried to save Marie. He failed.

Marie had been driving on the Mississippi River bridge in Baton Rouge when a truck tried to change lanes and clipped her rear bumper. She spun and crashed into the railing, the grille crumpling all the way into the back seat, crushing her. The truck had never been found, and for a long time, Raymond wept and thought about the vanished vehicle and its faceless operator and drank himself to sleep. It was as if God himself had plucked the driver and the truck off the earth. Witnesses could not even agree on whether the truck had been maroon or navy blue or black, brand-new or an early '90s model. Raymond had no one to punch, no one to shoot, so he dove into every bottle of booze he could find. He took cabs to Armstrong Park at 2 in the morning and

sat against the statues, watching the ebb and flow of forgotten people
with no place else to go. Friends told him it was just a matter of time
before he joined Marie in the family mausoleum.

Well, yeah, he thought. *That's the point.*

Still, no matter how blackout drunk he got, the dream visited him
at least three times a week. In it, he stood on the bridge as traffic zipped
by. He leaned against the railing, the same one that would drive the
engine block through Marie's abdomen. The winter wind screamed off
the water. The night sky was pitch black. When Marie's Pontiac shimmered into view, Raymond recognized the truck that would kill her,
even though it was never the same one—sometimes a Ford, sometimes
a Chevy, sometimes an amorphous blob. He tried to warn her, but nothing ever worked. His feet were lead, fused to the bridge, and his arms
might have weighed three tons each. His voice disappeared, too. No
matter how he tried to shout, nothing came out except a shrill whine.

Tonight, as he stood on the dream bridge again, Marie's car appeared
just as the truck, dark green this time, struck it. She spun and careened
straight for Raymond, her face floating above the steering wheel. Just as
she was about to run him down, she opened her mouth and said, Ray.

When he jerked forward, awake and roaring, tears on his face,
LeBlanc had already reached him. The big man gave him a bottle of
water and rubbed his shoulders and held him as he wept, until he fell
asleep again.

A week later, after Raymond returned to work, he studied some financial documents at his desk. LeBlanc goofed around on the computer.
It was nearing five o'clock. They would have to grab dinner soon, or

LeBlanc might start eating the drywall.

Raymond dropped the papers on his desk and sighed, rubbing his bleary eyes.

I can't look at this shit anymore, he said.

LeBlanc did not look up. You called Rennie lately?

Raymond stood up and stretched. Not since the last time you made me.

Reckon you better in the next day or two.

She's still callin you.

Don't get mad. She's worried.

That's an understatement. She's been scared half to death. I reckon C.W.'s gonna punch me in the nose the next time I see him.

Raymond and his brother-in-law used to call each other twice a week. They fished the Louisiana waters and Texas rivers and ponds, hunted squirrel and duck and deer, made idiotic wagers every time the Saints played the Cowboys—loser must dye his hair the winner's team colors for a week—that sort of nonsense. But once Raymond's drinking spiraled out of control and Rennie cried herself to sleep enough times, Roark's phone calls ceased. The few times he answered the phone, his responses were curt, bordering on hostile, and when Rennie came to the phone, she sounded tense.

I need to check my email one more time, LeBlanc said.

Do it on your phone, Raymond said. I got a hankerin for a catfish po' boy. I'm buyin.

LeBlanc grinned. He shut down the computer and stood up. Now you're talkin my language. I could eat a horse.

CHAPTER FIVE

May 8, 2015—Comanche, Texas

M orlon Redheart finally seemed happy. *He's sick of landscapin,*
C.W. Roark thought, *and Silky's gettin too old to drag pallets
around Brookshire's. They* need *this.* The contractors had installed the
new front walk and lights and windows and an alarm system but left
the depot's more picturesque scrapes and dings alone. They laid a small
concrete parking lot but didn't bother with a light pole. The ambient
light from Austin Street would suffice.

As the renovations progressed, Roark sometimes stopped on Austin
and watched, leaning against his truck with his arms and ankles crossed.
*Gotta make sure Red gets a good picture when it's finally time to run his arti-
cle.* The newspaperman had decided to make it part of a group. Other
photos would show Old Cora—the authentic frontier cabin that had
served as the original county courthouse and now squatted on the town
square as if a bored god had scooped it out of the past and dropped it in
the twenty-first century—and the Fleming Oak, the old gnarled tree in
which a white boy had once hidden from a Comanche attack. *Tourists
eat that kind of shit for breakfast, especially the ones who think every town
west of the Mississippi used to be like Dodge City or Tombstone.*

As for the outbuilding, they installed no extra lights and protected it with only a padlock. Why bother with much else, when the best any thieves could hope for might be a big can of corn or a broken stool? Morlon had ordered the workers to toss all the old shit into the courtyard, where he stuffed smaller items into trash bags, larger ones into the bed of his pickup. He planned to haul it all to the dump.

One day, Roark stopped by as Morlon was dropping half a dozen pewter plates into a Hefty.

Hang on, the Mayor said. He pulled out the plates and then dug through the bag. He found a few more dishes, a set of tarnished forks and knives, a pair of busted cowboy boots, and a gun belt that looked older than Moses. Both the boots and the belt were stained with what might have been mud a century old. Roark spread these items on the ground. You find any other stuff like this?

Nope, Redheart said. Just trash.

Get somebody to clean these up, the mayor said, indicating the dishes and cutlery. Maybe we can hang 'em around the diner. Give the place more authenticity.

What about that cowboy shit?

When Roark picked up the boots and gun belt, he shivered. His arms broke into gooseflesh despite the heat. He dropped the junk and wiped his hands on his pants. *Felt like stickin my hand into ice water. Maybe I'm comin down with somethin.*

Redheart raised his eyebrows but said nothing.

Just put 'em back on a shelf, Roark said. I'll figure out a place for 'em.

Redheart shrugged and resumed loading trash.

Roark left. *Tomorrow, I'll call around and see if anybody works on leather that old.*

The next day, however, meetings took up most of his time. When he got home that night, he was exhausted, and he had forgotten all about the boots and belt.

After the building passed inspection, Roark announced the grand opening of the Depot Diner. It seated about as many people as your average Waffle House and served authentic Texas and Mexican cuisine, from family-recipe *posole* to Americanized dishes like chili cheeseburgers. The mayor and his family attended opening night, as did every Comanche bigwig Roark could beg, harass, or threaten. By the time these people brought their friends and neighbors, cars and pickups filled the parking area and the grass lot, with many more lining both sides of Austin Street. Patrons stood on the walk or sat on the new backless benches as they slapped mosquitoes, bullshitted, and waited for their tables.

No one paid any attention to the wind that sometimes kicked up when certain townsfolk stepped onto the depot grounds. And if the patrons noticed the way the air shimmered near the storage building, none of them spoke of it.

CHAPTER SIX

May 23, 2016—New Orleans, Louisiana

Raymond sat on his front porch, watching the oak's shadow stretch its bony fingers across the yard. He held a glass of sweet tea in his lap, the condensation dampening his trousers. These days, he drank enough tea to make him diabetic, as if water or Coca-Cola would cast him back to rock bottom as effectively as straight whiskey. Those drunken months had probably damaged his liver, and all this sugar could not be good for his kidneys. Would it always be like this— exchanging one addiction for another, one kind of harm for something just as bad?

He had left LeBlanc in the office around three. They had just finished one of those divorce jobs that made Raymond feel like a piece of shit in a broken-down outhouse, and now he badly wanted a whiskey, a beer, anything to dull the knife edge in his brain.

The wife had hired the agency to follow her husband, who led them to a motel on I-10. This fellow went inside one of the rooms and exited an hour later, his clothes disheveled. Raymond snapped some photos and stayed put, keeping his camera trained on the door. Ten minutes later, the man's companion left, running her fingers through her hair and adjusting her bra straps. She could not have been more than fifteen.

Raymond took more pictures as she descended the concrete-and-metal staircase and passed under the breezeway, out of Raymond's sight, out of his life. Ever since, he had felt dirty just for having been there, for not trying to save that girl from whatever life she led. Even Travis Bickle had done more than watch. But saving her had not been the job. Besides, who was he to fix anybody else's life? Hopefully, the wife would use the pictures to take everything that son of a bitch had, maybe put him in jail for statutory rape, where he would find out firsthand what it was like to be used.

On such days, Raymond ached for Marie so deeply it felt like illness. In the old days, whenever he came home feeling slimy, he took off his shoes, cracked his toes, and stretched out on the couch, his head in her lap. If she asked him about the job, he told her. If she did not, he just closed his eyes as her fingers worked his temples, his sinuses. The tension and filth drained away. Sometimes he would drift off to sleep for twenty minutes or half an hour. When he awoke, he saw her face, and if that could not make him feel better, nothing would.

But now she was gone.

Take a real vacation, LeBlanc kept saying. *Get outta the city. Go fishin. Take some long naps. You want me to come with?*

That sounded good, but if he walked away for even a week, he might never come back. He might find a shack on the beach or a cabin near a lake and let the world pass him by. He was not ready for that.

What was Betsy McDowell up to these days? Her charms, like Marie's, made the world seem lighter.

LeBlanc had reintroduced them back in the summer of 2013. Expecting a flighty, annoying fraud, Raymond found her both charming and capable. She had consulted on six or eight cases since then and often stopped by the offices to shoot the shit. While her histrionics resembled every other medium's he had ever seen—the trancelike state, the muttering of information just specific enough to hook you, head lolling, eyes that shut tight or opened wide and refused to blink—he had never felt like she played anyone false. In fact, as far as he could tell, she was genuinely uninterested in money. Her presence made people feel better, just as LeBlanc had said.

Plus, there was the way LeBlanc looked at her when he thought she was not looking back. If Raymond had any right to give advice, he would have told LeBlanc to stop wasting time. Life was short.

Reckon I ought to call Rennie tonight. But not until after supper. I don't want to get yelled at on an empty stomach. Hell, maybe I'll even cook.

That last part was a lie. He kept very little food in the house these days. It gave him a reason to leave. Otherwise, he would stay here, alone with his pain and his guilt, and one night he would find a bottle in his hand. Better to leave and come back only when exhausted enough to fall straight into bed. Somebody else could make the gumbo or the stuffed red snapper.

He sighed and took a drink. His crotch was freezing. Soon enough, the sun would go down, and then he would have to fill the long evening.

CHAPTER SEVEN

July 4, 2016, 7 p.m.—Comanche, Texas

Red Thornapple—owner, editor in chief, publisher, and staff writer for Comanche's local paper, the *Warrior-Tribune*—set in motion the events leading to the first death. In prepping his long-promised article about the Piney Woods Kid and the local descendants of the men who killed him, Thornapple had researched the outlaw, dug in to old family documents, and used an online ancestry program to create family trees. At least one direct descendant of each man who had handled the Kid's body still lived in town. The McCorkles and Johnstones had left Comanche in the early 1900s, but one of them came back and planted seeds in the town's soil—the McCorkles in the fifties, the Johnstones in the midseventies. For every other family on the list, some members had moved on—as close as Stephenville and Granbury, as far away as Fargo, North Dakota—but someone had stayed. A small miracle.

Roark had asked for a picture and a fluff piece about the diner, but Thornapple smelled a real story—a historical think piece about how these families had been tied together through violent Old West justice. It took quite a bit of effort to gather the descendants together, especially when you had to get the mayor in the same room, at the same time, with a long-haul trucker and a shift worker like Benny Harveston. In fact, it had proved impossible. Thornapple found a day when everyone but Harveston could make it, and he scheduled the interview for that evening—the Fourth of July. Harveston sent his daughter, Lorena, in his place.

Everyone arrived around 7 p.m.—Thornapple, the Harveston girl, Mayor Roark, Sue McCorkle, Adam Garner, John Wayne and his wife, Pat, and Joyce Johnstone. The town no longer provided a fireworks display, so there was nothing to see in the sky except the occasional arc of someone's Roman candle or bottle rocket. Inside the diner, the juke-box played classic country and country pop. McCorkle flirted with the men, while Garner and Wayne, old high-school friends, spent half their time arm wrestling or laughing at each other's jokes. Joyce Johnstone sat near Thornapple, answering questions with grace and humor. He returned to her over and over and ignored some of the others, like Sue McCorkle, too often.

John Wayne showed genuine interest in their shared history. The mayor seemed bored.

In the following days, though, Thornapple would mostly remember Lorena Harveston, who was not even supposed to be there.

It started with a question he asked her just after Garner and Wayne recounted several amusing but useless stories about their days playing football for Comanche High, their nights prowling the back roads with a bootlegged case of beer, and their literal pissing contests. Thornapple laughed and pretended to take notes. Then, as Wayne turned to the mayor and began a lecture on why the town should hire fewer Mexicans, Thornapple looked to Lorena Harveston and said, So. Tell your daddy we sure do wish he could have come.

She sipped her Coke. He's workin twelves. He's either at work or in bed.

Tell me about you then. What's kept you in town?

She ate a French fry. The University of Miami.

Pardon?

I'm twenty-six and livin with my parents.

Okay.

I used to hate it here. There's nothin to do. So when I got a full ride at the U, I thought I'd never see this town again, except on holidays. But I didn't even last two years.

Thornapple took one of her fries and dipped it in gravy. How come?

Because I majored in vodka and minored in smokin blunts with frat boys. I was on academic probation after my freshman year. Daddy like to killed me, so I settled down. Took a couple of summer courses, came home for six or seven weeks, and headed back in the fall. One day, I got invited to a party. Figured, what the hell, I've been good. They had enough Jell-O shots to get most of Dallas drunk. I barely remember the rest of that semester. They suspended me for the spring, but I could tell I'd never make it there. Too much temptation. So I came home and worked at Brookshire's for a year and a half. Got into Tarleton and majored in nursin. After graduation, Community Hospital hired me. And you know what? I'm happy. I like my job. I know most everybody. And I love the cheeseburgers here. They'll probably put me in my own ER one day.

She smiled. Her teeth were white and straight, her skin tan. Her long, dark hair spilled over her shoulder.

Thornapple took a long swallow of tea and then said, So what do you think about this business with our ancestors?

It's pretty cool that somethin happened in this town once.

The mayor shook hands all around and excused himself. John Wayne tapped Garner on the shoulder and launched into a dirty joke about a Baptist minister, a farmer, and an automatic milking machine. Garner laughed so hard, his belly shook the table. Pat Wayne rolled her eyes and started a conversation with Joyce Johnstone. A few minutes later, Thornapple joined them. Wayne eventually turned back to her husband, but Thornapple and Johnstone kept chatting. At some point, Lorena Harveston left, too. Red Thornapple did not think of her again until he heard her scream.

CHAPTER EIGHT

July 4, 2016, 9:05 p.m.—Comanche, Texas

Lorena Harveston left the diner alone, with her purse slung over her shoulder. She had not wanted to spend her off evening with people at least twenty years older than her, but their stories and their laughter had been entertaining, even though that Thornapple guy had barely written down anything she said. The big truck driver—Garner? Garland?—and that John Wayne guy, whose parents must have hated him if they saddled him with that name, had made her cackle and blush with their awful jokes. The woman named Joyce had complimented Lorena's skin and earrings. Even the mayor, who cut out early, seemed nice enough.

Overhead, the waning moon was a great piece of chipped marble. A few clouds drifted across the sky. Fireworks shrieked nearby, shrill and earsplitting as trains' brakes must have been. The July air was hot and smelled of gunpowder. She smiled. Not so long ago, this kind of evening would have made her long for a big city near an ocean, a place as different from Comanche as possible. Funny how things changed, what kinds of evolutions your life wrought.

Lorena stopped and turned back toward the diner. Framed by a window's drawn curtains, a couple bent over their food. A waitress passed behind them and appeared in the next window, this one otherwise empty, before moving out of sight again. Three evenly spaced carriage lights illuminated most of the porch and two or three feet of the grounds. A Kenny Chesney song blasted from the jukebox the Redhearts liked to crank up after dark. *When my friends at college asked me what small-town Texas was like, this is the kind of picture I wish I had painted, instead of makin us all sound like redneck ignoramuses.* She turned back toward the lot. The streetlamps along Austin provided plenty of light.

She reached the end of the concrete walk before they flickered. A cold breeze passed over her. Gooseflesh broke out on her arms and legs. She shivered and looked about.

The hell?

In front of the diner's storage building, something moved. All the lights in the diner dimmed and then went out. The muffled music from the jukebox cut off midsong. From inside, cries of surprise and dismay.

Lorena peered into the shadows. A man stood in front of the building. He did not move or speak. His arms dangled at his sides.

The lights, that weird wind, this guy—it was all a little too much like a scene from a bad horror film. He was so *still.* She had never considered how often people shift or twitch, even when standing in one place. Nobody just let their arms hang. They clasped their hands at the waist or stuffed them into pockets. This man seemed more like one of those life-size cardboard cutouts of famous people.

Screw this. Lorena turned on her heel.

When she reached the grass, the figure moved out of the shadows, ten feet in front of her.

How did he get over here? Nobody's that fast. Yet there he stood. She backed onto the concrete lot. An icepick stabbed her lungs.

Don't panic. Don't you dare run.

He came forward as she backpedaled, keeping perfect pace with her, always ten feet away. She looked about. No one in the lot, on the street, on the diner's porch.

You come any closer and I'll scream, she said. Go on now. Leave me alone.

She struck an SUV, the front bumper hitting the backs of her knees. She managed to stay upright and leaned against the grille, heat radiating from the engine. The man stopped, too.

Her voice trembling, Lorena whispered, What do you want? Her throat and mouth had gone dry.

The man said nothing. He just stood there, watching her.

I'm not waitin on him to jump me. I'm callin the cops.

She dug through her purse, fingers slipping over her keys, through loose change and lipstick and mascara and eye shadow, until they found her phone. She yanked it out and dropped the purse. It hit the concrete, and everything spilled out like the guts of a dead animal someone had left in the middle of field dressing. She dialed 911, willing her hands not to shake. But before she could even raise the phone, it exploded. Tiny pieces of plastic and metal shrapnel, hot and sharp, scraped her arms, her torso, her face. She screamed and clawed at the wounds, her hand numb from the impact. The phone's misshapen remains, gnarled like a fragment of a crashed airplane, clattered to the concrete. She wheezed. The world began to go gray.

Harveston slapped herself across the face as hard as she could. Her head rocked to one side, her teeth clicking together, and the parking lot swam back into focus. The man stood there, ten feet away. In one hand, he held a gun big enough to kill a rhino. It was aimed right at her. He was so pale, he practically glowed, like a television tuned to a dead station.

Jesus Christ. He shot my phone. He shot it right out of my hand.

She ran for the diner, sprinting as if all hell were after her, heart hammering in her chest.

If I can just make it inside. If I can just make it inside.

A bang, and pain exploded in her right thigh. She fell to her knees and onto her chest and face, skidding between an old Buick and a Chrysler with rusting white paint, her head near the Buick's front tire. A nail protruded an eighth of an inch from the tread. Dried mud had caked on the car's undercarriage.

Her face and chest ached. She touched her nose, and her hand came away bloody.

If I can just make it inside. If I can just make it inside.

Six or eight people emerged from the diner. They were talking, though she could not make out the words. Then one of them, a woman, raised her voice and said, I'm tellin you, I heard somebody scream.

Probably a firecracker, said a man's voice.

Help, Harveston screamed, her chest aching. Using the Buick as a crutch, she pulled herself to her feet. With every heartbeat, fire raced from her leg to her chest.

There she is, in the lot, someone said. Come on, fellas.

The pale man still stood ten feet away. He looked like someone's black-and-white drawing come to life. Only that was not exactly right. He was *gray*, as if age had consumed all the natural hues, leaving only shades of blacks and whites. His hair spilled from under his wilting cowboy hat in long, greasy jags. His body was slender but strong. He wore what appeared to be jeans, chaps, a shirt made of some woven fabric, a leather vest, a gun belt festooned with bullets, and holsters slung low on each hip. One holster held a gun. One was empty. He still aimed that pistol at her. If she stared into its cavernous barrel long enough, she might fall headlong into its depths. Her leg throbbed and pulsed.

Footsteps on the concrete. Beyond the apparition, three shadowed forms made their way down the walk and among the cars on the paved lot.

Where are you? one of them called.

Look, said another. You hurtin a woman, shithead?

Lorena opened her mouth to cry for help again, but as soon as her lips parted, another shot thundered—the sound seemed to come from inside her head—and then her guts exploded.

One of the men cried out.

What the hell was that? shouted another.

Lorena gripped her abdomen and moaned. When she pulled her hands away, she expected them to be covered with gore.

They were scraped and dirty but otherwise bare.

Her head spun. Her stomach churned. She looked at the man who had shot her and found she had no capacity for surprise left when he faded before her eyes. She could see right through him.

A ghost. A ghost shot me.

The apparition disappeared. Lorena closed her eyes.

The pain seemed to be lessening. Perhaps the ghost took it with him. Or maybe she had not seen him at all, had not been shot. Maybe she had stumbled in the lot and hit her head, and the rest had been a concussion-induced dream. But then nausea struck again, and she vomited a column of blood. It coated the Buick's dirty, leaking tire. The footsteps had gotten much closer now, but she no longer cared. She felt tired, sleepy.

Men surrounded her, their faces blocking out the stars. Red Thornapple, the trucker whose name might have been Garland, the Indian man who worked the grill. They looked frightened.

The grillman leaned over her. From a thousand miles away, he said, Aw shit—hey, you okay?

Strong hands grabbed her arm and shook her, but she closed her eyes, too tired to talk.

Hang on, lady, the cook said. I'm callin 911—yeah, hello, this is Morlon Redheart down at the Depot Diner. There's a woman hurt in the parkin lot. Looks like she's in bad trouble. Naw, I can't see nothin. Look, just *send* somebody, okay? I ain't a goddam doctor.

CHAPTER NINE

August 12, 2016—New Orleans, Louisiana

Raymond groaned and sat up, rubbing sleep from his eyes. His new alarm clock could double for an ambulance siren on its day off. Its puke-green digital readout said it was 7 a.m. *Wonder if I can get away with a couple more hours?* He sat for a while, his phone in one hand, ready to text LeBlanc some excuse.

No. You already missed too much work.

He got up and went to the kitchen, where he made coffee and drank a cup, pouring the rest of the pot into his silver thermos. Then he showered, brushed his teeth and tongue, and got dressed. No need to shave. Given all the pulp fiction and film noir most people had consumed, his customers would look with suspicion or outright distrust on any private detective without a five o'clock shadow. Besides, even one more task seemed like too much. *Maybe it's depression. I hear that makes you feel tired all the time. I wonder if it makes you feel old, too.* Raymond Turner was only forty-one years old but felt twice that age, like a man who has outlived his family and most of his friends.

That goddam picture.

💀

He had found the photo in his office desk while cleaning out a drawer a few weeks back, and it had hit him like a sledgehammer between the eyes—a years-younger Raymond and Marie standing in front of the old capitol building in Baton Rouge. Seeing it somehow underscored his loneliness in a way even the empty house did not. Back then, they had still believed they would have children, three or four at least. So much hope in the photograph, two lives stretching out and intertwining, hope that had survived the discovery that Raymond was sterile, that local adoption agencies disapproved of his transient and dangerous profession. He had seen them all in that photo—Marie and the children who never were—felt the vacuum of their absence, and then he had made some piss-poor excuse to LeBlanc and left, dropping the photo, not even thinking about where it might land or who might see it. On the way home, he bought a case of Shiner Bock and felt only mild surprise when LeBlanc was waiting on his porch. The big man had unfolded himself from the swing and stood with his hands in his pockets as Raymond hesitated, afraid to take out the beer, afraid not to.

Might as well bring it on in, LeBlanc said. Using the spare key Raymond kept under the welcome mat, he let himself in.

Raymond followed him, carrying the beer and wondering if he would weep when LeBlanc resigned from the agency and left.

This about that picture I found on the floor this afternoon? LeBlanc said.

Yeah.

LeBlanc sighed. I get it, but we're not doin all that shit again. Hand it over.

I wish Betsy McDowell was here. She always made Raymond feel better, just like she did with the clients.

LeBlanc poured the beer down the sink and stayed until bedtime. But Raymond had awakened from dreaming of the bridge every night since.

Now, he locked up the house and got in his car. Then he looked at his left hand and saw his ring finger was naked. He got back out and went inside. In his bedroom, the ring lay on his nightstand, where he had left it before taking his shower. It was a silk-fit gold ring filigreed with palm leaves and tiny doves—Marie's idea, to remind him of the inner peace everyone should seek. He picked it up and slipped it on, as he had done every day for sixteen years, thinking, as he always did, of the words *'til death do us part*.

He intended to do better than that.

CHAPTER TEN

August 27, 2016—Comanche, Texas

M orlon and Silky had gone home at five. The staff planned to close around ten. Of course, sometimes *around ten* became one in the morning when the truckers and shift workers rolled in, and while the night cooks and manager liked the extra hours, both servers rolled their eyes and griped to each other. They never gave back their tips, though.

At 9:30 p.m., John and Pat Wayne pulled into the parking lot. It seemed like a slow night—only seven or eight cars, most of them probably the workers'. John smiled. Perhaps he and Pat would get their food faster than usual and be home in time for the news. Beside him, Pat looked skittish, probably thinking about how that poor Harveston girl had died not five minutes after saying goodbye. That had been sad and strange, and the cops had no leads on the man spotted in the lot that night. John had come back to the diner since then, but this was Pat's first time.

He drove his brand-new Ford Mustang GT, royal blue with gray interior. He had driven the old one until you could damn near see through parts of the chassis that had rusted away. He had bought that car as a kid and had kept it up as best he could over the years. He had driven it to his senior prom and to his wedding and to the hospital when Pat miscarried the only child they ever conceived; he had picked up his first date in it and lost his virginity in its back seat and drove Pat to Dallas for what they called a honeymoon, squirreling away a little money every month toward his next Mustang. John Wayne paid his bills on time and owned a nice house, a bass boat he pulled behind his crummy work truck, a savings account, a sixty-inch television, and a growing retirement fund. When the old Mustang had finally decayed beyond his powers to repair it, he took a big chunk of his savings and paid almost a third of the $32,000 price on the spot. The salesman had nearly choked.

Now John parked on the lot's fringe, sure that if he pulled in next to another car, someone would back into the 'Stang or sit on it and leave their ass prints on his hood. He killed the engine, and they got out, the night's heat descending on them like a wave. The recently mown grass clumped around their feet. *Shit fire. I just washed her, too.* As he walked away, he trailed his fingers down the length of the car.

If you're thinkin of makin love to it, I'd advise you not to use the exhaust pipe, Pat said.

John laughed and put his arm around her. She had always made him smile without resorting to the usual jokes about his name. If they had lived in a big city, he would have advised her to try stand-up insult comedy, like that old fella Rickles. But they lived in Comanche, so she practiced her art at Pat's Hair and Nails, her own little shop. Humor had helped them stay together during the tough times when bills and work and Texas summers upped the everyday tensions of their lives. Except during the most serious of crises, she always cracked the first joke.

Pat slipped her arm around John's waist and hooked her thumb into his Wranglers' back pocket, and together they stepped out of the grass and onto the parking lot proper.

The streetlights along Austin flickered.

When they reached the walkway, John saw movement in his peripheral vision. He stopped.

A figure stood beside the old storage building—a man dressed in Old West garb, complete with pistols. He slumped as if exhausted and looked somehow bleached, as if he had walked out of the *Llano Estacado* and brought half its sand and dust with him.

He watched them.

I think I've seen that fella before.

Pat clutched his arm. Come on, she said, tugging him. Let's get inside. Her voice carried an edge that John registered in some part of his mind. She tugged harder.

John stared at the figure. He could not seem to stop. He shivered and felt the hair on his neck stand up.

Now Pat was practically yanking his arm out of its socket.

Yeah, you're right, he muttered. Let's get inside right now.

They took three steps before the man appeared in front of them, just popped out of nowhere like one of those holograms on *Star Trek*. Over on Austin, the streetlights buzzed like angry insects and then winked out. The diner's overheads strobed and crackled. The jukebox cut off. From inside came a cacophony of outraged voices. Pat moaned and gripped John's arm. He was sure her long nails would break the skin.

Just like that night the Harveston girl died. Oh, shit. Oh, shit.

The man stood perhaps ten feet away. John was over six feet tall and weighed 240 pounds, and he had gone toe to toe with even bigger men in honky-tonks across central Texas. It had never frightened him. But now, standing in front of this short, skinny, grayish man in the cowboy getup, John Marion Wayne nearly pissed himself.

Get hold of yourself, you pussy. He cleared his throat.

Mister, you're scarin my wife. Best you step outta the way.

Pat trembled. John wondered if those pistols were functional. They sure looked real. *We heard gunshots that night.*

Let's go back to the car, Pat said.

I mean it, mister, John said. Don't make me tell you again.

But the cowboy did not move.

I wanna go home, Pat said.

John's fists clenched. *Jesus, it's just some jackass in a cowboy suit, not the goddam boogeyman.* He pulled away from Pat and assumed a boxer's stance.

All right. I don't know how you got over here so fast or why you're wearin that getup, and I don't care. Move your skinny ass, or I'll move it for you.

He took two steps toward the gray figure.

The cowboy raised his head. His visage was haggard and gaunt and stubbled, the cheekbones prominent. His eyes, already gray and faded, sunk into his head, and the Waynes screamed as they gazed into the his skull's empty sockets.

The cowboy snarled. Pat's voice rose like the whistle of a teakettle.

And then, faster than John could follow, the cowboy drew his pistols and fired twice. Something punched John in the gut, and he flew backward five feet, landing on his back, his legs in the air. Then he rolled onto his side and lay still, groaning.

Pat ran to John and grabbed his shoulder with both hands and pulled him onto his back. His eyes were wide open, his teeth clenched. He opened his mouth. She leaned in close. And then John vomited blood, hitting her in the face. It streamed into her shirt and burned her eyes. Some ran into her mouth, gagging her, yet she kept on screaming, clawing at her eyes, flinging ropes of gore into the grass. By the time she could see, John was dead.

The cowboy stood ten feet away, guns holstered, arms hanging slack at his sides as if he had never moved.

You killed him, Pat said. You son of a bitch.

People poured out of the diner, their footfalls like the muted thud of faraway horses' hooves. The cowboy ignored them. Pat got to her feet, hands hooked into claws. Let the cowboy blow her head off. If he did not, if she could get close enough, she would dig her fingers deep into those gray sockets and see if she could find something soft.

Behind the cowboy, a white man and two Latinos arrived and fanned out.

What the hell's goin on here? one of the men said.

The cowboy ignored him.

Pat advanced, her arms outstretched, John's blood dripping from her fingers.

But just as she got close enough to rip his face off, the cowboy disappeared. He did not move or fade. He winked out of existence.

Pat stumbled toward the men, not seeing their puzzled, frightened expressions. The white man caught her before she fell. She tried to scream again, her abused vocal chords not up to the task. She beat at the man's face, blood spattering onto the other two as they tried to pull her away.

Jesus, she's as slippery as a greased pig, the first Latino man said.

What happened to her? said the other.

What I wanna know is where that sumbitch in the cowboy hat went.

The white man wiped streaks of blood off his face with his shirttail and trotted to John's body. He put two fingers under John's upper jaw. Then he put his ear to John's chest and listened. The other men watched, silent. Pat had collapsed in their arms. She hung there like a puppet without strings.

This fella's dead, the white man said. Somebody call the cops. Anybody know these people?

I don't, one of the Latino men said. Maybe somebody inside does.

Sirens warbled in the distance. In the back of the parking lot, the Mustang sat in darkness, where the police would find it minutes later, still perfect but for a bit of dust and cut grass sticking to its undercarriage.

Bathed in the pulsing reds and blues of police and ambulance lights, C.W. Roark stood over John Wayne's body. The eyes were open, the mouth pulled down in a horrible rictus. Nearby, Bob Bradley, the chief of police, conversed with the county coroner. Deputy Roen interviewed three men who had come out to help. Every other cop on the payroll worked crowd control. That had never been much of a problem in Comanche, but when two people were killed in the same place only seven or eight weeks apart, the townsfolk tended to gawk. Or piss themselves. They might even tell their friends and relatives to stay away, and right before the annual Pow Wow.

Roark squinted against the lights. A pounding headache formed on top of his skull. Will was out there, leaning against his truck and shooting the scene with his phone. *Hell and damnation. Gotta go make him delete it, or it'll be up on the YouTube before I get home.* Roark started to move. Then, as if he needed more problems, Rennie arrived.

She parked on Austin. The streetlights—burning bright, though the three witnesses swore they had gone dark during the killing—reflected off the hood and roof of her car. She got out, her red hair pulled back in its usual bun, and spotted Will. Pausing long enough to glare at him, hands on her hips, she said something Roark could not make out. The boy scowled, put the phone in his pocket, and got in his truck. As he drove away, Rennie ducked under the police tape, ignoring the calls of the deputies to stop, to get back on the other side of the barrier. Roark sighed. They all knew her and would not restrain her, though who knew whether they feared losing their jobs by his hand or their heads by hers?

Rennie trooped past the chief and the coroner, who stopped talking long enough to watch. The coroner shook his head and laughed. The chief did not. Rennie stamped up and regarded C.W., hands on her hips, her head cocked to one side, as if he were their son come home two hours after curfew with liquor on his breath. Roark steeled himself for the onslaught and hoped his temper would hold.

C.W., she said, I wonder if you understand what this means.

He frowned. I understand we've had two people dead in our goddam front yard. You shouldn't be here. You ain't a town official.

I don't give a rat's ass. Is that really John Wayne over yonder?

Not the one you're thinkin of. He's been dead a lot longer.

That's about as funny as a broken knee. We're in trouble here.

He snorted. Don't I know it. Sayin this is bad for our business is like callin Niagara Falls a campground shower. Plus, we can kiss the Pow Wow goodbye if we don't catch this fella. And if I can't keep the Pow Wow goin, I might as well clear out my office, because our merchants will remember next Election Day.

I couldn't care less about the diner or the Pow Wow. Or your job either.

Then what?

She reached into her purse and pulled out a newspaper clipping and handed it to him. He took it and stepped closer to the street-lights, pulling his reading glasses out of his shirt pocket. It was Red Thornapple's article on the Piney Woods Kid. Roark looked at the black-and-white photograph with the names under it. He saw himself and Garner, the big truck driver, and the Johnstone lady, who was, if memory served, somebody or other's secretary. The sluttish McCorkle woman, whose pants had been tight enough to trace the creases in her ass. Red Thornapple himself. The young girl, dark hair falling past her shoulders—Lorena Harveston. And John Wayne.

Rennie's point was obvious, but why would anybody target the folks in that picture? Most of them had done little in their lives beyond ordinary living. Only he was of any particular importance to the community. Only he and Thornapple had money. No one could be jealous of their publicity; the *Warrior-Tribune* did not exactly enjoy national circulation. Rennie was seeing connections where only happenstance existed, but he did not have that luxury. Not now, when his town needed him and would remember, for better or worse, how he handled this crisis.

He folded the article. If you're tryin to show me two people in this picture have died here, I kind of noticed.

She touched his arm. I heard those men say the killer disappeared. Like he was a ghost.

Oh, for God's sake.

Listen to me, she hissed. I don't know what those people saw, but how did he get away? How did he do it *twice?*

We don't even know if it was the same person.

She groaned. Are you really arguin we should worry less because maybe there's two killers in town? We gotta call somebody. Bob Bradley don't know how to deal with a serial killer. Maybe the state police or the FBI—

Damn the state police, he said. This town needs every single dollar we can get, and to attract more dollars, we need the Pow Wow. If anybody so much as hears the words *serial killer*, we can kiss it goodbye. And if the diner goes under, we'll lose our investment. Is that what you want?

I told you. I don't give a damn about that. I'd rather be the wife of a live ex-mayor than a widow.

Bradley and the coroner stopped talking and glanced at them. So did some of the deputies.

Keep your voice down, C.W. urged. People are lookin. I'm tellin you, this town can't afford to let this shit go statewide. This killer ain't no goddam ghost or a criminal genius. He's just a man, and he'll slip up. So we're gonna handle this ourselves. I mean it, Rennie. If you so much as breathe a word to any law enforcement official—local, state, or federal—you and me are gonna go round and round.

They scowled at each other, their eyes locked. Finally, C.W. looked away. Rennie could stare down a rabid bull when she put her mind to it.

Then she poleaxed him by saying, What about Raymond? We could call him.

Anger welled up in C.W.'s throat like acrid vomit. His expression hardened. What's he gonna do? Drink the killer under the table?

He's been sober for months now. You know that.

What I know is that he near about broke your heart and probably gave himself cirrhosis while he was at it.

Rennie looked like she could rip out C.W.'s liver with her teeth. Marie died, she said. She was his whole world. He's human.

He's weak is what he is. No. We ain't callin Raymond. He'd just muck things up even worse. Now please. Get on home, and let our people earn their salaries.

He walked away. *I never talked to her that way before. I'll be in the doghouse at least a week.* She tromped back toward the car. The deputies backed away like she was a grizzly bear.

Rennie pulled into her driveway and killed the engine, yanking the keys out of the ignition and slamming the door behind her. On the drive home, one thought flashed like a neon sign: *God, that man can be an ass.* She unlocked the front door and dropped the keys on the coffee table while passing through the living room. In the bedroom, she sat down and leaned against the headboard, looking at the family picture on her nightstand—her, C.W., and Will, all sitting on a bench in front of an oak tree. Everyone looked happy.

She dug her phone out of her purse, opened her contacts, and selected *Raymond*.

He answered on the second ring. What's wrong? he asked.

CHAPTER ELEVEN

August 29, 2016—New Orleans, Louisiana

When Raymond reached the office, he had already sweated through his clothes, which felt fused to his skin. He had not eaten breakfast. The agency's waiting room, on a busy day, looked like a doctor's office, with prospective clients reading old magazines. Today it was empty. Good. Anytime the sun glared down like the wrathful eye of God, slow days felt like a blessing. He opened the heavy oak door and walked into the office proper.

Raymond's desk sat near the far wall in front of a framed Dali poster. To its right stood the door to the back rooms—storage, a restroom, and sleeping quarters he and LeBlanc sometimes used and sometimes hid their clients in. His desk looked sloppy as hell—papers spilled everywhere, a dirty coffee cup on one corner, an empty in-and-out box, a laptop buried somewhere. Two padded red chairs faced it. Two more stood in front of LeBlanc's desk near the left wall. LeBlanc sat behind it, snoring, his feet planted on the burgundy carpet, his head tilting over the back of his chair like the lid of a teapot. Raymond laughed. LeBlanc, a good six inches taller and sixty pounds heavier than Raymond, looked like a grown-up in a third grader's seat.

Raymond tiptoed into the room and shut the door. Then he rooted around until he found a phone book. He walked over to LeBlanc and savored the big man's peaceful look before slamming the phone book down with a sound like a shotgun blast.

LeBlanc's eyes flew open, and he overbalanced, his arms pinwheeling, his mouth open in a surprised yawp that doubled Raymond over in laughter even before LeBlanc fell onto his right side. He jumped up, eyes wild. Raymond stepped away in case LeBlanc took a swing before all his senses returned. But when his eyes focused, LeBlanc just said, You asshole.

You should have seen your face, said Raymond, still laughing.

LeBlanc glowered a moment longer, and then his mouth twitched upward and his eyes softened. Soon he was grinning. One of these days, I'm gonna get *you*. He sat back in his chair and tossed the phone book across the room. It fluttered like a wounded bird, landing near Raymond's visitors chairs.

Raymond sat on the edge of LeBlanc's desk. LeBlanc eyed Raymond's ring.

Still wearin it, I see.

You feel like eatin?

LeBlanc stood up and gestured toward the door. Age before beauty.

Smartass.

They both ordered a shrimp po' boy with fries and tea, despite the early hour. At their table facing Decatur, LeBlanc read a printout of the article from the *Comanche Warrior-Tribune*. At the top were two pictures. On the left, a grainy photograph of an old gunfighter standing on an empty street, his hat tipped back, his expression inscrutable, both thumbs tucked into his gun belt. The caption read *The Piney Woods Kid c. 1884*. The other showed several people sitting in a restaurant booth. Their names were listed: Mayor C.W. Roark, Sue McCorkle, Adam Garner, Joyce Johnstone, Red Thornapple, John M. Wayne, and Lorena Harveston.

So. It's an article about your sister's new business, LeBlanc said.

Raymond took it back and folded it. Two people in that picture are dead. Lorena Harveston and John Wayne. Both died right outside the diner, the girl on the very night they took that picture.

I can see why Rennie's concerned. Any other connections between the victims?

Nope.

So the question's whether they died because of the diner or their ancestors, LeBlanc said.

Can't imagine there's much about the diner worth killin for. It just started up.

Maybe C.W. crossed a mob contractor or somethin.

Raymond laughed. If they were in New Jersey, maybe, but I doubt even the Dixie Mafia's ever heard of Comanche. Besides, C.W. wouldn't get involved in somethin shady. Some folks got a stick up their ass. C.W.'s got a whole tree.

LeBlanc took a huge bite of his sandwich. Mouth still full, he said, So no problems with gettin the land or anything?

Rennie said somethin about the county historical society wantin it, but those ain't generally the kind of folks that resort to killin nurses.

But the posse angle seems pretty thin, too. I mean, this is Texas we're talkin about. Somebody in your family tree had to be part of a posse at some point.

Or the one the posse chased.

Where the hell is Comanche anyway? Is it closer to Dallas or El Paso? Or goddam Lubbock?

Closer to Dallas than them other two, Raymond said. Oh, I haven't even told you the best part. Eyewitnesses say the killer wasn't human.

That surprised the big man so much, he almost stopped chewing. What was it then? A coyote or a Bengal tiger? What lives in Texas?

Raymond sipped his tea and, just for fun, waited until LeBlanc bit off another hunk of sandwich before he said, Word is a ghost killed 'em.

LeBlanc nearly choked. He sputtered and coughed, crumbs and bits of half-chewed shrimp and tomato and lettuce spewing onto the table and Raymond's fries. Raymond frowned and pushed his plate away.

Are you serious? LeBlanc croaked.

I'm just tellin you what Rennie told me.

LeBlanc drained his glass and signaled a server for another, his face still red, crumbs dotting his chin. A ghost. Just when you think you've heard everything.

Maybe we can get us a ghost-huntin TV show.

They already got a few of those. They all suck.

Don't I know it.

They stopped talking while LeBlanc ate. They would take the case, of course, even though they were not licensed in Texas. With all the worry Raymond had put Rennie through, he owed her that much, and more. He would miss New Orleans, though. He had visited Comanche before and had seen no sign of beignets and po' boys and crawfish and shrimp and beer and strippers and shitfaced tourists taking their pants off in the streets. In fact, it was hard to remember just what he *had* seen—a hardware store, maybe, and some car-repair joints and a motel or two. If he and LeBlanc had to stay more than a few days, how would they stand it?

LeBlanc commandeered the rest of Raymond's sandwich and wolfed it down. He finished another glass of tea.

Well, he said as he came up for breath, when do we leave?

ASAP.

Does C.W. know we're comin?

Nope. In fact, he pretty much ordered Rennie not to call anybody. I reckon that was his first mistake.

LeBlanc needed to piss, so he excused himself.

C.W.'s gonna breathe fire and spit broken glass, Raymond thought. *And that's before he finds out we're there to poke around in his business.*

Maybe Betsy McDowell could help with that. Whenever she stopped by or consulted, she added something Raymond had not even realized was missing—a soothing voice, a third perspective that juxtaposed with his and LeBlanc's more jaded viewpoints. Theory-swapping sessions in the office, late nights in stakeout cars, greasy pizza and Chinese takeout and cold po' boys on stale bread—it reminded Raymond of what life was like when Marie's friends and whomever LeBlanc was seeing at the time would join the agency boys for beers and gumbo, and they would stay up all night, laughing and joking. Beyond that, McDowell could calm you down with a touch and a few words. She might even affect a grumpy bear like C.W. Roark.

Raymond had barely seen her in a month. Her tarot readings and such did little good with divorce cases. But something like this ran right up her alley. Two deaths, two grieving families, even a ghost.

Plus, a few months back, she had mentioned reading for a professor of folklore at the University of Louisiana at New Orleans. A guy like that might make a good source of information about a gunfighter from the late 1800s—and ghost legends, if it actually seemed relevant. McDowell already knew the man, so they could help each other while Raymond and LeBlanc did the legwork.

LeBlanc and their server returned at the same time.

Did you gentlemen save any room for dessert? the server asked.

Yeah, LeBlanc said. One key lime pie and one bread pudding. You want anything, Ray?

Sure. Bring me another shrimp po' boy. Some asshole ate most of mine.

When the new order arrived, Raymond watched LeBlanc destroy the desserts. *If we take Betsy, maybe spendin that much time with her will spark Darrell's kindling. God knows he deserves a little happiness.*

LeBlanc wiped his mouth with his napkin. About our nonexistent Texas license, he said. If we ain't takin a fee, then we're just concerned private citizens helpin out your family.

I reckon that's how we'll play it. But C.W. loves to throw his weight around. We're gonna have to be political.

LeBlanc groaned. Can't we just hog-tie him and throw him in the trunk until we're done?

Raymond laughed. Call Betsy while I finish this sandwich. Ask her about that folklore guy at ULNO.

LeBlanc grinned.

CHAPTER TWELVE

August 30, 2016—New Orleans, Louisiana

They gathered in the Turner Agency offices at 10 a.m. Raymond had made an 11 a.m. reservation, but LeBlanc had already rooted in the cupboards of their shoebox-sized kitchenette five times. The problem with LeBlanc's hunger lay not so much in its omnipresence but in his accompanying attitude. Whenever his blood sugar dropped too low—in other words, if he had not eaten in two hours or more—he snarled when spoken to and tossed furniture when questioned or teased. Despite that, Raymond said, Darrell, everything in that kitchen was in there the first four times you looked.

LeBlanc came back into the office, muttering dark words, and leaned against the wall near Professor Jacob Frost and Elizabeth McDowell, who were seated in Raymond's visitors chairs.

Frost looked different than Raymond had imagined. Thin and just under six feet tall, he wore faded blue jeans and a wrinkled powder-blue button-down shirt with the sleeves rolled up to his elbows. His light brown hair was flecked with gray at the temples and had not seen a brush all day. His brown eyes were bloodshot.

In contrast, McDowell looked radiant and celestial. Her long blond hair cascaded down her back in four braids. Her bright blue eyes sparkled, as did her skin, which seemed speckled with glitter. In a deep-purple tie-dyed T-shirt, she might have stepped out of 1968. She wore a short skirt and high-heeled sandals, her legs crossed right over left. When she smiled at LeBlanc, some of the clouds around him seemed to lift.

Frost was nodding off.

Darrell and me appreciate y'all comin down, Raymond said. We fly out tomorrow. If you're comin, we gotta make the arrangements.

Frost sighed and looked at the floor. Because life had taught him what disappointment bordering on depression looked like, Raymond knew the professor would say no, even if it hurt. Back at LSU, Raymond had been an all-Southeast Conference strong safety, drafted in the fifth round by the Green Bay Packers, but, when leaping for an interception during his very first training camp, he had landed awkwardly and obliterated every ligament in his right knee. Aimless, his life's plan as shredded as his medial collateral, and holding a criminal justice degree, he joined the New Orleans Police Department. He rehabbed the knee, pushing harder than anyone thought advisable, and still the injury almost disqualified him from joining the academy. As he had watched his first career implode and then nearly missed his second, Raymond had seen an expression similar to Frost's in every mirror he passed.

I really appreciate the offer, Frost said. And I *want* to come. It's as close to field research as I'll probably ever get. A murderer who dresses like an Old West gunfighter? That's the stuff of urban legend. Folklore in the making. But the fall semester just started. I can't leave.

Well, Raymond said, I'm sorry to hear that. But we understand.

I'll be happy to help with any research from here.

Thanks. We'll take you up on that. Don't worry about it.

Frost nodded, but he still looked like he might step on his own bottom lip. Based on the five minutes Raymond had known him, Frost seemed like a good man. But only LeBlanc was essential, and of the other two, McDowell would likely prove more useful. In the past, some of their conservative clients and suspects had assumed she was just a hippy-dippy weirdo, but soon enough, they were offering her a bowl of jambalaya and asking about rates. Those people skills could prove invaluable. Raymond turned to her.

What about you, little miss? You game for a trip to the land of cowboy hats, cowboy boots, and Dallas Cowboys?

She grinned. Her teeth were even, a little yellowed from the coffee and tea she drank every waking moment.

I reckon folks around here can live without me for a while.

LeBlanc beamed. If his smile stretched any wider, the top of his head might fall off. He saw Raymond watching, and the smile disappeared. He cleared his throat and sat up straighter, tugging at his open shirt collar.

Well, LeBlanc said. Now that that's all settled, let's go. I'm so hungry, I could eat a raw nutria.

Forty-five minutes later, the foursome sat at an outdoor table in Brennan's, LeBlanc slurping turtle soup while they awaited their Eggs Bayou Lafourche and crabmeat omelets. Frost still looked crestfallen. He had barely glanced at the menu and seemed most interested in drinking glass after glass of red wine, despite the hour. Raymond patted him on the arm. Frost looked up with watery eyes—exhaustion, the wine, or both? He pushed his glass away but said nothing.

He's really takin it hard, Raymond thought. *Reckon his no came after a lot of lost sleep. I don't often meet folks who love their work this much.*

LeBlanc finished his soup. He wiped his mouth with his napkin. When McDowell smiled at him, his eyes lit up like his brain was on fire. Raymond had not seen so much red-faced grinning since junior high.

He turned to Frost. Look at it this way. At least you probably won't get shot at.

It just would have been nice to see the lore take root, Frost said.

Maybe next time.

The hell of it is, I think I could have helped. And it would have been a damn interesting line on my vitae.

I reckon so.

The professor made a *the hell with it* expression and drained his wineglass again. A word of warning, he said, setting the glass down. The killer won't be your only problem. From what Betsy tells me, you and Mr. LeBlanc have spent your entire lives in cities. Things are different in small towns—the food, the values, the attitudes, even the weather. The phrase *fish out of water* comes to mind. And I have no idea what they'll make of Betsy.

Raymond laughed. I've been on jobs in half the parishes in this state, from New Orleans to places you'd miss if you blinked. I ain't never stepped in a pile of shit I couldn't wipe off my shoes.

Central Texas isn't south Louisiana. And then there's the Piney Woods Kid.

What about him? In case you ain't heard, he's dead.

Frost picked up his napkin and spread it across his lap. Yes. Your case may have nothing to do with him.

I sense a *but* comin.

The professor leaned closer. *But* I saw a History Channel documentary on him a few years back. He was a mean, murdering bastard. If

what happened at this truck stop—

It's a diner.

If what happened at this diner was perpetrated by somebody modeling themselves after the Piney Woods Kid, you might need a life jacket to float through all the blood you'll find.

That's damn poetic and all, but we're goin to Comanche, Texas, not Baghdad.

You're probably right. But watch each other's backs.

One server refilled Frost's glass as another arrived with the food. Plates were distributed as Raymond felt the same tickle in the back of his brain that vacationers feel when they forget to feed the cat or turn off the iron. But then McDowell laughed, and as he took a bite of andouille in hollandaise sauce, he decided he would have plenty of time to think about it in Texas.

Later, they exited onto Royal Street, Raymond and Frost chatting, McDowell and LeBlanc hanging back ten yards or so, dodging map-carrying tourists and street peddlers. Occasionally, their arms touched. They probably looked like a couple in the early stages of infatuation, too nervous to speak much, unaware of each other's rhythms. By the time LeBlanc found his courage, they had reached the intersection of Royal and St. Phillip. Raymond and Frost had gone ahead.

McDowell started to turn left toward the office when LeBlanc took her arm. She raised her eyebrows. Around them, pedestrians ebbed and flowed. A tourist in a Cadillac stopped at the intersection and rolled down her window, asking passersby if they knew the quickest way to the Garden District. From somewhere nearby, a trumpet burst into life, a jazz tune LeBlanc had never heard before. His face burned. He had grabbed McDowell like she had stolen something, and now he was acting like a sheepish teenager sliding into second base for the first time. She watched him with curiosity and something like amusement.

Finally, she took one of his hands in hers and said, Don't be so nervous. I won't bite.

LeBlanc swallowed hard, trying to unstick the words that had lodged in his traitor throat.

I don't know why I'm actin like such a doofus, he said. But look. I was wonderin if you'd like to get a drink with me sometime. Or maybe dinner.

She looked coy. You mean another business meetin, Mr. LeBlanc?

You know what I mean. Just you and me.

McDowell smiled and twirled one of her braids. I'd like that. What took you so long, anyway?

And just like that, LeBlanc fell for her. Not love yet, but not just lust either. A kind of deep affection and a sense of propriety, as if he had made a pact with an honorable personage. She had surmounted his defenses so easily she had not even needed to try—so discomfiting, so glorious.

I reckon I'm just slow, he said.

McDowell slipped her arm into his. I'm sweatin through my shirt. How about escortin a lady back to the air-conditioning?

Yes, ma'am, he said. Maybe by the time we get there, your friend Jake will feel better.

They set off down St. Phillip, arm in arm.

CHAPTER THIRTEEN

September 1, 2016—Central Texas

McDowell woke with a jolt, her head banging against the window hard enough to make her ears ring. Her vision swam, the pain sharp as an icepick. In the front seats, the men shouted at each other. She, Raymond Turner, and Darrell LeBlanc were driving over a bumpy road somewhere in Texas. Emanating from the front seat, nervous energy mixed with edgy, bordering-on-angry humor. Whatever happened had been brief but intense. She rubbed the right side of her head. No blood.

Her voice still thick with sleep, she said, What's goin on? I about fractured my skull on this window.

From the passenger seat, Raymond turned, looking concerned. Sorry. We need to get you looked at?

Nah. But it sounds like y'all might need a time-out.

Raymond turned back around. We were just havin a difference of opinion about what makes a good driver. Darrell's definition seems to be whatever he's doin at the time, while mine steers more toward somebody who watches the goddam road instead of the scenery.

From the driver's seat, LeBlanc growled, I *was* watchin. It ain't my fault if nobody tends to this highway.

A lot of Louisiana roads looked like they had been shelled by heavy artillery, but McDowell let the remark pass. Besides, she knew what LeBlanc meant. Most of the road looked fine, pavement the color of faded blue jeans lined with bright whites and yellows, but sometimes they swerved around a pothole big enough to swallow a tire or rumbled over patches of black asphalt, which stood out like oil stains on a white shirt. LeBlanc must have hit one of the potholes. The resulting jerk had banged her head on the window and, if she imagined the situation correctly, yanked the wheel out of LeBlanc's hands for a split second. She doubted they had ever been in real danger, but Raymond hated any sort of hiccup whenever someone else controlled his fate. She had seen it on the approach into Dallas/Fort Worth International, when their 727 hit some turbulence and shook them hard enough to rattle teeth. Raymond had cursed darkly and threatened to beat the shit out of the pilot. Luckily, he kept his voice down, or they would all still be at DFW, cuffed and stuffed and trying to prove they were not terrorists.

They had rented a 2012 Toyota Corolla the color of a ripe red plum. They passed flat fields and light poles, remnants of crops, the occasional herd of grazing cattle or horses, single-story houses with peeling white paint and two-tone cars in the yard, two-story homes with wraparound porches overlooking farmland, low and rolling hills full of thick, waving grass set beside acres of brush and mesquite, and bare patches like desert. As if a tornado had blown through and shuffled the landscape. Everything looked, in other words, like central Texas.

So how much longer? she asked.

LeBlanc shrugged. Maybe fifteen minutes.

Good. I'm starvin. I hope one of you boys will buy a lady a burger.

Soon they drove into town on Central Avenue. They spotted their hotel, a Best Western, and pulled in. Raymond went inside to make their arrangements while McDowell and LeBlanc parked the car. They got out. LeBlanc locked the doors and opened the trunk. Then he and McDowell dug out six bags. They struggled into the hotel just as a tall, rail-thin desk clerk with a whisper of a mustache handed Raymond their keys.

They set the bags on the floor. Raymond took his. LeBlanc wiped his brow. God, it's hot.

We're on the second floor, Raymond said.

He handed LeBlanc a room key and gave two to McDowell. She handed one back. In case I lose mine, she said. No sense misplacin 'em both. Just don't come bustin in without knockin. You never know when a lady's steppin outta the shower.

LeBlanc reddened and looked away.

Raymond winked. We weren't raised in a barn. I reckon we'll knock.

If we don't all melt first, LeBlanc growled. Then he stalked off, carrying his bags.

Wait'll he finds they ain't turned on the air yet, Raymond said.

The hotel elevator was busted, so they dragged their luggage upstairs. McDowell opened the door to number 216, stowed her things, and turned on her air conditioner. Then she opened her side of the doors that connected the two rooms and waited for the men.

The room looked like every other Best Western room she had ever seen—short hallway with a bathroom and closet. Stark white walls decorated with paintings of bull skulls half-buried in desert landscapes and lone Native Americans—Comanches, she assumed—looking over water. Two queen-size beds with triple white sheeting and turquoise coverlets at the bottom, pillows piled against the headboard like models of cumulonimbus clouds. Striped carpet that looked as if it cost five dollars an acre. Between the beds, a night stand with a beige telephone and a clock radio, probably a phone book, a Bible, and some stationery in the drawers. A couple of chairs, one stuffed, one straight-backed. A desk with enough space for a laptop and your wallet, keys, spare change. Black mini-fridge, microwave oven, coffee pot big enough to hold a half cup or so. Curtains pulled together.

Raymond opened their side of the connector, and McDowell stepped into an identical room. On the bed nearest the window, LeBlanc lay sprawled out with his head on a pillow, dozing, his mouth open, his shoes off. Sweat stains expanded from his armpits. One hand was tucked behind his head. The other lay across his stomach. Raymond's duffel sat on the other bed.

Watch this, Raymond said. Then he turned to LeBlanc and shouted, Hey!

LeBlanc's eyes snapped open. He sat up, eyes wide, a thin line of drool hanging from his mouth like a spider's web. He stared at Raymond and McDowell for a moment, uncomprehending. Then his eyes focused, and he wiped his mouth with the back of his hand.

You asshole, he said, running his hand through his hair and straightening his shirt.

Man, McDowell said, you must have been exhausted if you fell asleep that hard and that fast in this oven.

Flyin does it to me. Don't matter if I'm in the air thirty minutes. I crash as soon as my head hits the pillow.

I wouldn't say *flyin* and *crash* that close together, Raymond said. Then he patted the bed. Relax, Betsy.

McDowell sat on the end of the bed, cross-legged.

We should check out Rennie's diner, LeBlanc said. I could eat a horse right now.

You could *always* eat a horse, Raymond said.

LeBlanc gave him the finger. McDowell pulled open a nightstand drawer and found a phone book only marginally bigger than a pamphlet. She turned to the Yellow Pages and looked up restaurants. Raymond flipped channels.

We got a Subway, a Dairy Queen, a pizza place, a couple of chicken joints, and a Mexican restaurant, McDowell said. No diners. Guess it's too new.

Well, LeBlanc said, why not kill two birds with the same double cheeseburger?

Raymond shook his head. I need to touch base with Rennie first. Besides, I've had enough of that car for one day. What's closest?

McDowell shut the phone book and put it back in the drawer. Sonic it is.

How do you know it's closest?

Well, we passed it on the way in.

In the hall, they passed no one, heard nothing. They might have been the only people on the second floor. When they reached the lobby, two men stood near the front desk. One wore a police uniform. The clerk looked like he might shit himself. He said something to the two men. The newcomers turned, and the taller one scowled.

Hello, C.W., Raymond said. How'd you know we was here?

We're on the lookout for any outta-towners.

Roark wore a gray suit that looked too hot for the weather. Beads of sweat had formed on his brow. Occasionally one would break free and streak down his face, merging with shallow wrinkles and curving across his cheeks so he appeared to be crying. *Look at that hair and that suit*, Raymond thought. *He looks like a movie wise guy. Somebody ought to tell him he lives in Texas.*

The other man stood six or eight inches shorter than the mayor and a good thirty pounds heavier, most of it in his belly. His dirty-blond hair receded from his sunburned forehead and face. His black uniform looked new and stiff.

The two groups met in the center of the lobby. Raymond shook hands with Roark, who let go as soon as decorum allowed and wiped his hand on his trousers, and then turned to the cop.

I reckon you're the chief of police, Raymond said.

Bob Bradley, the cop said. They shook. Bradley's grip felt strong but sweaty.

This here's my partner, Darrell LeBlanc. And our associate, Elizabeth McDowell.

My friends call me Betsy, McDowell said as everyone shook hands.

Roark looked at her clothes with distaste, as if he had never seen a tie-dyed shirt before. She looked him straight in the face until he turned away.

Thatta girl.

The chief opened his mouth to speak with McDowell, but a glance from Roark quieted him. The mayor's eyes were chips of slate sharp enough to cut bone. Raymond held his gaze. Roark was used to getting his way, cowing people with his power when he could, intimidating them physically when politics failed. But Raymond had spent his adult life dealing with criminals, junkies, prostitutes, adulterers, thieves, murderers, and the New Orleans Police Department. His brother-in-law did not scare him in the least and never had.

We know why y'all came, Roark said.

That should make things easier, Raymond said.

No. It won't. You're my wife's brother, so I've gotta put up with you, even after all you've done. Visitors are welcome to shop in our stores and eat in our restaurants. But as for what's goin on at the diner, we don't need help. If that's all the business you got, you might as well pack up and head back to DFW right now.

The chief looked at the floor. He thrust his hands in his pockets, cleared his throat, shuffled his feet—everything but take Raymond by the lapels and beg for help.

He's outta his league, and he's got enough sense to put away his pride, Raymond thought. *We need to get him away from C.W.*

LeBlanc kept silent and crossed his arms, expressionless. McDowell smiled, as if they were discussing kittens or babies.

Nobody's sayin you can't handle your business, Raymond said, careful to keep his tone neutral. But Rennie thinks a fresh eye might help. That's all.

Roark stepped closer to Raymond, sneering. LeBlanc started to move in, but Raymond motioned him away.

If you butt in, you'll get acquainted with our jailhouse bunks, Roark said. Obstruction of justice and whatever else we can think of.

Harsh words and anger swelled in Raymond's mind like a blister about to burst. *You stubborn jackass. You'd rather somebody else die than work with me.*

He was about to mention the newspaper article, the linked deaths, when a sharp, high-pitched voice cried, C.W. Roark, you better quit it.

They all turned, wincing. Rennie approached, looking madder than an old wet hen. *God, I'll never get used to her mad voice if I live to be two hundred.* Her red hair was pulled back in a bun. She wore rimless glasses and bright red lipstick, a free-flowing taffeta dress the color of arterial blood, red high-heeled shoes. *She looks like a movin wound.*

You stay outta this, Roark said.

She shook her finger at him. We ain't seen Ray in two years. You ain't runnin him off.

The mayor glared at her. They ain't here to visit. And I know who called 'em.

Rennie poked him in the chest with one bony finger tipped with a long red nail. And I'd do it again since you've lost whatever sense God gave you.

Roark looked away, hands on his hips like a parent trying to reason with a petulant child. They're just gonna get in the way. Besides, they got no jurisdiction. Hell, they ain't even licensed.

Raymond cleared his throat. This ain't our first rodeo. We can poke around without makin you trip over us.

The mayor turned on Raymond. You got a lot of nerve. Rennie's been trippin over you ever since Marie died.

Something twisted in Raymond's gut. Keep my wife's name outta your mouth.

Then stay away from mine. You done enough to her already.

Stop it, both of you, Rennie snapped.

Raymond's fists clenched. His jaw tightened. He stepped toward Roark.

The mayor's face turned deep red, as if someone had chopped his head off and sculpted a new one out of the world's largest beet.

Don't bother actin indignant, Roark said. We both know you got no shame.

You gonna do somethin, Raymond said, or am I just waitin for your fat head to explode?

Roark came at him.

Bradley stepped between them, grabbing the mayor around the waist.

Come on, C.W., he said. I reckon your blood pressure reads like an SAT score.

Roark kept clenching his fists and gritting his teeth, eyes blazing.

Raymond, Rennie said.

He sighed and backed up a step. I don't wanna fistfight you in a hotel lobby, C.W. Or anywhere else. We're family, even if you are a puckered asshole.

Roark stared at him. Then his shoulders sagged, and his bloodshot eyes lost their intensity. The redness drained from his face. Rennie took his arm and pulled him backward three steps.

That's good, Bradley said. I don't see horns or cloven hooves on these folks. I reckon the town will survive 'em.

Roark looked weary. He nodded. Let me loose. I need to say somethin.

Rennie locked eyes with him. Then she nodded once and let him go, watching him like a schoolmarm who expects her students to hurl spit wads as soon as she turns her back.

We're under a lot of pressure here, Roark said. We got the Pow Wow comin up. Just stay outta our way, and keep a low profile. People are scared. Don't make it worse.

Like I said, this ain't our first rodeo. Raymond still wanted to fracture Roark's jaw. We was headin over to the Sonic. You're welcome to join us.

I got business, Roark said. He turned to LeBlanc and McDowell. You look well, Darrell. Nice to meet you, ma'am. Sorry for the dustup.

I've seen worse, McDowell said.

Stone-faced, LeBlanc said nothing.

Roark turned and headed for the door. Rennie squeezed his shoulder as he passed. Then she embraced Raymond. It's good to see you, she said.

You, too, said Raymond.

She kissed his cheek. I need to go mend some fences. I'll call you.

Okay.

She followed the mayor outside.

McDowell exhaled. LeBlanc's eyes were still cold. *If C.W. had swung on me, Darrell would have mopped the floor with him and his police chief. I gotta keep my temper.*

The chief stood there with his hands still in his pockets. He looked embarrassed.

You boys sure do know how to make a body feel welcome, LeBlanc said.

The chief smiled without humor or mirth. *He's the boss. If he wants me to back his play, I gotta do it.*

He looked around the empty lobby and saw the clerk watching them, his eyes wide, leaning so far over the desk he seemed in danger of tumbling onto his head. The chief grunted.

Raising his voice a bit, Bradley said, Y'all stay outta trouble. You got that?

Sure, Raymond said.

The chief nodded. Then he turned and walked across the lobby and out the door.

What kind of read you get on that guy? LeBlanc asked.

I think he's okay, Raymond said.

How come?

Because he slipped me a piece of paper when we shook. Raymond raised his voice. Come on. Let's go get Betsy that hamburger.

I could use a beer, LeBlanc said.

Me, too, Raymond said.

You can have some sweet tea or ice water.

Water? Raymond said. Now you're goin too far.

Back in the room, Raymond had barely gotten his shoes off when his cellphone rang. He took it out of his shirt pocket and answered it.

Hey, Rennie said.

Hey. He turned down the television. Behind him, LeBlanc grabbed some clothes from his suitcase and went into the bathroom, closing the door behind him.

Sorry about this afternoon, said Rennie. C.W.'s never been much for lettin things go.

No shit.

Don't be too hard on him. He's doin the best he can.

So am I.

I know. I just wanted to tell you I'll keep him off your back as much as I can. And how much I appreciate you doin this.

I'll always come when you call. Can we get together? Talk? Maybe spend some time with Will?

Soon. After C.W. calms down.

Okay. How is Will, anyway?

He's a teenage boy. It's all I can do not to wring his neck.

He know I'm in town?

Yeah. C.W. wishes he didn't.

I'm unlikely to corrupt him in one visit.

Like I said. Give it time.

Okay.

Soon LeBlanc came out of the shower, wearing only a pair of shorts. He combed his hair, water dripping down his torso.

Everything okay?

As much as it can be.

While LeBlanc brushed his teeth. Raymond lay on his bed, staring at the ceiling, hands linked behind his head. Tomorrow he would have to go out and hunt a killer. Rennie sounded strained, as if she had been fighting off tears. And his brother-in-law wanted to kick his ass.

Nothin's okay, but it don't pay to say so.

CHAPTER FOURTEEN

September 2, 2016—Comanche, Texas

At 3 p.m., the Depot Diner served mostly truck drivers and kids trickling in from school and people passing through on their way to bigger places. McDowell and LeBlanc sat in a booth near the back, looking over a menu featuring bright pictures of too-perfect-to-be-true entrées, two pages printed on both sides and laminated. Across the table, Raymond fiddled with his notebook and pen. He had taken six pages of notes so far, none of which seemed related to the case.

They had first come by the diner around 9 so he could interview Morlon and Silky Redheart. Morlon had loomed over the counter, barrel chest bulging against his wife beater and stained white apron. When Raymond introduced himself, Redheart nodded and said nothing, stoic. They went over the usual background questions, Redheart answering in monosyllables and grunts. They talked about the diner, its construction, whether anyone had noticed anything odd. Then Raymond asked about the deaths.

I ran out there when we heard the Harveston girl scream, Morlon said. We all saw a white fella standin by the road, but I didn't see him do nothin. Next thing I knew, he was gone.

What about Wayne? Raymond asked.

We were home that night. I drove up here after I heard what happened, but the cops didn't tell me shit except I had another corpse in the parkin lot.

Any idea why somebody might target these folks?

Nope.

Why go after 'em here?

Who knows?

Can you elaborate?

How?

Never mind.

Silky had been just as elusive. She might have stood five feet tall if you spotted her two or three inches, and she outweighed Morlon. She grimaced all the time. Rennie had mentioned a lower back problem stemming from years of dragging full pallets of groceries around the Brookshire's storeroom—and wore an unfortunate orange-and-black shirt that made her look like a basketball with legs.

When Raymond mentioned Lorena Harveston and John Wayne, she shook her head and said, Shame what happened to them folks, but I don't know anything.

So what about this Piney Woods Kid business?

Never met him.

Raymond had poked around a bit more, sidling up to a booth full of old-timers and striking up a conversation, but when he brought up the murders, they glanced at each other and shut their mouths like a passel of snapping turtles. Perhaps they had come to the same conclusion as Roark—that such doings were best kept in-house. After striking out with the breakfast crowd, Raymond and the others retreated to their hotel long enough for the old patrons to skedaddle and the new ones to get comfortable. Then they drove back out, parked in the grass near the concrete lot, and took the corner booth.

Silky Redheart brought them water in red plastic glasses. McDowell and LeBlanc rolled the straw wrappers into balls and tossed them at each other like schoolkids. Silky raised her ticket pad.

Somethin else to drink? she asked.

Coffee all around, please, ma'am, Raymond said.

Silky nodded and went away. A few booths over, five old-timers—not the same ones from that morning, though their John Deere caps and faded pants and ragged button-down shirts made it hard to tell—sat discussing the day's events in too loud voices. Raymond considered trying them, but one was holding court, telling a convoluted tale about a swap meet where a vendor had cheated him. *Doubt they'll appreciate an interruption.* So he got up and went to the jukebox, where a middle-aged woman wearing gray polyester pants and a bright blue shirt plugged quarters into the slot. He sidled in and leaned against the box, studying the selections. She glanced at him and nodded. He nodded back.

I hope you like country music, mister, because that's all they got, she said. I never saw so much George Strait in one place.

Raymond chuckled. I'm a blues man. Jazz, too.

She scrutinized him with narrowed eyes. You ain't from Texas.

I'm from the great city of New Orleans.

Never been there.

You should go.

She laughed. I don't like hurricanes.

Well, they don't stay all year. Besides, word is y'all had some trouble of your own, right here at this restaurant.

The woman looked sad. I knew the Harveston girl's family my whole life. She was a nurse. The Wayne fella was real nice, too. I reckon bein from New Orleans, you're used to folks killin each other, but it don't happen here much.

You never get used to killin, Raymond wanted to say. *And it ain't like I walk out my front door and trip over bodies.* But he let her comment pass.

I hear the circumstances were weird, he said.

She laid her hand on his upper arm and squeezed. You durn right. Folks are tellin some crazy stories.

Silky Redheart walked by carrying a tray piled high with greasy cheeseburgers and mounds of steaming fries. The woman at the juke-box picked a song. Raymond steeled himself for a four-and-a-half-minute assault of twanging voices and fiddles and lyrics about rodeos and cowboy boots. Then the music started, and he recognized it, a song about a vengeful woman and her philandering man, sung by one of those kids who won a TV reality show.

Raymond smiled at Polyester Pants. Good choice. That girl sure can sing.

The woman winked. You ain't tellin me nothin I don't already know. What were we talkin about?

John Wayne and poor Lorena Harveston and the stories goin around. Though I reckon that's rude talk among strangers.

Raymond looked about, as if making sure no one was listening. I like a little rude talk.

The woman reddened and grinned, hiding it behind her hand. She slapped his arm. Oh, you.

Tell me, he said. I'm hard to scare off.

She considered for a moment. Then she leaned close, as if to whisper in Raymond's ear. He leaned down to accommodate.

Folks say their insides looked like they got shot, only there wasn't no bullet wounds.

Raymond tried to look surprised, though Rennie had already told him that.

Well, that don't make no sense, he said in a hushed tone. What killed 'em if not bullets?

Nobody knows, the woman whispered.

No theories at all?

She looked pained, as if she were about to divulge a dark family secret.

I don't even wanna mention what people are sayin.

I love gossip.

She sighed. You'll think this town is nuts.

Try me.

Well, some folks—the ones with too much time to flap their gums and not enough brains to stop, if you ask me—some folks claim the Piney Woods Kid shot 'em.

The which? Raymond asked.

An old outlaw. The Kid and John Wesley Hardin made a lot of noise in these parts back in the 1800s. Some say the Kid was worse. The legend goes that after the Kid died, townsfolk saw him around the depot.

Raymond let out a low whistle. I'll be damned. So you're sayin this town's got a killer ghost.

Not me. But if you threw a rock, you'd probably hit somebody sayin it. The cops tried to hush it up, but you know small towns.

I sure do.

Silky Redheart had made her way back around to their side of the restaurant and stopped by the jukebox.

Y'all okay? she asked.

Doin fine, Polyester Pants said. Just passin the time.

Silky looked at Raymond. Your friends are ready to order, mister.

She walked away as Raymond turned back to Polyester Pants. I reckon I better get back. Good meetin you.

The woman's gold incisor winked in the afternoon light. Always nice to meet a gentleman.

Raymond walked back to the booth. LeBlanc and McDowell sipped their coffee. He slipped into his seat and picked up his coffee cup. They watched him, waiting.

Finally, LeBlanc said, So. When's the wedding? Can I be your best man?

Raymond flipped him off, and then Silky Redheart appeared again, ready to take their orders.

Later, McDowell went back to her room, while Raymond and LeBlanc sat on their beds, LeBlanc watching a Rangers game, Raymond studying the paper that Chief Bob Bradley had slipped him the day before. A phone number had been printed in a tiny, neat script. Raymond squinted. *If Bradley ever gets tired of police work, he could write secret messages for spies. You need a goddam electron microscope to read this.* When he finally puzzled out the number, he programmed it into his phone and shredded the note.

Gonna make a call, he said.

Uh-huh, LeBlanc said, watching the game.

In the hall, Raymond dialed the number. It rang twice before the chief said, Hello.

This is Raymond Turner.

Hang on.

Sounds in the background—phones ringing, muffled voices,

laughter, a low clunking that might have been a stapler crunching through thick documents. *Sounds like he's at the station.* Bradley mumbled to the people on his end, probably some excuse for leaving. Soon Raymond heard cars on asphalt, the occasional diesel engine roaring in the distance.

Any day now, he muttered.

You there? Bradley asked.

Yeah.

Sorry about that. I had to step out. If the mayor finds out I'm talkin to you about this case, my ass is grass.

I'd think y'all would welcome the help.

Some of us do. I'm okay at my job, but this one's got me stumped, and I don't cotton to seein no more bodies.

But my brother-in-law handcuffed you.

He's worried about tourism.

Raymond walked to the nearest window and looked out on a parking lot with a half dozen cars in it. Beyond, yellowing grass stretched into the distance. The other window revealed a stretch of nondescript road and a few buildings, more grass in between. A town with a couple of grocery stores, a smattering of fast-food places, not even a goddam Walmart.

Tourism? Raymond asked, trying not to laugh.

I know what you're thinkin, the chief said. But the mayor's tryin to jump-start it. Got a town website and everything. Plus, we got the Pow Wow. That's a festival we have every year. Got a barbecue cook-off and a car show, some Old West cowboy shit, Indian dancers, and such. It's more popular than you might think.

And C.W. thinks the murders will ruin all that.

Right.

I can understand that. Well, like I told y'all before, we're here to help. We ain't callin CNN.

Bradley sighed. Might not matter anyway. People are makin up their own stories and spreadin 'em like bedbugs.

You mean this ghost hogwash.

People are dead, and we got no suspects. I guess any explanation will do in a pinch. Me, I don't care if we're after a ghost or a man or Wile E. Coyote. I just wanna keep my people safe.

Good to know somebody in this town's got sense. What can you tell me about the case?

What did you hear at the diner?

Raymond laughed. Jesus, remind me not to kill anybody while I'm here. I reckon you can't fart in church without everybody knowin about it by dinnertime.

That's a small town for you.

I heard the victims' insides got torn up, even though they didn't have external wounds.

Yep. Weirdest damn thing I ever seen. I'd like to know how that information got out.

Like you said. Small town. Raymond had no intention of revealing to anyone in authority that Rennie had told him about the wounds.

You hear about the article?

Rennie sent me a copy. Anything else connectin the victims?

No phone calls or emails, except between Adam Garner and John Wayne. They were old buddies from way back. No canoodlin in the sheets with each other's wives or husbands, no financial red flags. It's like somebody killed 'em just for bein in that article, and it don't tell you anything you couldn't find out yourself at a library.

This Garner—you looked into him, I guess.

Yeah. He was drivin his truck up north when Wayne got killed. And he was one of the folks that found Lorena Harveston. He ran outta the diner with the others.

I'll need to talk to all of 'em.

If C.W. finds out you're buttin in, he'll order me to run you outta town, brother-in-law or not. Hold your water till I can figure out the best way forward.

But—

Mayor's callin. I gotta go. I'll call you when I can, but don't tell nobody we talked or that you've got this number.

Bradley hung up before Raymond could reply. Raymond stuck the phone in his shirt pocket and leaned against the wall. What kind of weapon or accident could tear up a person's insides and leave the outside untouched? *It's like they were shot with a goddam science fiction ray gun. Or a magic ghost bullet, I reckon.* He shook his head and walked back to his room, where he learned the Rangers were four runs down in the bottom of the eighth.

So what's our next move? LeBlanc asked.

Raymond thought for a moment. We check out the diner grounds. Maybe the locals missed somethin. After that, we talk to the families, as soon as Bradley's ready to hold our hands.

He went to brush his teeth. LeBlanc turned back to his game. Eventually, they went to bed. Raymond slept like a dead man.

CHAPTER FIFTEEN

September 3, 2016—Comanche, Texas

Raymond studied the diner's clientele. Small-town, lower-middle-class people. Lots of white folks and people who might have been Latinx or Native American or *mestizo*. Some worked office jobs, judging from their clean clothes, their dress shoes, their ties. Some looked like truck drivers and mechanics. But they seemed at ease with each other and friendly. No one seemed suspicious, and if McDowell was feeling any odd vibes, she did not say.

The chief walked in. Bradley nodded to Raymond and sat at the counter. Silky Redheart brought Bradley a cup of coffee. He said something to her. She laughed and slapped her thigh. The chief spoke again, and she disappeared into the kitchen. A moment later, Morlon Redheart came out and talked with the chief. Redheart looked toward Raymond's table and said something to Bradley. The two men shook hands, and then Redheart went back to the kitchen. Silky reappeared and set a plate in front of Bradley.

Wonder what that was all about, LeBlanc said.

Us, said Raymond.

If they don't get we're here to help, screw 'em.

They aren't mad, McDowell offered. They're afraid.

She had a better handle on other people's emotions than Raymond had on his own. But in the end, it mattered little. The Turner Agency would do its job. He drank his sweet tea and finished his chili cheeseburger, which tasted of poblanos. He mopped up the excess chili with his fries. McDowell picked at the remains of her food and alternated between her fourth glass of tea and her third cup of coffee.

Fifteen minutes after his food arrived, Bradley paid his check. He took a toothpick from the clear plastic dispenser on the counter and stuck it in his mouth as he approached Raymond's table.

Afternoon, he said.

Raymond nodded. Chief Bradley.

McDowell sat against the wall on her side of the booth, so Bradley squeezed in beside her.

Okay. I spoke to Morlon, Bradley said. Told him y'all were helpin me out on the sly. He won't lie for us, but he won't run and tattle either.

Good, Raymond said.

McDowell's voice was like tinkling silver bells. We'll be discreet.

If you cost 'em one customer, C.W. will hear about it, and then we're all in a world of shit. Pardon my French, ma'am.

Don't worry. I got a dirty fuckin mouth, too.

Bradley laughed and shook his head. By the way, C.W.'s gonna be in his office all afternoon. If you wanna swing by and talk to Benny Harveston, now's the time. Just remember, if C.W. catches y'all out there, I don't know nothin about it. He stood up and stretched, his hands in the small of his back.

Don't worry, Raymond said. I've been round and round with C.W. before. If it comes to that, I'll take all the heat.

Bradley seemed at ease. Holler at me if you find anything my people missed, you hear?

We will, said Raymond.

The chief looked at them a moment longer. Then he turned and walked out of the diner, waving to Silky Redheart as he went. She waddled around the counter and up to their table, where she folded a ticket in half and tore it off the pad and laid it down next to Raymond's plate.

Y'all want anything else?

Raymond patted his belly. No, ma'am. That was the best chili cheeseburger I ever ate, and I live in a town that takes its food mighty serious.

'Preciate it. Y'all come back. She turned and walked to her register, stopping by each table and booth to check on her customers.

Raymond unfolded the check. Inside it lay a key on which someone had Scotch-taped a white label reading *Strg. Bldg.* Raymond pocketed it and said, Come on. Let's go get hot and sweaty in yonder desert.

An hour later, they had completed a sweep of the porch, the parking lot, and the outlying fields. No one had paid them much attention. They found nothing of note: dried and crumbling footprints from the last rain, discarded trash, tire tracks, all business as usual at a diner, all of it so mashed together that not even a TV detective could draw any conclusions. The only hope lay in the storage building. If nothing presented itself there, it would be time to interview witnesses, which would lessen their lead time exponentially.

Raymond whistled and waved McDowell and LeBlanc to the storage building. It was about the length of a railroad car and made of ancient, rough-hewn boards. It had been painted red last summer to match the diner, but somehow the new coat seemed to have aged. The place looked like a deep bruise. As far as Raymond could see, no one had installed an electric light. The ash-gray curtains on the other side could have been decades old. Only the windowpanes looked new.

I don't wanna go in there.

From behind him, her voice shaking, McDowell said, This place is *bad*.

Raymond did not look at her. If he did, he might take her by the elbow and pull her away, because he felt it, too—a tickling at the base of his skull, swelling and itching like an infected mosquito bite, worse than the voice that had told him to drink after Marie died. The storage building seemed like one of those places where danger slept in every weakened board and vicious splinter protruding from the walls like broken teeth. He had seen a lot of those places in south Louisiana. He had even gone into some of them. And he had hated it the whole time, feeling as if the very air pressed down on him like a malevolent hand.

He would have to enter this one, too. The job required it. So he forced himself to stand in front of the door.

Up close, the knob and lock looked new. Raymond fished in his pocket and dug out the key. *Jesus. It feels like my throat's closin up.* Still, he stuck the key in the hole and turned, hearing the tumblers clack. He took the key out and put it back in his pocket and turned the knob, hating the feel of it, oily and warm like rotting meat.

I reckon it's too late to be roofers or somethin, LeBlanc said, his voice strained.

Raymond pushed open the door, took a deep breath, and stepped into the dim, hot interior.

The northern wall was lined with shelves that were empty save for a pair of ancient boots and some kind of belt. Wooden folding tables were stacked in the middle of the floor. On these lay bulk-wrapped packages of paper towels, toilet paper, and napkins. On the floor to the east, gallon-size cans of corn and beans and tomatoes and pie fillings in towers of irregular heights, grouped according to content. Around the tables and cans, extra chairs and disassembled booths. Nothing appeared interesting or helpful.

From behind him, LeBlanc said, You gonna let us in, too?

Betsy, see what you make of them boots over yonder, Raymond said. Darrell, you take the right side. I'll take the left, and we'll meet in the middle. Remember we're lookin for anything unusual.

You mean like an expired can of purple-hull peas? LeBlanc asked. I mean, I don't even get why we're in here. No sign of forced entry.

Maybe the killer had a key, Raymond said.

That would mean somebody at the diner's our man, LeBlanc said.

Let's try to rule it out.

They spread out. The windows provided some illumination, but LeBlanc left the door open for extra light. He and Raymond poked around their areas, picking up cases of plastic and metal cutlery, moving stacked cans around, kneeling to inspect every inch of the floor before walking on it. Nothing seemed out of place, or, rather, everything seemed haphazard, so they could not know one way or the other. Sweat poured from Raymond's brow. LeBlanc huffed and puffed like a marathon runner in the last quarter mile. Their curses filled the air as they tripped over bric-a-brac.

McDowell had not made a single noise.

After ten minutes, during which he stubbed his toe three times and cut his finger on the edge of a can, LeBlanc stood to his full height, the top of his head only inches from the ceiling, and said, Well, this sucks ass. Nothin more interestin than that box of glow-in-the-dark condoms. And they expired in 2003.

Raymond straightened up, his spine aching. Only thing I've found is my tolerance for heat and bad air, which, as it turns out, ain't too high. Betsy?

McDowell stood at the back wall, staring at the items on the shelves, not moving. LeBlanc raised his eyebrows. They began picking their way around the clutter.

When they reached her, she was staring at the old, scuffed boots. They were splotched with dark stains that might have been blood or ancient mud or some of the Redhearts' barbecue sauce. No insects or vermin had chewed them up over the years, a minor miracle for something that old. An ancient gun belt lay coiled around the boots like a snake sunning itself on a rock. It was covered in those same crusty splotches.

LeBlanc started to touch McDowell's shoulder, but Raymond stopped him. Her eyes were wide and unblinking and distant. Raymond had seen this before, when she read for clients. He had always believed her trance to be an act, but if that were so, where was the audience now? Her bottom lip quivered.

He leaned in close. What is it, Betsy?

So *angry*, she whispered. So much *pain*.

Whose pain?

McDowell did not reply.

Raymond motioned for LeBlanc to step back. They maneuvered their way to the front wall and watched her, speaking in whispers.

Jesus Christ, Ray. I ain't never seen her this intense before, LeBlanc said. What do we do? Poke her? Leave her alone?

Hell if I know. Whoever them boots belonged to, they wasn't happy.

You thinkin the Piney Woods Kid?

They look old enough.

That'd be weird, LeBlanc said. The Kid's shit at the murder site.

Weird, yeah. But proof that he's back from the dead and killin folks with his ghost revolvers?

I didn't say that. Can't we pull her away from there now?

Whatever she's feelin might be useful, Raymond said. She's always handled herself before. We gotta let it play out.

They leaned against the rough, splintery wall. LeBlanc shifted from foot to foot, clenching his fists. *He'd chew through steel to protect her.*

Come on, Betsy, LeBlanc muttered.

Easy, Raymond whispered. This is what she does.

Minutes later, though, she still had not moved. *Hell with it.* He motioned LeBlanc forward.

She looked exactly as she had before—eyes wide, mouth working as if she were struggling to form words. Then her brows knitted. She scowled. She trembled as her eyes filled with tears.

They cut and chop and slice like they're slaughterin a pig, she whispered. They got no respect. They wanna damn the spirit to wander the earth, but they got no idea what real hate can do. And if they knew, they wouldn't care. *This is a bad place.*

LeBlanc goggled. Raymond shivered, as if his spine had been stroked with the tip of a feather. He wanted a drink, and not a beer, either—whiskey, at least a pint, maybe even a gallon.

McDowell trembled harder. And then a single drop of blood oozed out of her right eye and mixed with her tears, thin streams of red cascading down her face and dripping onto her shirt.

What the hell? LeBlanc said.

Raymond grunted. He had never seen anything like that, had never even heard tell of it. He grabbed McDowell by the shoulder and turned her around. Blood dripped from both her eyes.

Raymond shook her. Betsy. Snap out of it, darlin, he said.

LeBlanc's eyes bugged. Is she okay?

Wake *up*, Raymond said. Come on back.

McDowell's eyes focused. Then she burst into sobs. She fell against LeBlanc, turned, and buried her face in his shirt. He held her and stroked her hair and made shushing sounds as she gasped and wracked tears up from the deep well of her soul, smearing blood and sweat all over LeBlanc.

We're leavin, LeBlanc said.

Yeah, Raymond said. Come on, Betsy. Watch your step.

Screw that, LeBlanc snapped. He picked her up and carried her, kicking pieces of booth and disassembled stools out of his way. He toted her out the door, and Raymond followed them back into the light of the Texas afternoon.

Everyone was thirsty, and LeBlanc insisted they take McDowell away from the diner, so they drove to Dairy Queen and bought her a Coca-Cola and a Blizzard. Raymond sat across from her, sipping Coke. LeBlanc took the seat beside her. He watched her as if she might burst into flame. The air conditioner blasted out of the vent over their heads, and a couple of ceiling fans twirled nearby, but the heat still pressed them like an iron. The décor hardly helped. With its mix of what Raymond hoped were fake cow skulls and potted cacti and warm-hued paint, it looked like a desert. Raymond reached over and patted LeBlanc's right hand. The big man nodded but did not relax.

McDowell spooned the Blizzard into her mouth with metronomic regularity. How long before she got brain freeze? After a while, she put down her plastic spoon and smiled.

Much better, she said. Felt like I was about to melt.

LeBlanc still looked stricken. You sure you're okay? We were really worried about you.

I'm fine.

LeBlanc seemed unconvinced. And McDowell did seem out of sorts. The fear in her voice, the blood dripping from her eyes like something from a horror film—what had they witnessed?

Betsy, Raymond said. I hate to ask you—

It's okay. I can talk about it.

LeBlanc glanced at Raymond. We can do this later.

She shook her head. Now's better, while it's still fresh. Though I can't tell you much.

Whatever you can give us will help, Raymond said.

McDowell pushed her hair behind her ears and drank more soda.

The boots, the belt—it was like a black swarm of bees hung over 'em and buzzed around my head, McDowell said. This high-pitched whine that tickled my throat just under my ears. And the feelin—like a wall of pure hate. The anger—no, more like rage. It felt *murderous*. Somethin bad happened in that storeroom. And we better hope it ain't connected to our case, because if it is, we're in for some rough times.

LeBlanc wanted McDowell to stay in the hotel while he and Raymond talked to Lorena Harveston's family. But as they wound through town following Google Maps, McDowell drove. After she showered and changed her clothes, she had argued her skills were best used in situations like this. LeBlanc had gritted his teeth and complained, but it was McDowell's decision. Besides, she was right. They had brought her along to help deal with people, and in any murder case, you had to look at the family. According to Bradley, the Harveston woman's mother and father still lived in the house where she had grown up. The agency had to persuade the parents to talk.

Soon they pulled up to the curb of a white house with flaking paint and a rusty pickup in the drive. A grill sat in the middle of the yard, wisps of smoke curling from the vents on top and carrying the sweet smell of barbecue. They walked through the front yard, and as they passed the grill, LeBlanc raised the lid and waved away the smoke and steam. Leg quarters and a couple of breasts.

If I can do this without a beer, you can get your mind off your stomach, Raymond said.

LeBlanc stuck out his tongue. McDowell laughed.

The temperature had not abated. Even the ankle-deep grass felt hot. At the front door, they arranged themselves strategically—McDowell in front, Raymond behind her, and LeBlanc with his imposing figure in the rear. McDowell knocked. From within, the sound of a television turned to deafening levels. McDowell knocked again, harder this time. Nothing. Finally, LeBlanc stepped past her and rapped on the door hard enough to shake it in its frame. The television volume decreased. A moment later, the door opened, a blast of cool air washing over them. The man who stood before them looked to be in his midfifties. He wore a short but ill-kept beard, a white T-shirt with drops of barbecue sauce on the chest, and a pair of bright red shorts. He held an open Shiner Bock, the bottle sweating in his hand. Raymond licked his lips.

Benny Harveston looked them over and said, I already took a copy of *The Watchtower* this week.

McDowell favored him with her 200-watt smile. Mr. Harveston, I believe Chief Bradley told you we'd be stoppin by.

Harveston's eyes narrowed. He might have.

Well, sir, first of all, I hope you'll accept our condolences—

Hold up, Harveston broke in, looking at each of them as he spoke, his eyes cold. I ain't speakin about Lorena with strangers unless I know what you want. And if you're startin a sales pitch for some goddam magazine article, you'll have about a two-minute head start before I can fetch my shotgun.

LeBlanc tensed. Raymond shook his head, hoping LeBlanc saw him. McDowell reached out and took Harveston's free hand in both of hers. The man's face went slack. His eyes widened. McDowell was sending now—sympathy, calmness, whatever—and it seemed to be working. Harveston's watery red eyes softened.

We ain't journalists, McDowell said, her voice gentle. And we would never disrespect your daughter's memory. We want to catch whoever took her away from you. Will you let us help?

Harveston looked at McDowell for a moment more, then at Raymond and LeBlanc. He blinked as if he had just noticed them.

Scuse my manners. We done had too many buzzards flappin around. And forgive the mess. We ain't been much on housekeepin since Lorena passed.

Harveston led them into the living room—a couch and glass-topped coffee table, an easy chair, a flat-screen television on which the Houston Astros were beating the Cincinnati Reds 4-1. Harveston took one end of the couch and set his beer on the coffee table. He did not use a coaster.

Y'all have a seat, he said. My wife's at the store.

McDowell sat on the other end of the sofa. Raymond and LeBlanc stood.

Raymond made the introductions. I'm Raymond Turner. These are my partners, Darrell LeBlanc and Elizabeth McDowell. We're private detectives.

Harveston's brow furrowed. Who hired you?

Raymond glanced at LeBlanc. Somebody who wants to make sure nobody else gets hurt. We'd like to ask you some questions.

Harveston looked at McDowell. She nodded.

All right, Harveston said. But let's get this done before my wife gets back. She's been through enough.

Raymond nodded. Can you think of anybody that might have wanted to hurt your daughter?

Harveston ran his fingers through his unkempt hair. Like I told the cops, I can't think of a single person. The folks she worked with liked her. She hadn't dated since she came home from school.

LeBlanc took notes. McDowell focused on Harveston.

All right, Raymond said. Did anything unusual happen around the time of your daughter's death? Any strangers in your neighborhood, any prank phone calls?

Naw. Nothin we don't see and hear every goddam day.

Raymond pretended to think for a minute while LeBlanc scribbled. Then he asked, You got any opinion on this Piney Woods Kid business? I've been private eyein for a long time now, and I never heard somethin so far-fetched.

Harveston gestured dismissively. It's disrespectful. Crazy bastards. It ain't like my daughter was the first person that ever got killed in this town. No, that shit's spreadin because them folks out at the diner's got too much imagination. And because of my family's connection to the Kid.

Tell us about that.

My great-great-granddad, name of Roy, was a member of the posse that killed the Kid and brought him back to Comanche.

Raymond looked at LeBlanc. Huh.

Only reason I know what Roy did was because of that article Red Thornapple wrote.

Thornapple. Seems like I heard that name before, Raymond said, hoping Harveston would tell him something Bradley had not discovered.

Red runs the town newspaper. He's the one that got everybody together at the diner. Took their picture. I was supposed to be in it, but I had to work that evenin, so Lorena went instead. If I'd been there instead of her, she'd still be alive. My little girl.

Harveston wiped his eyes. LeBlanc wrote.

It's not your fault, said McDowell. The only person to blame is the killer.

Harveston snuffled. If it wasn't for the Wayne fella dyin there, too, I'd say some tweaker needed money and Lorena was just in the wrong place. I mean, why would somebody come after us? We ain't done nothin. We ain't *got* nothin.

And your wife doesn't have any ideas about why… Raymond said.

Harveston's expression darkened. No, he said. And I won't drag her through the whole thing again.

I understand. We're just lookin at every angle.

Well, you'll have to look at this angle without my wife.

Ten minutes later, they were driving back to the hotel. Heat shimmered off the pavement. Kids played in yards and splashed in plastic swimming pools. One man in a swimsuit washed his truck in his driveway, the sudsy water snaking into the street.

Betsy, Raymond said. Anything?

Grief. Pain, McDowell said from the back seat. Some anger when you asked about his wife. Survivor's guilt.

There's gotta be somethin more that connects these people, LeBlanc said.

Yeah, said Raymond. Two descendants buy it on damn near the same spot the posse brought the Kid's body. It can't be a coincidence.

Well, what next? McDowell asked.

Three things. One, we call the chief and see if he's got our copies of the case files yet. Two, we talk to the other descendants. Maybe one of 'em knows somethin, even if they don't know they know. Three, we find out everything we can about the Piney Woods Kid. Our connection might be in the history.

From what I felt earlier, McDowell said, I'd say there's a really good chance you're right.

LeBlanc glanced at Raymond. Time to call Betsy's friend Jake?

He wanted to help, Raymond said, and professors *like* libraries.

CHAPTER SIXTEEN

September 5, 2016—Comanche, Texas

Raymond sat in a booth at Dairy Queen, eating a basket of steak fingers. *God, I miss New Orleans.* He had never gone so long without eating dishes filled with bell peppers and onions and celery. He wanted a steaming bowl of gumbo, heavy on the shrimp and okra and andouille; some crawfish etouffee; a real po' boy, not a cold ham sandwich on a hoagie roll. He wanted some spice. Perhaps tomorrow LeBlanc might grab some takeout from that Mexican place south of the diner, because if Raymond had to eat one more meal deep-fried in vegetable oil, he might just puke.

Bradley had called that morning, waking Raymond from a sound sleep in which he had dreamed of eating stuffed fish and key lime pie in the Quarter with Marie. In all their years of marriage, they must have eaten that meal hundreds of times, always seeking a table near the windows or on the patio, mosquitoes and humidity be damned, the seafood varying from night to night but the pie a constant. Marie could have lived on key lime pie. Raymond always ordered two pieces, and he would eat his own first, hoarding both slices on his side of the table, moaning with pleasure as he chewed and swallowed, slapping her hands when she tried to grab hers, pretending not to hear her

good-natured protests, her laughter, recurring moments in his past
now mere ghosts flitting through his dreams more often than he could
stand. He woke from those dreams with tears on his pillow, the pressure
of her hand on his. He never dreamed of how he used to feed her the
first bite, a delicate forkful, filling and crust and a brushing of whipped
cream, the way her eyes would close in pleasure as she tasted it, how
he would pass the saucer to her and watch her eat until every crumb
was gone. He never dreamed it, but he never forgot. Moments like
that followed him about, haunted him, kissed him like a breeze. And
whenever it happened, he wanted a drink.

He wanted one now, but instead of drinking himself into a dayslong
stupor, he ate something resembling fried steak and waited for the chief.
The second murder victim's autopsy results had come in.

When Raymond had asked for details on the phone, Bradley said, I
ain't got time to get into it. C.W.'s here and breathin fire like a goddam
dragon. I'm callin you from the shitter. Be at the Dairy Queen this
afternoon after one, and I'll bump in to you there.

Bradley had hung up, leaving a fuzzy-brained Raymond to wonder
if he had heard the chief correctly. He was supposed to go sit in Dairy
Queen from one o'clock until when? How many cups of Coca-Cola
could he drink before he had to piss, which, according to his luck,
would be exactly when Bradley arrived? And was he supposed to come
alone, or could he bring LeBlanc and McDowell? Raymond had cursed.
Then he had gotten up and showered and started the coffee. LeBlanc
had not awakened, his snores rhythmic.

Raymond sat in the restaurant for an hour and a half before Bradley
arrived.

The chief did not look into the dining room. Instead, he walked to
the counter and ordered something, bantering with the pimple-faced

teenaged girl taking orders in her grease-stained shirt. Then he stood at the counter near the frozen cakes, scratching his ass until his order was ready. Taking the dog-dick-red tray and carrying it to the dining room, selecting the table across from Raymond's booth, he sat down, scooted the chair up until the table's edge rested against his gut, and unwrapped a double cheeseburger.

The chief took a bite, chewing with apparent gusto. Then he cut his eyes at Raymond and, his voice low, said, Sorry for the wait. C.W.'s been followin me around like a lost puppy.

What's up?

Bradley turned away, staring straight ahead. He ate a couple of fries and took a drink.

Tox screen won't be back for a while yet, but we know why Wayne died. His insides looked like he swallowed a live grenade.

Like the Harveston girl.

Yeah. Stomach and intestines in pieces. One kidney exploded. It looks like somebody gut-shot him with a goddam Howitzer. But since there ain't any entry or exit wounds, the coroner can't call it a gunshot. We don't know what the hell did it.

The chief ate. Raymond picked up a steak finger and dropped it back in the basket. The coroner's report told them nothing new.

I need to talk to Wayne's wife, Raymond said. She saw the whole thing, right?

Bradley munched fries and looked around, making sure no one was listening.

We interviewed her in the hospital the night it happened. They had to sedate her. She's home now, and I'm hopin she'll make more sense. If you care to show up at her house in about fifteen minutes, I'm headin over there as soon as I finish my lunch.

Sounds good. But what do you mean? What did she say the first time?

Bradley swallowed, his expression somewhere between amusement and disgust.

She claims John got shot by a gray-lookin man dressed in Old West cowboy clothes. Folks at the scene say the son of a bitch disappeared into thin air.

Raymond groaned. More to himself than to the chief, he muttered, Of *course* they did. Shit.

Bradley stopped to speak with an old-timer on his way out, so Raymond beat him to the Waynes' house and parked on the side of the road, his right tires in someone's ditch. He left the car running and tried to find a good radio station, sweating despite the air-conditioning. He had almost resigned himself to a country station playing oldies like Patsy Cline and Hank Williams when Bradley's cruiser passed him. It pulled into the Waynes' driveway. Raymond killed his engine and got out and walked down the street.

Bradley leaned against the radio car. If anybody asks, you just happened to show up when I did, and I decided to keep an eye on you.

You think that'll fly with C.W.?

No. But it's better than admittin I invited you.

They walked up the driveway and turned onto the little walk. Piles of recently cut grass lay at the concrete's edges. A black welcome mat sat before a screen door trimmed in white. The heavy wooden door beyond it was also white. Overhead, a porch light hung in its globular cover, the shadowed corpses of bugs visible at the bottom. Bradley opened the screen and rapped on the door. Soon they heard soft footfalls on creaky boards. The latches and locks clicked, and the door opened. Patricia Wayne stood there in her housecoat, hair frizzed, face pale, eyes as red as a radio tower beacon. She looked at Bradley and Raymond without surprise and snuffled twice, wiping her nose on her housecoat sleeve.

Hello, Bob, she said.

Bradley laid a hand on her shoulder. Pat. May we come in?

She looked at Raymond. Who's this?

Raymond stepped forward and extended his hand. I'm Raymond Turner, ma'am. A private detective.

His hand hung in the air. She didn't even look at it. The neighbors keep sendin their kids to mow my yard, but ain't nobody picked up the house, she said, turning on her heel.

Raymond lowered his hand and followed Bradley and Pat into the dim house. The wooden floor creaked under their feet. Crumpled tissues littered the place. Empty glasses and cans of Bud Light sat on every flat surface. Pat sat on a green couch and picked up a remote control and turned down the television. An old, comfortable-looking La-Z-Boy recliner sat on one side of the couch. On the other, a wooden end table held a lamp and more empty cans. The place smelled like sweat and beer and despair. Raymond recognized it because his own house had smelled precisely the same way for weeks after Marie's accident, for long months after her death, if you substituted the beer smell for hard liquor. He rubbed his wedding ring with his thumb. Every image here could have come from his life. The curtains pulled, as if sunlight might reveal your haunted visage. The thundering silence of someone's absence. The almost tangible emptiness on the sofa or their side of the bed. He still wandered his house expecting to run into Marie, still ached when he did not, so he knew what Pat Wayne felt in a personal and specific way. Yet the scents also reminded Raymond of every death house he had ever entered, the aromas of various foods assaulting the nostrils instead of tantalizing. Through a doorless entry in the far wall, half the kitchen table and some counter space had been covered with casserole dishes and bowls.

Bradley sat on the couch near Pat and patted her knee. I was hopin you had thought of somethin we missed the other night. Maybe somebody mad at John, or anything out of the ordinary from the last few months.

Pat took a battered pack of Marlboros and a lighter from her pocket. She offered them to both men, who declined. She lit one and blew a plume of smoke at the ceiling, where it wafted and disappeared like fog.

No. John didn't have enemies. He's punched out a few guys in bars over the years, but most of 'em were his best friends, and they hugged like a married couple the next day. The rest were folks we never saw again. Most people liked him just fine.

Raymond took out his pocket notebook and a pen and scribbled in his own shorthand.

Now, think hard, Bradley said. Did you see anything that might help us? Somethin the man said, somethin he wore, anything?

Pat took another long drag and eyed Bradley with something like contempt.

You mean other than what I already told you? That the son of a bitch looked like he stepped outta 1870 and didn't have a drop of color on him? How many guys like that can there be in this goddam town?

She looked hopeless, disinterested, as if none of this mattered. She dropped her cigarette in a beer can. It hissed as it went out. Yes, Raymond had seen rooms like this before, and not all of them had belonged to grief-stricken wives or to widowed private eyes. Some of them had housed plain old drunks who defined alcohol abuse as the failure to finish a drink. If Patricia Wayne had not been an alcoholic before her husband's death, she would be one soon if she did not snap out of her funk.

But Raymond was no therapist.

Ma'am, I hope you don't mind me askin, and I hope the chief will forgive me if I'm outta line, Raymond said. But you say this fella looked colorless. I'm not sure what that means.

Pat sighed and favored him with an expression that seemed half patience and half consternation.

It looked like somebody cut out a person from a black-and-white picture and pasted him into the world, she said. You seen them old pictures of cowboys with dust all over 'em or a Rebel soldier in his gray uniform? This wasn't like that. It was like the sun had bleached him out. Not just his clothes. His skin and his hair, too. Even them guns he shot my John with. All of him.

Raymond looked at Bradley and raised his eyebrows.

I can see usin makeup to hide your face, Bradley said, but I don't know why anybody would do that to his guns.

Pat turned to him and sat up straight.

It wasn't no fuckin *makeup*, Bob Bradley. It was just *him*. Hell, I don't know what you want from me. I done told you who killed John. Or what.

Raymond looked at Bradley. The chief's face reddened.

Now, Pat, you know that don't make sense. He turned to Raymond. She believes the Piney Woods Kid killed John.

Pat Wayne scoffed. Then she got up and walked down the hall, her footfalls thudding on the bare floor. Then the sounds of drawers opening and slamming shut, of Pat's muttering. Raymond and Bradley stood there, unsure what to do. Raymond shifted from foot to foot. When Pat came back, she carried a newspaper clipping in her hand. She walked over to Bradley, nearly bowling Raymond over, and thrust it in his face, her other hand on her hip.

You fellas wanna know what that motherfucker looked like? she said. His picture's right here. You can copy it onto your wanted posters or whatever the hell you use these days. I'm tellin you. The Piney Woods Kid killed my husband, and I don't care how it sounds.

Bradley did not take the clipping.

We already saw that, he said. But we need a *live* suspect to investigate, some motive. There just ain't no way to track down and question a fella that's been dead over a hundred years. And we can't find another connection between your husband and the folks in this picture. If there's anything else you might know—

Pat crossed her arms and scowled. I don't know anything else. And I don't know how to make that any plainer. Two folks in that picture are dead. It's your job to figure out the rest.

But we already looked—

I don't give a damn! she shouted. You just get out there and catch that piece of shit. Find a priest or call a goddam psychic. I don't care how you do it. Don't let him get away with this. She put her hands on Bradley's shoulders, her face inches from his, her voice low and deadly and sad. You hear me? *Don't you let him get away with it.*

Outside, they stopped beside Bradley's cruiser. Raymond put on his sunglasses and mopped his sweaty brow with his shirtsleeve.

She's right, Raymond said. We gotta be missin somethin.

I'm tellin you, we've gone at this from every angle. Bradley pulled out a handkerchief and wiped his face.

Everybody in this picture's a suspect *and* a potential victim. You got enough men to watch 'em all?

Not full time, and not if we're gonna keep catchin speeders and meth heads and such. You know C.W. He ain't gonna let us slack off.

They stood in silence for a while. Some masochist's lawn mower sputtered to life. A dog barked.

Finally, Raymond said, You got them case files?

Comin soon, Bradley said. I gotta make copies when nobody's around, which is practically never. If I don't, C.W. will know.

We need to talk to him about all this sooner or later. Probably sooner. I'm pretty sure Rennie's the only reason I haven't seen him since the hotel lobby, but that won't last.

Yeah. Bradley got into his cruiser. But I'd rather catch my nuts in a mousetrap than get him started again.

Raymond walked back to his car as the chief pulled away. He got in and started it up, the air blowing full blast. He leaned his head back against the seat and waited for it to cool off.

CHAPTER SEVENTEEN

September 8, 2016—Comanche, Texas

Raymond, LeBlanc, McDowell, and Chief Bradley stood in C.W. Roark's office at 9 a.m., watching the mayor's face turn an ever deeper shade of red.

Bradley had stopped by the hotel on the sixth, bearing files. Raymond and LeBlanc had spent that night and most of yesterday going through them and found nothing new. They still had no alternative logical explanation for the similarities between the two killings, for the mysterious witness testimony and Pat Wayne's certainty a ghost had gunned down her husband. The one conclusion they had reached—the diner would need to shut down. *Take away the prey and the hunting ground,* Raymond had said, *and maybe the killer moves on or makes a mistake.* Still, they had nothing to give Roark but their fears and suppositions.

When Bradley escorted them into the office, the mayor had, to his credit, tried to stay calm and treat the agency with courtesy. Now you could practically see smoke rising from the man's ears. Roark stood behind his battered desk, papers falling off and drifting to the floor, and looked at Raymond, LeBlanc, and McDowell with a mixture of anger and disappointment, a strict parent regarding a child who has broken all the windows in the house. Bradley kept shifting from foot to foot and clearing his throat, but C.W. Roark did not intimidate Raymond. McDowell appeared to be thinking about something else entirely, and LeBlanc towered over them all, his face an unreadable mask.

Let me get this straight, Bob, Roark said. You've been workin with them after I ordered you not to. And you want me to shut down my restaurant because Pat Wayne believes a ghost shot her husband.

I didn't say that, Bradley protested. I said I ran into Mr. Turner outside Pat Wayne's house and let him sit in. I figured you'd like that better than if he just waited till I left and talked to her alone.

Roark glared at Raymond. You should have locked him up like I told you to. Mr. Turner is not part of the Comanche PD. I shouldn't have to remind you of that, since you run the place.

Look, I got a half dozen deputies and three shifts to cover. Think about the logistics here. Bradley ticked off the numbers on his fingers. Red Thornapple. Sue McCorkle. Joyce Johnstone. Adam Garner. And you, Rennie, and Will. That's seven possible targets. Then there's the rest of the town, which might go to pot while we're sittin on your house, waitin to see whether some freak dressed like a gunfighter shows up. We need help. You think the state patrol would commit any manpower here when we got no real suspects except a guy that's been dead for 130 years? And would you want the Staties here anyway, with the Pow Wow and all?

Roark sat down and rubbed his temples as if the conversation had given him a headache. Perhaps it had.

Bradley looked at Raymond and shrugged. They had revealed their information and made their pitch. Bradley had promised to keep the agency in the loop, no matter what, but things would be easier if Roark listened to reason.

The mayor leaned back in his chair and looked at Raymond, his upper lip curled.

Go home, Raymond. This clusterfuck don't need your help to get worse.

But before anyone could move, a man burst through the door, the mayor's secretary close behind, saying, You come back here. He's busy.

I don't give a rat's ass, the newcomer growled. This is a goddam First Amendment issue.

He stopped short when he saw the office filled with people and looked at them as if they were zoo animals that had somehow wandered into his living room. The man appeared to be in his early forties and stood perhaps five feet, eight inches, a bit overweight for his height, suggesting a white-collar job and too much fast food. His red hair was parted to one side, but the heat and his sweat made it look like a bad toupee. It matched a three-day scruff of reddish beard. A sweat-stained white shirt, an ugly paisley tie, loosened, and a pair of blue jeans suggested he might have gotten dressed three days ago, perhaps in the dark. In his shirt pocket, a small spiral-bound notebook and a pen, both of which he took out.

Might as well let him in, Janey, Roark said. Hell, everybody else in town is already here.

Janey retreated as the disheveled newcomer shouldered his way past Raymond and Bradley, saying, I got your voicemail.

Look— Roark said.

You're puttin money ahead of people's lives, and the goddam Constitution, too. Or am I wrong? It sounded like you're threatenin to cut me outta the loop if I print any more stories about the murders.

Roark glanced at his guests. He fidgeted, drumming his fingers on his desk.

I never said that, Red.

I can't give you any information if I can't trust you is what you said. Jesus, C.W., your name's on that list, too.

Roark stood up again. I know that, damn it. But if you call this nut a serial killer, half this town will hightail it outta here, and our only tourist dollars will come from sicko murder groupies and ghost chasers. Besides, we got two dead. That ain't serial murder.

Accordin to the FBI, it is, Thornapple said. Bob can tell you the definition if you ain't looked it up.

He's right, Bradley said.

Am I the only one here who cares about this town? Roark said.

Thornapple said something about freedom of the press and the public's right to know, but Raymond was not listening. Lorena Harveston and John Wayne, both dead. C.W. Roark and his son, Will, who was, what, seventeen years old? Red Thornapple, newspaperman. Sue McCorkle, a housewife and mother. Joyce Johnstone, a law-office secretary. And Adam Garner, a long-haul trucker. According to Bradley, Garner would probably be gone another week, but he ate at the diner several times a month, so once he came back, he would be a prime target. The rest were already in town. So many people to watch, investigate, protect, or avenge. And still, C.W. stood there blustering, as if they were planning a public-relations attack campaign to destroy Comanche's reputation. Somebody needed to grab him by his lapels and yank him across the desk and shout in his face that as long as people were dying, nobody gave a shit about his beautification projects or where you could shop.

God, Raymond needed a drink. Maybe a dozen.

In all the years I've known you, Thornapple said, I never thought you'd piss on the First Amendment, especially with your own ass in the sling.

Well, unlike you, I ain't just worried about my own ass, Roark said. The town's economy is at stake.

You think I'm worried about my paper? Thornapple cried. Goddam it, I already got all the circulation I'm ever gonna get. But it's my job to tell those people the truth, not get you their votes. Or are you just worried about your diner?

Roark came around his desk, ready to deck the much smaller Red Thornapple. The chief grabbed Roark, while LeBlanc bear-hugged Thornapple from behind and pulled him away. Raymond stood between them, his arms outstretched like a referee trying to hold back two fighters until the opening bell. Janey the secretary pressed herself against the wall, her face as white as a cotton ball, while McDowell leaned in a corner, hands pressed to her temples. *All their shit is hittin her like a tidal wave.*

After a moment, Roark shook loose from Bradley and walked back around his desk. He sat down, the leather chair creaking, and slammed one fist on his desk. LeBlanc put Thornapple down. The newspaperman shook his head in disgust.

All right, Raymond said. If you two are through, we need to figure out what to do here.

You ain't in this, Roark said.

Raymond started to reply, but McDowell touched his arm and shook her head, so he said nothing.

Bradley edged past Raymond and LeBlanc and put his hands on Red Thornapple's shoulders and looked him in the eye.

I ain't askin you to kill any story. But I'm hopin you'll sit on it a while. C.W.'s right about some things. If you start talkin *serial killer* this and *Piney Woods Kid* that, we'll have all the TV reporters, half-ass bloggers, and conspiracy nuts in the Southwest hangin off every lamppost and tree limb in town. Give us some time.

Thornapple looked hard at the chief. It seemed he might tell Bradley to go to hell. But then he took a deep breath and exhaled.

I can't hold off forever. A week, ten days, tops. After that, I tell people what I know. And if there's another killin, all bets are off.

Bradley looked at Roark. That sounds fair to me. How about you, C.W.?

Roark frowned and flapped a hand at them. Why ask me? I'm only the goddam mayor.

As he talked, Rennie appeared in the doorway, wearing a sea-green skirt and blouse, her hair in a bun. She stepped past them all and stood in front of her husband, who groaned.

Oh, great. Fine. Now we're bringin people in off the street to tell me how to do my job.

Raymond coughed. The chief held up his hands in surrender. LeBlanc looked away.

Rennie put her hands on her hips. Ain't this a meetin of the minds, she said.

We're a little busy here, C.W. said. Whatever it is, it can wait till I get home.

Seems like every time I walk into a room, you're yellin at my brother, she said. So let me save you some wear on your ulcer. Bob and his department will work with Raymond.

That ain't your call.

Maybe you're willin to play Russian roulette with your life, but you won't do it with our son's. He's a descendant, too. Or did you forget that while you were chasin tourist nickels?

Roark's face reddened again. He looked murderous, as if he might reach across the desk and backhand her.

Don't you dare, Raymond thought.

The police should handle town business, C.W. said. There's more at stake here than just us.

Rennie walked around the desk and took his hand and patted it, like a mother comforting a small child. I know there is. But Ray and Darrell ain't the FBI. I want you to let him do what he does.

Why would I? After all he's done to you?

Because I'm askin it. And because we gotta do anything we can to keep Will safe.

Roark looked into her eyes. He seemed to deflate. Then he turned to Raymond, LeBlanc, and McDowell as he restacked some papers on his desk.

Fine. I'm done fightin this. But if y'all make things worse, it's on your heads, not mine.

Then he stood up and walked out of the office, bumping Raymond on the way out. He did not excuse himself. Janey the secretary trailed after him, waving some papers he needed to sign. He ignored her. They turned the corner.

Everyone stood in the office, unsure of what to do.

Ray, Rennie said, turning to him. Find this son of a bitch. Keep my family safe.

She hugged him. He put his arms around her and closed his eyes and kissed the top of her head. She let go, turned on her heel, and walked out, leaving Bradley, Thornapple, Raymond, LeBlanc, and McDowell standing in the mayor's office.

The phone rang. Bradley glanced at it and then at Janey's empty desk. He picked up the receiver.

Mayor's office, he said, opening a drawer and taking out a pen and notepad.

Raymond and LeBlanc followed McDowell out of the room.

Who the hell were those folks? Red Thornapple said.

For three days, Raymond, LeBlanc, and McDowell poked around, interviewing witnesses. Those who seemed most credible had seen nothing at all.

Others claimed to have witnessed events that failed to match the cases' details. One man said the Kid rode a fiery horse. He was either lying or drunk, possibly both. A woman stated she had seen the Kid's Comanche companion, but nobody else had.

As for those who had run into the parking lot just before or after John Wayne's death, their accounts matched almost perfectly, a real oddity with eyewitnesses: a gray-looking fellow in old gunfighter clothes had thrown down on Wayne, who had flown backward. They all claimed to have heard a gunshot but had no theories as to why the body had been unmarked.

Roark avoided Raymond's group, and they saw little of Bradley, who had apparently decided distance might be necessary for a while. No one else got shot, perhaps because Bradley had, with the mayor's grudging approval, ordered the diner closed until further notice. Bright yellow crime scene tape bordered the lot and the buildings, while patrol cars swept the area to run off curious citizens and kids taking a break from *cruising the Drag*, local teenage parlance for driving back and forth on Central Avenue. In the evenings, Raymond, LeBlanc, and McDowell ate restaurant food and drank store-bought sweet tea from gallon jugs.

But on the third day, as Raymond lay in his room dozing under the air conditioner, his cellphone buzzed. He sat up and rubbed his eyes.

Then he picked up the phone from the bedside table and punched the Accept button.

Turner, he yawned.

You guys have really stepped in it, Jacob Frost said.

Raymond's head ached. The sunlight streaming through the window sent sharp slivers of pain into his skull. Perhaps a migraine.

Professor, he said. You got somethin?

Frost sounded both excited and worried. I've been working genealogy websites and looking up records. As far as I can tell, everybody mentioned in that article falls in the direct line of descent from the men who killed the Piney Woods Kid or handled his body on the night he died. Even that newspaper guy, Thornapple. If I've counted back through the generations correctly, his great-great-uncle P.D. ran the depot that night. P.D. Thornapple would have been responsible for storing the body.

Raymond yawned. Yeah. That matches what we've found here. Our killer's obsessed with the Kid. Just when I thought I'd seen every brand of crazy.

Look, now that we know there's a connection to the local legends, maybe I can get somebody to cover my classes for a couple of weeks.

Sounds great. We need all the help we can get.

Raymond hung up. Frost seemed far too eager to fly halfway across the country just to piddle around in the county courthouse archives, but they really did need help. In a town this small, the citizenry would not need press leaks to know what was happening and to whom. And word of mouth worked both ways. He had not even looked at a copy of Thornapple's little paper and had said little to Bradley since leaving the mayor's office, but he knew C.W. wanted the diner open again. The Roarks were losing income every hour.

Raymond dialed Bob Bradley's number.

Silky and Morlon Redheart lived in a small ranch-style house on Highway 67 near Hasse. The city boy in Raymond pissed and moaned about how Comanche rolled up its sidewalks at nine o'clock every night, but he had to admit the area had its attractions: the variety of trees and landscapes, which reminded him of southeast Louisiana; how a new house might be built on a run-down lot with two or three cars rusting in the yard, or the way a brand-new Lexus might be parked in the driveway of a tumbledown shack; the little café up by the square with the excellent coffee and pie; and, of course, the Depot Diner, which had the best hamburgers he had ever eaten, plus some damn good chicken fajitas.

Bob Bradley turned his cruiser into the Redhearts' long gravel drive-way, Raymond in the passenger seat, gauging the height of the pecan trees growing on either side. The yard had been cut recently, the grass a uniform two inches. The trees threw angular shadows on the shingled roof. A silver pickup sat in the carport, a fiery red Toyota Camry on the lawn. A dog the approximate size of a horse lounged on the porch near two rocking chairs and a side table piled high with paperback books. Bradley killed the engine, and they got out. Birds chattered in the trees. A squirrel scampered across the yard, an old and dusty-looking pecan in its mouth. The dog raised his ears and watched it but did not pursue. He regarded Raymond and Bradley with open curiosity, muzzle on his paws. His tail thumped the porch boards.

Raymond and Bradley climbed the two rickety wooden steps and crossed the porch, the splintered boards creaking. Raymond must have looked worried because Bradley winked at him and said, She's solider than she looks. Or sounds.

The chief pulled open the screen, the hinges squealing like an old car's worn brakes, and rapped on the faded red door. Behind them, cicadas' electric hums filled the air, setting Raymond's teeth on edge. The sound of bugs, the absence of car horns and streetcar rumblings and motorcycles tearing down the streets—it took him back to Marie, as so many things did. Before her accident, they used to stroll along the Riverwalk and talk about what they would do after he retired, where they might go. In one of their favorite scenarios, they would buy a little cabin overlooking a bayou, where they would spend their evenings drinking sweet tea on a screened-in porch, watching the water flow, spotting the turtles and the fish and the occasional gator breaking water. Perhaps they would hold hands, side by side on their porch swing, and breathe the fresh air, let the day's heat or cold settle into their bones, and listen to the birds, the buzzing mosquitoes, the croaking frogs, the cacophony of the evening rising around them like an orchestra, the whole world a stage, the play just for them.

His breath hitched as if he were about to burst into tears. Marie had ambushed him again, jumping out from the corners of his memory. He turned his head and pressed a hand into his eyes, willing the emotions away. He had not thought of their little bayou dream since her death. It came to him now like a spirit someone careless and stupid had evoked.

You okay? Bradley said.

Yeah. Raymond cleared his throat. Heavy footsteps thudded toward them. He glanced at Bradley, who was digging a pinky finger into his ear canal and snorting. His eyes were red and watery. What's the matter with you?

Allergies. I stop up like this every time I come out here. All this damn mesquite.

You live in Texas, and you're allergic to mesquite?

Yeah. I reckon I got a taste for irony.

Silky Redheart opened the door. She had taken down her braids, her coarse hair flowing past her waist. She wore a deep blue muumuu and house shoes. Her face looked as blank as a raw concrete wall. As they squeezed past her, Raymond's chest knocked against the enormity of her breasts, which bounced like pudding-filled balloons. Silky did not seem to notice or care. The house smelled of onions, cabbage, and frying meat, a not unpleasant aroma that made Raymond's stomach rumble. He had not eaten lunch and wished for a diner-style chiliburger.

Inside, Silky turned right and disappeared through a closed door, where she stomped around, rattling pots and pans and scraping something that sounded like a spatula on a cast-iron skillet. Raymond's stomach gurgled again. Before them lay the Redhearts' den. A deep brown leather couch faced a flat-screen television mounted on the far wall. Morlon Redheart sat watching TV, only the back of his head and his broad shoulders visible, his hair straight and free. A jet-black cat damn near as big as a bear cub lay on one of the couch's arms. Did they feed their pets growth hormones? A recliner sat next to the couch. The walls had been painted a mélange of deep summer colors. Potted plants grew in each corner. A concrete fireplace dominated the left-hand wall, the blackened hearth clean and swept. Almost straight across from the front door, a dark hallway led deeper into the house. Bradley and Raymond walked around the couch and faced Morlon Redheart, who glanced at them and then resumed watching a program in which four or five blustery talking heads debated the relative merits of college football teams. Redheart was drinking a cold bottle of beer.

What I wouldn't give for one of those.

Morlon, said Bradley.

Chief, Redheart said. You gonna let us open?

Can't do it. We need your help on somethin.

Redheart picked up the remote control. He turned off the TV and nodded at the couch. Bradley took a seat. Raymond remained standing.

Silky offer you boys anything to drink? Morlon asked.

We're good, Bradley replied. We won't take up much of your time.

Suit yourself.

Did Lorena Harveston and Johnny Wayne eat with y'all much?

Silky appeared and handed Raymond an opened bottle of beer. He took it out of instinct and then stared at it like it was an alien artifact. *Shit.* Beads of moisture had already formed on its neck. As he watched, one trickled down the surface and onto his hand. Like the bottle itself, the condensation felt ice-cold. Perhaps an eighth inch of head inside. *Don't take so much as a sip. Don't you dare.*

The Harveston gal came in maybe once every week or ten days, I believe, Redheart said. I seen Wayne more than that. Reckon his wife ain't much of a cook. They might have stopped by after we went home sometimes. You'd have to ask the employees.

Bradley nodded. All right. How much do the rest of these folks eat with you?

He handed Redheart the article. Redheart took it and studied it. Then he sighed and handed it back to Bradley, who folded it up.

I'd estimate at least once a week. Adam Garner eats breakfast every day when he's in town. I remember the day they took this picture. They tipped Silky enough to get her nails done in Fort Worth.

Raymond gripped the beer in his hand. *Can't give it back now that I took it. That would be rude. But I can't drink it. I can't. Don't drink it, you asshole.*

They're all in danger, the chief said. We need your help to keep 'em away from the diner until we catch the killer.

Redheart leaned forward, elbows on knees. How? Am I supposed to run off my own customers or what?

We're keepin your place closed till we can contact everybody in that article. After that, you can open, but we're gonna have somebody sittin on your place day and night. Until we get evidence to the contrary, we gotta assume your parkin lot is this sumbitch's huntin ground.

I still don't see what you want me to do.

When these folks come in, call the station. In case the deputy on duty misses 'em. That's it.

Redheart sat back and relaxed. I reckon we can do that much, even if the mayor has a fit.

The aromas from the kitchen grew thicker. Raymond half expected a fog to roll in. Redheart turned on the television again and belched. He did not ask Bradley and Raymond to stay for supper. On their way to the car, Raymond poured out the beer.

Raymond pulled into the hotel parking lot and left the engine running. He took out his phone and dialed Frost's office. The question he was about to ask made him feel like an asshole.

Frost picked up on the second ring. Raymond took a deep breath.

How do you fight a ghost?

Who is this? asked Frost. You could practically hear his smile.

I'm serious. We got some weird shit goin down here. I'm startin to put more stock in the theory that our guy might believe he's a ghost. Wouldn't hurt to know what might scare him.

Wow. Okay. Well, these myths vary more than you'd think. Some legends say ghosts can't cross running water. Others feature ghost ships and ghost rafts and ghost canoes. Some say you can repel a ghost with cold iron or rock salt. Some claim that ghosts appear only at night, but there have been plenty of daytime sightings over the years. Then there's exorcism.

Raymond shuddered. He had seen that movie, and he had no desire to live it.

So basically, I gotta come up with some iron and rock salt or find myself a good priest.

I'll research Texas lore. Your man might be operating under a specific set of rules. Frost cleared his throat. Raymond could hear that smile again. Or maybe he's just trying to make people think he's a ghost, like in the cartoons.

Raymond groaned. God help us, I didn't even bring a talkin dog or any teenagers.

Well, I wouldn't recommend splitting up, just in case. What else? Ghosts are usually associated with unfinished business and a specific location. You've found the place and made a tenuous connection between the victims. I assume you've tried to find any descendants of the Piney Woods Kid, right? I can't find any records online.

Raymond turned up the air conditioner. Nobody's come forward.

Keep it in mind. Maybe there's a Hatfields-and-McCoys thing the locals aren't telling you about.

The folks that run the diner for my sister—they're descended from the Kid's Comanche runnin buddy, but I can't think of a reason why they'd sabotage the place they work. And neither of them's the killer. Their body types are all wrong, if the eyewitness accounts are anywhere close to accurate, and they were on duty when the Harveston girl died.

Well, you know the situation better than I do. In the meantime, I'd also suggest finding out what happened on the night the Kid died. We've heard the bones of the story, but we need the meat. I'll do that part. Sound good?

Yeah. Thanks, Jake.

Raymond hung up and killed the engine. He did not like where this case was going. All roads led back to the diner and that storage building, and McDowell's spell had frightened Raymond worse than he let on. Not just the trance—her goddam eyes had bled. She had talked as if something terrible were whispering in her ear.

He opened the car door and stepped into the heat, wishing he had a gallon of cold beer and one of those portable fans the tourists carried around the Quarter.

CHAPTER EIGHTEEN

September 11, 2016—Comanche, Texas

R aymond was supposed to meet Bradley in the afternoon. They had planned to visit Sue McCorkle. But that morning, Rennie called and asked Raymond to stop by her house. Before, she had asked him to stay away until C.W. calmed down, so something must have been bothering her a great deal. *It won't hurt to take Betsy along. She'll be better for Rennie than a fistful of Valium, and healthier, too.*

When Raymond asked LeBlanc to partner with Bradley for the day, he had shrugged.

Sure. If it's after lunch.

That was LeBlanc all over—still thinking with his stomach.

McDowell said nothing. She seemed distracted.

When the time came, they walked outside. Bradley waited in his cruiser. LeBlanc got in and waved as the radio car pulled away. Raymond fed Rennie's address into the rental's GPS and drove away. McDowell stared at the dashboard all the way over, grunting when spoken to. Her brow was wrinkled, her eyes distant.

What is it? Raymond asked.

She looked out her window and chewed on a fingernail. I've been thinkin about that building. I don't wanna go back there.

Raymond patted her hand. Don't worry about that now.

Still, he felt as if someone had squeezed his guts with a vise. If the investigation took them back to the diner, as it almost certainly would, McDowell would have to go. Whatever she had felt meant something. It was, in fact, the only thing resembling a lead they had found.

Raymond pulled into the Roarks' driveway ten minutes later.

The house stood two stories high, with a wraparound porch and healthy shrubs. The wood and brick were well tended, though a few shingles on the roof needed repair. A three-year-old silver Cadillac sat under the carport. Raymond had not seen the interior since a year or so before Marie died, but he would have bet his team and buggy it would look exactly the same. McDowell seemed to be studying the live oaks and pecan trees planted around the house, lending shade here, allowing a view there. Raymond killed the engine and got out. Sweat beaded on his forehead and upper lip. McDowell followed and slammed her door. Blackbirds flew out of a nearby oak.

They ascended the porch steps. At their feet, a woven doormat sported a scrolled letter *R*, merging the practical and the ornate. A black iron knocker hung on the door, while a button was mounted on the wall at waist level. Raymond ignored both and rapped with his knuckles.

Rennie answered. She had pulled her hair back into another skin-ripping bun. *Does she keep it that way all the time?* Raymond wondered. *It looks like somebody stapled it to her scalp.* She wore faded blue jeans and a button-down shirt that must have belonged to C.W., since it hung to her knees. She was sweating, the shirt clinging to her.

Been doin some housekeepin, she said. Mind the mess. They followed her into the house, which seemed dim after the afternoon sunlight. I'll get y'all some tea. She left them in the den.

I was wrong. Some things have changed.

Everything looked neat and clean and organized. Ceramic roosters perched on some of the flat surfaces. They were new. In other places stood photos and knickknacks that had been there ever since Raymond could remember. Framed cross-stitched proverbs and more photographs hung on the walls. Handmade quilts draped the furniture. Raymond sat on the couch. McDowell joined him, displacing several throw pillows bearing pictures of cows and horses. The air smelled of Pine-Sol and strong potpourri, an odor that lodged itself in the back of Raymond's throat. Rennie bustled in the kitchen, opening and closing the fridge. Ice clinked into glasses. Soon she returned, carrying three tall glasses of iced tea on a tray. She set her burden on the wooden coffee table. Someone had decoupaged a set of family photos in a spiral pattern. The table's distressed wood gave it the appearance of an antique, though Raymond doubted C.W. Roark would cotton to pasting photographs onto anything worth money.

A bowl of lemon slices accompanied the glasses. Rennie took one and squeezed it into her tea and stirred with one finger. Raymond picked up the other two glasses and held one out to McDowell, who took it and helped herself to some lemon, dropping the slice into the glass.

Thank you, Mrs. Roark, she said. It's sure enough hot out there.

Rennie smiled. You're welcome, honey. I try to be hospitable, even when somebody's comin to shit in my corn flakes. Y'all got bad news. I can see it in your faces.

McDowell took a long drink. She set the glass on the tray and wiped her mouth with the back of her hand.

That's awful good. I wish I could make tea that way. Mine's always too strong.

You gotta watch it while it steeps. If it sits there too long, you're sunk.

McDowell smiled and nodded as if this were the most enlightening advice in the world. Next, she asked Rennie about the coffee table decorations. Rennie spent fifteen minutes explaining her technique and what each picture meant. Then McDowell moved on to quilting and from that, to the general décor. Raymond sat back and marveled at the skillful way McDowell put Rennie at ease. It was not just the conversation. Anyone else who tried this tactic might have left with his balls in a sling. The rest could be chalked up to whatever mojo McDowell carried. Even Raymond felt happier.

But now it was time for business. When the conversation lagged, Raymond leaned forward and said, So far, we haven't found anything you don't already know. We won't give up, but in the meantime, stay away from the diner. You, but especially C.W. and Will. In fact, y'all might wanna take a little vacation. Just in case.

Rennie sighed. Then she stood up and walked to the far wall, where a group of framed pictures hung. She took a photo down and studied it, her expression full of love and fear. She ran her finger across the glass.

I can do a lot of things, but I can't make C.W. leave.

Then you should go. Take Will with you.

Folks will remember that. It's liable to cost C.W., come the election.

It'll cost him more if one of you dies.

He's my husband, Raymond. Would you have left Marie?

All the arguments he had prepared flew out of his head. No, he said.

That's what I thought. What if I keep 'em away from the diner? Will they be safe?

Raymond looked at McDowell, but he found no help there. She

had no more answers than he did. He turned back to Rennie.

Nobody's been killed anywhere else, but that could change.

Rennie sat back down and handed Raymond the photograph. It showed a bullet-headed boy of about seventeen. The lines of the jaw and the eyes were unmistakably C.W.'s. Raymond had not seen a photograph of Will since he started drinking. The kid looked more like a man now. Raymond passed the picture to McDowell. Then he walked around the coffee table, knelt in front of Rennie, and took one of her hands in his. Her lacquered nails bit into his wrist.

There's somethin else, he said. I got a man workin on ways to fight a ghost.

Rennie raised her eyebrows. Did you get heatstroke?

We're worried this killer thinks he's the Piney Woods Kid. We're just tryin to think like him—what he's liable to do, what might keep him away. It'll probably come to nothin, but this fella's covered his tracks like a professional hit man. Better, even. We'd rather be safe than sorry. I just wanted you to hear it from me.

Rennie looked at Raymond for a long time. Finally, she said, Do what you think is best.

Raymond squeezed her hand. There ain't no promises worth makin in my line of work. But I can tell you this. We're gonna do everything we can to keep you and yours safe. When you're steerin your family away from the diner, though, I'd advise you to keep our names out of it, and don't mention a ghost.

She frowned. I'm not stupid. Right now if you said the sky's blue, C.W. would swear it's green, just for spite.

Don't I know it.

She put her free hand on his cheek. You be careful. You're my favorite brother.

I'm your only brother.

Still and all.

As Raymond and McDowell climbed into their rental, a cherry-red Ford F-150 extended cab pulled up, the driver hidden behind windows so tinted they had to be illegal. McDowell glanced at Raymond.

He shrugged. Better get in. In case it's C.W. or somebody he sent.

McDowell got in the car. She likely wouldn't stay there if trouble started, but at least the first blush of it would miss her.

The Ford's driver's-side door opened. Will Roark stepped out. He wore blue jeans and a Toadies concert T-shirt. His too-long hair hung in his flawless face.

Shit-fire. You'd think a boy his age would have at least one pimple. Raymond approached, grinning.

Will smiled. Hey, Uncle Ray.

Look at you. You've done growed like a weed.

Raymond stuck out his hand. Will shook it and then, without letting go, pulled Raymond into a one-armed bro hug, patting his uncle on the back precisely two times. When he let go, Raymond took him by the shoulders and held him at arm's length. Will punched him in the stomach just hard enough for him to feel the impact. They laughed.

It's good to see you, the boy said. It's been way too long.

It sure has.

Will raised his chin at the car. Who's your friend?

Wanna meet her?

Will raised an arm and sniffed his pit. Maybe later. I just got outta P.E.

What are you doin home this time of day anyway?

Run outta deodorant. They let me run home to get some. Reckon bein the mayor's son ain't all bad.

I reckon not. When you gonna come out to New Orleans?

Will looked at the ground. He cleared his throat. Um. Well.

I know. Your daddy ain't gonna let you near me. Still, the invitation's open. House has been too empty since your aunt Marie passed.

A pained expression crossed the boy's face. I'm real sorry about that. I wish I'd got to spend more time with her.

We would have liked that, too, son. It was nobody's fault. We lived in different states. It's hard when you're that far away.

Yeah. Well. Anyway.

Raymond squeezed Will's shoulder. I reckon I better let you get on, before the school sends out a search party. Maybe we can get lunch or somethin before I leave.

Will scowled. Yeah. If I can get away from Daddy. Y'all gonna find this killer or what?

That's the plan.

Well, be careful. You're my favorite uncle.

I'm your only uncle.

Like I said.

After Will had walked on and Raymond had climbed into the car, McDowell said, So. That's your nephew.

Yep. He's gonna break some hearts, if we don't let him get killed.

McDowell took Raymond's hand. Calm flooded him. His heartbeat slowed.

Come on, she said. Ain't no percentage in sittin here all day.

Ten minutes after leaving, Raymond and McDowell pulled into Joyce Johnstone's drive on Goodson Street. They had passed a sign for the Comanche Airport, which made Raymond laugh and wonder aloud if a good-sized meadow with a dirt track qualified as an airport in these parts. McDowell told him to stop being such a city boy, but sometimes he could not help himself. He missed New Orleans.

Johnstone's house looked about like what he expected of a Comanche secretary—a one-story crackerbox-shaped place with bare spots in the yard, an oil-stained carport and cracked concrete driveway, peeling paint, and three or four emaciated trees. He got out of the car and shut the door and strode up the driveway. McDowell stood to his left as he knocked. Crickets chirped in the yard. Overhead, birds bickered like old married couples. He knocked again.

They stood there a bit longer before Raymond said, Ain't nobody home. Maybe Bradley knows where else we can look.

LeBlanc and Bradley pulled into Sue McCorkle's driveway just as the lady in question stepped outside. She looked to be fifty years old and wore cutoff shorts that might have been melted on. Her tight shirt's neckline plunged to reveal breasts roughly the size of honeydew melons. She watched the men as they rolled up behind her gray Ford Taurus. Bradley killed the engine. LeBlanc let out a low-pitched whistle.

Yeah, Bradley said. She dresses like that all the time. Seems to think she's thirty years younger.

That don't bother me, LeBlanc said, staring at her cleavage, which could probably be seen from space. It's the way she's watchin us. That's a woman confident in her charms.

You sure you never met her before?

They got out. McCorkle leaned against her carport wall, thumbs tucked into her Daisy Dukes. Her skin was wrinkled and leathery. Too many sessions in the tanning bed. Too many days in a bass boat using baby oil for sunscreen. And yet she exuded sensuality in the cock of her hips, the pouty grin.

Quit it, LeBlanc thought.

She looked him over.

My, my. If I knew you boys was hirin somebody like this, I would have applied, too.

This here's Darrell LeBlanc, Bradley said. Him and his partners are consultin on a case.

The killins.

That's the one. We need to speak with you about it, and it's hotter out here than a snake's belly in July. Can we come in?

McCorkle winked at LeBlanc and opened the door. She swept her hand toward the house. LeBlanc imagined a plump spider waiting in the shadows while two flies buzzed into its web. He edged by McCorkle and stepped inside.

The door led into her den. A ratty sectional dominated the room, pointing toward a wobbly entertainment center that might have been rescued from a dumpster. An ancient Sylvania sat on it like a boulder, gray and blank save for numerous scratches gouged into its plastic shell. McCorkle sat on the couch and shooed away a tabby with a cataract in one eye. The last three inches of its tail were bare, as if shaved. LeBlanc grimaced.

Bradley sat, unmindful of the gray cat fur sticking to his pants. Sue McCorkle patted the other side of the couch and winked at LeBlanc.

No, ma'am, I'm good, he said. Been sittin all day.

This was a lie. Bradley pretended to stifle a yawn, but he was hiding a shit-eating grin. LeBlanc scratched his nose with his middle finger.

If Sue McCorkle knew what was happening, she gave no sign. Looking at LeBlanc, she said, Well, sugar, if you need someplace to lay down for a spell, you just come on over. I got a bed big enough even for you.

Bradley coughed hard, his face reddening. LeBlanc tried to keep his expression neutral. He refused to look at Bradley and could not bring himself to meet McCorkle's gaze, so he turned to the walls. They had once been painted a uniform off-white that had yellowed in places, especially around the baseboards. The cat had marked its territory well over the years, as had a series of smokers.

Now, Sue, you behave, Bradley said. We got serious business here.

She pretended to pout. Bob Bradley, you always were a party pooper.

LeBlanc studied a picture on the wall, one of those cheesy dogs-playing-poker numbers. He had seen a hundred of them in a hundred places, but here, subtle differences revealed themselves. All the dogs sported bright red erections, and their playing cards showed pictures of busty naked women and rock-hard penises the size of fence posts. LeBlanc turned away.

Bradley was saying, So. The murders.

McCorkle shook her head. That poor Harveston gal. So young. She ain't even been back in town that long.

Bradley reached into his shirt pocket and took out a photocopy of the *Warrior-Tribune* article. He handed it to McCorkle. She glanced at it and passed it back, wiping her hands on her shirt as if the paper were contaminated. She looked from Bradley to LeBlanc and back again, serious now.

You think somebody's after the folks in that article, she said.

Includin me.

I reckon it's occurred to you, too, Bradley said. You heard about them folks claimin a ghost shot Johnny Wayne?

Yeah.

Then you also heard it's supposed to be the Piney Woods Kid. Crazy as it sounds, the killer's playin dress-up and coverin himself with somethin gray. Maybe some kind of pancake makeup. Whatever it is, he looks the part, and we still don't know how he's killin folks. It's like they were shot, but there ain't a mark on 'em.

McCorkle stood up and paced, crossing her arms as if she were cold. She stopped in front of LeBlanc. Her eyes moist, she said, What do you think, mister?

LeBlanc hooked his thumbs in his pockets and tried to sound comforting.

You'd be safer someplace else. We can take you there.

McCorkle looked defiant. I've lived in this house thirty years. I reckon I'll live in it till they haul me out to Siloam.

It wouldn't be forever, Bradley said. Think of your boys. You still got the two at home, right?

She wiped a tear from her cheek. Yeah. My oldest joined the Marines, and my second oldest is takin classes up at Tarleton. But Johnny and Mack still live at home.

As LeBlanc wondered how old Johnny and Mack might be and what they made of that dog painting, Bradley said, Well, that no-account ex of yours won't help 'em if somethin happens to you. Your cousin still lives in Stephenville, right? McCorkle nodded. Then go stay with her until we get this sorted out. Spend time with your college boy. And when you're in Comanche, stay away from the Depot Diner.

McCorkle sniffled and nodded. All the flirtation had vanished. Now, she just seemed like a frightened middle-aged woman with far too much on her mind.

They pulled out of McCorkle's driveway five minutes later. Bradley turned up the air full blast. LeBlanc watched the house in the side mirror until they turned right at the first stop sign and headed down a narrow residential street with cars parked on the curb and trees overhanging the asphalt.

So, LeBlanc said. That wasn't so bad. One less for us to worry about.

Yep, said Bradley. Let's just hope that Adam Garner's home.

But Garner's rig was gone. They pulled into his empty drive anyway and spent two or three minutes banging on the door, but no one answered. Bradley cursed and went back to the car.

LeBlanc followed, pulling his sweat-soaked shirt away from his torso. *I've probably lost ten pounds in water weight this afternoon.* Back in the car, he said, Well, what now? Get on a CB? Dig up his cell number? Grab a cheeseburger and fries from the DQ?

Nope, nope, and nope. Gotta touch base with Red Thornapple and make sure he'd rather live than get a good picture for the *Warrior-Tribune.* You might as well get your people to meet us out there. He may be the hardest one to convince.

Bradley backed out of Garner's driveway, the tires crunching gravel. LeBlanc took out his cell and called Raymond.

The route to Red Thornapple's house took Raymond and McDowell north of town, and when they turned off the highway and saw the place, Raymond double-checked the address. A man running a once-a-week small-town newspaper should not live in a two-story home sitting on enough acres to cover downtown New Orleans, but Bradley's cruiser was parked near the house. Where did Thornapple get his money? Did it have anything to do with the killings? Maybe his ancestor P.D. had gotten some of the Piney Woods Kid's loot and passed it down over the generations. Or maybe someone in the family had gotten rich in the oil booms or the cattle industry or train robberies. Raymond pulled up beside Bradley's car and killed the engine. They traversed the concrete driveway and knocked on the front door.

Red Thornapple answered it, a bottle of Bud Light in one hand.

Howdy, he said, holding out his hand. Red Thornapple. Sorry I didn't introduce myself the other day.

Ray Turner, said Raymond, shaking his hand. This is Betsy McDowell.

Ma'am, I'd like to apologize to you twice over. My manners left me that day.

Don't worry about it, McDowell said. Mayor Roark seems to bring that out in folks.

Thornapple grinned. He surely does. Y'all come on in.

They followed Thornapple through the foyer and into a great room that might have been hosting a yard sale. Piles of books stood in the corners and on the end tables near a deep brown leather couch. A woman sat on the sofa, her back to Raymond, curly blond hair cascading over her shoulders and poofing a good six inches outward like something from a 1980s heavy metal video. Her feet rested on a thick wooden coffee table. An entertainment center sat against one wall, on which an enormous flat-screen television had been mounted. DVDs and

Blu-rays were piled on the center's top surface. Figurines and novelty plaques filled three curio cabinets against one wall. Six or eight piles of folded laundry had been stacked near a recliner that had seen its best days during the Ford administration. Bradley and LeBlanc sat in two straight-backed dining chairs, part of a set that had been brought in and fanned in a semicircle before the sofa and coffee table.

Y'all find the place all right? Bradley asked.

Yep, said Raymond. At first, I thought we took a wrong turn and wound up in Graceland.

Thornapple laughed. It ain't near that grand. He nodded at the woman on the couch. Raymond Turner, Betsy McDowell, this is Joyce Johnstone.

They shook hands all around. Except for that aging rock groupie hair, Johnstone appeared elegant and composed, her makeup flawless, her dress conservative and tasteful. *Like she takes dictation for Whitesnake or Guns N' Roses.* She had crooked white teeth and bright hazel eyes.

Red's opened his own branch of witness protection, Bradley said. I didn't know, or I would have saved y'all the trip to Joyce's house.

Thornapple sat next to Johnstone. He put an arm around her and pulled her close. She laid her head on his shoulder.

It's a little more than that, he said. We've been seein each other since that night at the diner.

Bradley looked surprised. Well, shut my mouth.

We've kept a low profile. You know how people talk. We didn't want 'em whisperin about us every time we went to town.

Now they're doin it anyway, Johnstone said. Because of the murders.

Well, it's good to know you're safe, Raymond said. We should all trade numbers.

I was just tellin 'em they ought to stay here until we catch this fella,

Bradley said.

Yeah, said Thornapple, frowning. Except I'm supposed to be workin the story.

And we don't intend to live like prisoners, Johnstone said.

Raymond gestured at the room. This hardly counts as a cell. Right now, this sumbitch is workin the diner grounds, but it's possible he'll break the pattern. You don't want to be around if he does. You got security here?

Alarm system, said Thornapple. Security cameras with a clear view of the grounds. Floodlights and motion detectors.

Standard, but better than nothin. Then I'd suggest followin the chief's advice. If you go anywhere, go together. That includes trips to and from work. Stay around as many people as possible. Then lock up tight when you get back. Call one of us if anything weird happens, and I mean anything. That sound okay to you, Chief?

It would sound better if they just left town.

Thornapple and Johnstone both shook their heads.

Can't do it, the newspaperman said.

Bradley sighed. Well, I can't make you. I'll have a car swing by every so often. And whatever you do, don't go to the goddam diner. Hell, stay outta the south part of town, period.

But— Thornapple began.

No, said Bradley. If I so much as hear a rumor you're within a mile of that place, I'll arrest you for bein hardheaded.

Thornapple looked at Johnstone. She shrugged. I reckon we can live with that, he said.

Johnstone kissed him on the cheek.

CHAPTER NINETEEN

September 13, 2016—Comanche, Texas

Adam Garner could barely keep his eyes open. He had slept ten hours over the last three days and wanted nothing more than a sandwich, a long piss, and fourteen hours in bed. And now, finally, he had almost reached home.

When Pat Wayne called him with the news of John's death, she had been in shock or hysterical or both, rambling about how a ghost shot John in the guts. Garner could not follow most of it and, in truth, could barely recall it now. He must have drifted off while she talked, remembering John in his high-school football uniform, on his couch with a beer in hand, at Cowboys Stadium when Dallas lost their first game there to the New York Goddam Giants back in '09. Garner had wanted to hightail it back to Comanche, but he had been driving through upstate New York on the way to Minneapolis. By the time he offloaded and headed southwest, he had missed the funeral. He called Pat and apologized, and then he phoned his boss, asking for another assignment. He needed time, just enough for the worst of his grief and anger to subside. Pat would need a good friend. He had picked up a load of electronics in Fargo and hauled it to Salt Lake City, and when that was done, he pushed on to Vegas and spent nearly a week at an off-Strip casino, playing poker and slots and drinking beer and watching the whole sad press of humanity rumble by. When he felt like he could look at Comanche without punching someone, he got in his truck and headed home.

Now, nearing his house in the rig's cab, he geared down and tugged on the wheel, every muscle in his arms and shoulders protesting. *Jesus God, I ain't never been so tired. Even my hair hurts.* He did not notice the squad car parked across the street and paid no attention when two deputies got out. As he killed the engine, removed his keys, and stumbled out of the truck, he did not hear them approach or when they called his name three times. Heading for his front door, trying to find the house key on his overloaded ring, Garner finally acknowledged the cops' presence when one of them tapped him on the shoulder.

He turned around, eyes bleary, bladder aching, and said, Huh?

He recognized one of the cops, a sawed-off little prick named Roen who had given him four speeding tickets over the years. *After that last one, I promised myself I'd break your little rat face if I ever caught you outta uniform, but here you are again, all dressed up. It's like you turn invisible or teleport to the moon as soon as you unbutton that black shirt. What the hell are you doin here at one thirty in the mornin?* The other cop, a Latino Garner had never seen before, stood a head taller than Roen and looked as if he could eat the little bastard for supper with room left over. But Adam Garner was bigger than both. His beer gut protruded well past his belt. His biceps were the size of country hams, his graying beard cascading down his chest so far that more than one truck stop hoochie had asked if he were one of those ZZ Top guys. Maybe that was why the little rat-faced cop kept glancing around, one hand hovering near his service weapon. Even the bigger guy looked like he would jump a mile in the air, if anybody said boo.

Now, lookahere, Garner said. I did thirty-five ever since I hit the city limits. And don't give me no bull about crossin the center line. I kept my eye on it all the way home.

Roen's hand rested on his service weapon's butt. Chief sent us to pick you up.

He grabbed Garner's arm.

The bigger cop held out one hand like he expected Garner to skip through a field of flowers with him. But Garner pulled away.

I ain't done nothin. Y'all got no right to drag me off my own porch unless you're chargin me with somethin.

We're takin you in to protective custody, said Roen.

Garner laughed. You? Protect me from what, bunny rabbits and rainbows?

The bigger cop pulled a can of pepper spray out of his belt. Garner stopped laughing.

If you try to use that on me, you're gonna get a pepper enema.

The man looked like he might try it anyway until Roen said, No. Put that up.

That made Garner stop and think. Roen had always exuded Little Cop Syndrome like stink off a landfill, the kind of guy who used the badge and gun to bully people who could have folded him up like a wallet. He never warned, always ticketed, and took every attempt at friendly small talk as disrespect. If a son of a bitch like that was trying to keep things calm, he must be under strict orders from the chief, and that could mean nothing good for Adam Garner.

The bigger cop put the spray back in his belt. Roen turned back to Garner and said, Look. The chief believes you might be in danger.

Garner sighed. Why don't you boys come in and let me take a piss before I gotta do it in public and get arrested?

The cops looked at each other. Then Roen said, Gotta be better than standin out here where any damn fool can shoot at us. But we're goin in first.

Adam Garner unlocked his door and stepped aside, bowing like a prince before a lady.

Bradley's bedside landline rang seven times before his wife elbowed him in the ribs hard enough to wake him. Helen muttered something about turning down the ringer and rolled over. He rubbed his eyes and grabbed the handset off the cradle.

Bradley, he said, stifling a yawn.

The voice of David Roen blasted out of the earpiece. Sorry to get you up, but I thought you'd wanna know Adam Garner came home.

All right. You told him the plan?

Yessir. He ain't exactly inclined.

Put him on.

Roen talked with someone, but Garner did not pick up for nearly a minute, during which time Bradley considered hanging up and letting the man take his chances. But Momma Bradley had raised her kids to finish their jobs and do them well, no matter the pay or the circumstance, so he waited as Helen snored beside him.

Finally, Garner's gruff voice said, Hello.

Mr. Garner. Officer Roen tells me you won't cooperate.

Well, now, he walked up on me when I was half dead. Plus, he won't explain why I'm supposed to go stay with Red Thornapple. It ain't like me and Red eat breakfast together.

I expect my officer mentioned our reasonin relates to the deaths at the diner. That would be a whale of an omission if he didn't.

He did. But I don't know what that has to do with me.

You knew the Harveston girl.

I spoke to her at the diner when they took our picture for that article. Some months back, she helped fix me up after I burned the shit outta my forearm changin my oil. That's how well I knew her.

And what about John Wayne?

Garner went silent for a bit. Then he said, We was good friends. Played ball together in high school. Worked on old hot rods when we could spare the time. Drinkin buddies. Garner's voice broke.

A second later, the big man was snorting and snuffling, the sound muffled as if he held the phone to his chest. A loud goose honk suggested he had blown his nose. Bradley waited.

Sorry, Garner said. I thought it was all out of my system. Don't reckon I can do much for Pat, cryin like a little girl every time I think about Johnny. I'd like to get hold of the sumbitch that killed him.

Bradley mustered all his sleep-deprived sympathy. I'm sorry for your loss. We think somebody's after the folks in Red's article.

Bradley told Garner as much of the story as he could, leaving out the ghost angle. He would not mock the man's grief.

When Bradley finished, Garner said, I got no plans to eat at the diner anytime soon. Not when I could probably look out the door and still see John's blood on the ground.

Bradley exhaled. Good, he said.

Did Pat tell you what she thinks about all this?

Bradley cleared his throat. Yeah. A lot of folks saw somethin weird.

A lot of folks think they've seen Bigfoot and flyin saucers, too. Don't make 'em right.

It sure don't.

I hope somebody's been out to check on Pat.

One of my deputies goes by there every couple days. As for you, it'd be best if you cleared out until all this blows over.

I'm too tired to run. And I ain't gonna hide out at Red's place either. If somebody wants to kill me, I got a little somethin for 'em in my gun cabinet.

Don't you do nothin stupid.

I'm not lookin for trouble. I'll be sittin right here until it's time to hit the road again. Good night, Chief.

Garner must have handed the phone back to Roen, who said hello again just as Bradley hung up. The chief slipped back under the covers and curled up. He would have to assign someone to patrol Garner's neighborhood, especially at night, until they closed the case. It would be a pain in his ass and his budget. But the CPD could hardly leave the man unprotected. With any luck, the killer would move on to somebody else's town or slip up, and if Turner's group caught the bastard, that would suit Bradley right down to the ground.

So thinking, he drifted off and dreamed of a ghostly face—haggard and soiled, stubbled and gray. It stared at him, unblinking, unmoving, its faded eyes mesmerizing. And when it finally opened its mouth, Bradley woke up screaming, pouring sweat. He turned on the bedside lamp and clutched his chest, his heart pounding, until Helen sat up beside him, one breast poking out of her nightgown. She watched him with eyes the size of silver dollars, her hands bunched in the bedclothes. When he finally found his voice, he patted her on the leg and told her to go back to sleep. It had just been a nightmare, one that would fade in the light of day.

The next morning, at Larry's Grill on West Grand Avenue, Raymond sat across from LeBlanc and McDowell, eating an omelet and drinking a cup of strong coffee, when his phone buzzed. He plucked it out and saw Frost's name on the readout.

Hello, Jake, he said.

A deep yawn from the other end. Morning.

You sound beat.

Sorry. I've been up all night researching the history of the Comanche Depot, and holy shit, did I find something.

Yeah? What?

Okay, so I've been using a couple of those public records search companies, right?

Raymond sipped coffee. Uh-huh.

Well, it took quite a bit of digging, but I found it, buried in a defunct Fort Worth paper from the late nineteenth century.

Found what?

An account of what happened to the Piney Woods Kid. That posse didn't just gun him down. They brought him to the Comanche Depot dead house. Then they fucking dismembered it. The body, not the building. They chopped it into bits.

Raymond's stomach flip-flopped. To LeBlanc and McDowell, he said, I gotta take this outside. LeBlanc nodded, looking puzzled.

Raymond stood and pushed his chair under the table. He walked out and leaned against the rough brick wall, took a deep breath, and said, I'm back. Who wrote that article—Stephen King?

The time period's closer to Poe, but I know what you mean.

Did it say what happened to the pieces?

No, but people saw the posse ride out that morning covered in gore.

Christ.

A lot of people believe blood is life. Look at Christian communion rites. Look at vampire lore. Even if those men hauled in tubs to catch the runoff, they would have almost certainly spilled some. If you've started to believe in ghosts, that might be enough to anchor one to the depot.

Raymond laughed without humor. I'm not ready to call in the Winchesters just yet. Did you turn up anything about a pair of boots? Maybe the Kid's guns or gun belt?

Several moments of silence elapsed before Frost asked, How did you know?

Oh, shit. Raymond shivered. Tell me.

The Kid's gore dripped all over them when that posse shot him. The people who ran the depot displayed them near the ticket window for years. Can you believe this shit? They talk about it in the paper like it's as normal as Sunday brunch.

What happened to the boots after that?

No idea.

Raymond thought about the stains on the old boots and gun belt in the storage building. About McDowell's reaction. About what she said—*this is a bad place*. He told Frost what they had seen.

Her eyes bled, Frost said. They actually bled, and you saw it?

I wish I hadn't. You said earlier they took the Kid's body to the dead house. What the hell's a dead house?

It's like a morgue. You often find them near older cemeteries. Some train depots from that period have one, since bodies were often transported by rail.

There's an old cemetery just a few blocks from the depot. We've passed it a couple of times. I didn't see anything like that.

Maybe it never had one, Frost said. Maybe it got torn down. Or maybe nineteenth-century Comanche just had the one.

You think the diner's storage building used to be a dead house?

I don't know what the hell I think. But it fits the narrative. It would be where the Kid's remains were desecrated. Plus, dead houses weren't exactly secure or sanitary by our standards. Rats, flies, and so forth could find their way in. If the storage building was a dead house, it probably saw a lot of corrupted remains. It's exactly the kind of place a ghost would haunt. And if your killer knows the building's history, it makes sense he'd focus on that location.

Raymond swallowed hard. Again, he felt like vomiting. They had stomped around in a bad place all right. And although Frost had no doctorate in criminal psychology, he was probably right. Somebody who wanted to be the Kid or his ghost, or sought revenge for whatever the hell, would know the history and home in on the diner. Plus, it fit the nut jobs' revenge theory of why the killer had come after the posse's descendants. But who in Comanche might hatch such an unnecessarily convoluted response to an obscure historical moment?

God, he needed a whiskey. Frost had cleared up some questions but raised even more.

Thanks, Raymond said. I'll be in touch.

He hung up and rubbed his temples. He wanted another cup of coffee and twelve Tylenol.

He walked back inside and sat down. Their waitress refilled his coffee. LeBlanc ordered a slice of apple pie. McDowell sat beside him, watching Raymond, her brow furrowed like a worried mother's. She fished in her purse and pulled out a bottle of Excedrin Migraine and handed it to Raymond. He opened the bottle and shook out three pills, not caring about the recommended dosage. He dry-swallowed them and dumped a couple of sugar packets in his coffee.

Finally, LeBlanc said, Well? You gonna tell us what he said, or do we gotta guess?

Raymond leaned over the table as far as he could and waved them in. They huddled, elbows on the table, and in hushed tones Raymond summarized his conversation with Frost. In the middle of the story, the waitress brought LeBlanc's pie. It sat untouched until Raymond finished. Then LeBlanc wolfed it down in three bites. When the server brought the check, Raymond paid it as McDowell and LeBlanc stood at the register behind him, silent. They exited the restaurant, Raymond leading them back to their rental. They got in, and he started the car but did not pull away from the curb.

Well, McDowell said. On the practical side, it sounds like our guy is doing what he thinks an angry spirit would do.

LeBlanc nodded, though Raymond suspected he would have agreed with McDowell if she had said Yankees had two heads.

If that's the practical side, Raymond said, I'd hate to hear the whacko perspective.

I'm more open to the idea of spirits than you are. Back home, I've felt some things I can't explain. Not just on the ghost tours they advertise to the out-of-towners, either. Things that happened, people that lived and died—they leave echoes, some piece of themselves and whatever they felt. Pride, anger, love, desperation, guilt. And if the emotions are still there, then how much of a stretch is it to believe somethin's generatin those feelings? We're probably dealin with a man—a sick one, a vicious one, but just a man. Still—what if it *is* somethin else?

LeBlanc just about nodded himself into a concussion. Better safe than sorry, he said.

They drove back to the hotel and went to their rooms. Raymond wanted to stake out the diner, now that all the descendants were accounted for. He did not know what else to do. But given nothing had happened in the daytime yet, he felt reasonably safe in lying down for an hour or two, just long enough to get rid of his headache. After that, he supposed they would have to organize watches. The CPD lacked manpower. The Turner Agency would have to take up the slack. And he would not send McDowell alone after what had happened to her in the storage building. In short, the group would have to split up.

Shit, he muttered. This is more like *Scooby-Doo* all the time.

LeBlanc, lying on his bed and watching *SportsCenter*, said, Huh?

I said, I should have stayed in New Orleans. Wake me up in two hours, unless somethin happens.

He lay on his bed and settled in as an anchorman rattled off statistics from a ball game Raymond had not seen and did not care about.

After LeBlanc woke him, Raymond went to the bathroom and splashed cool water on his face. He combed his hair. *Too much gray. I'm gettin old.* It seemed like fifty years since Marie had died, and if she saw him today, she might mistake him for his father. He needed a shave and a bottle of whiskey and a goddam bowl of gumbo, and in Comanche, he would likely find only the shave. He took a long piss and grabbed an empty water bottle for the stakeout. No telling when a man might need to relieve himself, and the diner sat too close to the main drag to go behind a tree. Another problem—they had only the one car, meaning that the off man would have to leave the other to the elements or sit in the hotel with no way to get anywhere. The other choice—beg Bradley to lend them a vehicle. He certainly could not ask Rennie and C.W.

Raymond dialed Bradley and asked.

Brett Riley

I know where we can get you a low-profile ride. I'll meet you at the diner, the chief said.

The grounds were still cordoned off with sawhorses and police tape. Bradley leaned against his cruiser, parked on the west side of Austin, directly across from the diner. Behind it sat an early '90s Ford Ranger, black and beaten to shit, covered in mud. The back bumper was missing, the bed filled with junk and garbage—rusty spare parts, at least three rimless tires, loose bottles and cans.

LeBlanc pulled up behind the Ranger and got out, looking over the truck with disdain. Raymond joined him.

It looks like a burned-out Chevy took a shit, and that shit built this truck, LeBlanc said.

The inside was in only marginally better shape. The seat covers were split, the padding puffing out. An overflowing ashtray had spilled a fine coating of black ash all over the gearshift and the emergency brake. Raymond winced. He hated smoke even worse than divorce cases.

Someone sat in the passenger seat of Bradley's radio car, a balding, wispy man who looked about as happy as a pit bull with the clap. Raymond nodded in the little man's direction and said, That gent's truck, I take it.

Bradley grinned. That's Officer Roen. The truck belongs to his ex-wife. She wanted to sell it for parts but didn't have a title, so she hauled it to his house in the middle of the night and dumped it in his driveway. Nobody would suspect it for a stakeout car.

That's for sure, Raymond said. Looks like somethin a hobo wouldn't bother pissin in.

Bradley tossed the keys to Raymond. If you're lookin to watch both sides at once, you ought to stay here. Otherwise I'd park in the lot. If you see or hear anything, give me a call, and I'll come runnin.

He walked away. Roen never looked at them. When Bradley got in, Roen turned to him and said something. Bradley shook his head and started the car. Roen faced forward again. The cruiser pulled away.

Raymond and LeBlanc watched it go.

I wish he'd arm us, Raymond said. What the devil are we gonna use if the killer shows up? Irony?

LeBlanc grinned. He led Raymond to the rental's trunk and opened it. Inside were two 20-gauge pump-action shotguns and two cartons of shells. Raymond raised his eyebrows.

Borrowed 'em from Thornapple while you was nappin, LeBlanc said.

Raymond whistled. Jesus. I bet he owns stock in Lockheed Martin.

Nah. I think Texans are legally required to stockpile shootin irons.

LeBlanc picked up one of the guns and loaded it and handed it to Raymond. He left the second one in the trunk and gave Raymond a box of shells. Raymond walked back to the Ranger and opened the door. He climbed in and set the gun on the seat, its barrel pointed toward the passenger door. The smell of stale cigarettes assaulted him, making his nose burn and his eyes water. The ashtray would not shut.

I hate to do another man's work, Raymond said, but we need to clean this thing up. I'm scared I'm gonna catch hepatitis.

Yeah. Mrs. Roen must have been a real peach.

LeBlanc left Raymond at the diner and drove to Thornapple's place. Joyce Johnstone was napping. You could hear her snoring all the way down the hall. Thornapple reddened.

She had a rough night, so she took off work early, the newspaper-man said. She's, uh, got a sinus problem. Anyway, the shells I gave you ought to get y'all started. You can pick up more at the Stephenville Walmart.

We really appreciate everything you're doin, LeBlanc said. You and Joyce both.

Woman snores like a lumberjack, but God help me, I love her.

When LeBlanc returned to the hotel, he left the guns and shells in the car. He looked at his watch—6 p.m., enough time for a nap before he relieved Raymond at eight. They had something planned that they had not cleared with Bradley.

He had barely closed his eyes when someone rapped on the door three times, sharp and staccato. LeBlanc groaned and sat up, rubbing his eyes. When he opened the door, McDowell stood there holding a couple of Cokes. LeBlanc blinked, feeling stupid and thick. For the first time since they had gotten off the plane in Dallas, he had been too busy to think about McDowell. She had been stuck in her room all day, watching talk shows or soap operas or God only knew what, subsisting off whatever crap she could find in the vending machines.

Hey, Betsy, he yawned. I was just layin down for a nap.

She stepped past him into the room. Mind if I join you? I've been lonesome all day.

She grabbed the remote and turned on the television. Then she jumped onto Raymond's bed and rolled onto her stomach, her bare feet near the pillows, her arms tucked underneath her head. LeBlanc shut the door and went back to his bed. He sat down, back against the headboard. McDowell turned to an episode of *Dr. Phil*. The host sat between a crying mother and her thirteen-year-old daughter, who, according to the graphic on screen, had become sexually active and drank alcohol.

McDowell looked at LeBlanc over her shoulder. Can you believe the shit this kid does? What were *you* doin when you were thirteen?

At that age, LeBlanc had been a head taller than most of his classmates and skinny. He endured nicknames like Slim and Treetop and Ichabod Crane—a gangly and clumsy kid who had the passion and brains for playing football and basketball but also tripped over his own feet. When he ran, he looked like a cartoon character, arms and legs akimbo, all knees and knobby elbows. Around sixteen, he began to gain weight. Exercise produced muscle mass, and some of what he ate actually stuck to his ribs. If his thirteen-year-old self could see him now, the boy would probably jump for joy.

But why go into all that? It was over.

I hung out with my friends and talked about girls all day. What about you?

McDowell turned onto her side. I don't remember. Sometimes it feels like I've been this age my whole life. I've always sensed what other people felt, so I could never really tell what was mine and what was theirs.

You ever try to turn it off?

It just gave me a headache. She rolled off the bed and sat beside him on his. You know, we've been here all this time, and we've hardly been alone.

God knows I've wanted to. But we ain't even had that dinner we talked about. I—

She shushed him, putting a finger over her lips. Just kiss me.

LeBlanc obliged. They explored each other, hips and breasts and inner thighs. Soon they fell sideways and fumbled with buttons and zippers. The air conditioner hummed along as Dr. Phil dispensed advice in the background.

CHAPTER TWENTY

September 13, 2016, Near Sunset—Comanche, Texas

Raymond sat in the Ranger's cab, the windows rolled down for the faint breeze. He had sweated through his clothes hours ago and had drunk most of his water. Now he opened a bag of jerky and ate a piece. Jerky made his teeth ache like a seldom-used muscle being exercised. He checked his watch—7:09. LeBlanc would arrive any minute. They would perform their little ritual. And then, finally, he could grab a decent cheeseburger—assuming Dairy Queen or Sonic stayed open after eight—take a long shower, and fall into bed. In Comanche, you could walk for a few miles in any direction and find yourself in raw woods. New Orleans had seldom felt so far away.

He checked his watch again. 7:12.

The diner, the storage building, the grounds, the train tracks, the road—all that possibility, yet nothing had happened all day. Several cars had passed, most of the drivers craning their necks to look at the police tape, but no one had stopped. No trains passed, if any ever did. A stray dog had meandered by, giving the storage building a wide berth, stopping long enough to raise its leg and piss on the diner's porch steps, and that had been the day's most interesting event. Raymond should have been glad. No killer meant no victim. The shotgun was propped stock down in the trashy passenger floorboard. It was good to have some protection, but in truth, a 20-gauge seemed a bit excessive. Up close, it would practically cut the killer in two.

Fifteen minutes and another piece of jerky later, their rental turned down Austin. Raymond got out, stretching his legs, stifling a yawn, thinking, not for the first time, how doing nothing could exhaust you as much as keeping busy. Then he reached back in and grabbed a book of matches from the console, plus the shotgun, just in case. LeBlanc and McDowell got out of the rental and shut their doors.

As they approached, Raymond said, I started to think y'all weren't comin.

Sorry, LeBlanc said, reddening. Lost track of time.

Did you, now? Y'all ready, or should I turn around for three minutes?

McDowell nodded, though she looked paler than usual. Her smile seemed forced.

LeBlanc cleared his throat and said, Let's get it done. Then he went to the trunk and opened it. He took out an orange gasoline can and shut the trunk. The three of them crossed the street and ducked under the police tape. Overhead, the setting sun and broken cloud cover sailed through a sky the color of raw salmon. They had perhaps ten minutes of daylight left—plenty of time, without interruptions. What they planned was pointless in a practical sense. McDowell wanted to do it, though, and they owed her that much. As they walked toward the storage building, gas sloshed in the can.

Darrell, did you bring supplies? Raymond said. I went through damn near everything today.

They're in the car. Don't you run off before I get 'em out, you hear?

Raymond and LeBlanc had pranked each other many times over

the years, but never on a stakeout. You could not leave a man in a car for twelve hours without water or food. It was probably against the Geneva Convention.

Between them, McDowell walked in silence, laser-focused on the storage building. Now she took LeBlanc's free hand. He squeezed it.

It's about time. They've been circlin each other like seventh graders at their first dance. Maybe now Darrell can stop daydreamin and get more work done.

But Raymond's cheerful thoughts faded as they neared the building. He could feel the place. Dread emanated from it and settled in his balls and made him want to dash for the nearest liquor store. Could LeBlanc feel it, too? And if they could sense it, then McDowell would probably do well to stay conscious. What had Frost said—that the place had been a way station for corpses and that men who hated the Piney Woods Kid had hacked him to pieces in there? This really was a bad place. And they had to go back inside.

They reached the door and stood in front of it, shoulder to shoulder, like desperados facing down a sheriff on some dusty thoroughfare. *God, I ain't never felt so squirrelly.* Raymond Turner lived in New Orleans, once home to a major slave market, now host to one of the nation's highest murder rates. He had stayed in cheap hotels that had probably seen their fair share of suicides, rapes, overdoses, and insanity and had walked into those places with little thought of their histories. But now, here in Comanche, Texas, his spine wanted to climb right out of his skin. Eating the shotgun's barrel seemed preferable to walking back inside. He glanced at McDowell, who had closed her eyes and seemed to be whispering to herself. Or praying. LeBlanc still held her hand.

It's gotta be locked. And we don't have the key this time. Maybe we can just go back—

McDowell opened her eyes and turned the knob. She pushed the door open and stepped across the threshold.

Goddam Mayberry cops. Can't even secure their crime scene.

LeBlanc cleared his throat again. Then they followed her in.

The gloom seemed even thicker than last time. McDowell circumnavigated the junk on the floor and pulled back the smoke-colored curtains on the nearest window. The waning sunlight was pale and weak. Dust motes undulated everywhere. Raymond shuddered. He already needed fresh air. He needed a bottle of whiskey. He needed to be outside. They could be standing on the very spot where the posse had dismembered the Kid, taking impotent revenge on his remains like ghouls.

Raymond froze. So did LeBlanc. But McDowell stepped across the scattered cans and furniture and boxes of paper goods and took the boots off the shelf, holding one in each hand by her thumbs and forefingers, the way one might carry a dead rat by the tail. She winced. Now that they knew what those dark stains were, Raymond understood how she felt.

She moved past him, saying, One of you boys will have to get that gun belt.

She stepped out of the dead house and into the fading day as LeBlanc set down the gas can and made his way to the shelf. He grabbed the gun belt and stepped back over, picked up the can, and stumbled out the door. Raymond gripped the shotgun and followed, half expecting a pale figure in frontier garb to waylay them all.

He shut the door. McDowell and LeBlanc piled the boots and gun belt on the ground. The sun dipped ever closer to the horizon. It was harder to see now than it had been when they walked across the lot, as if they had spent half an hour inside, waiting for someone to make the first move. Raymond stepped up to the objects. McDowell stood ten feet away, arms folded across her chest. She seemed tired, as if the effort of carrying those boots had exhausted her. Raymond looked at LeBlanc and nodded.

LeBlanc tilted the can over the boots and gun belt. Gasoline gurgled over them, turning the dark, stained leather nearly black. Raymond handed LeBlanc the shotgun and pulled his sweat-soaked shirt over his nose. He could not afford to get high on the fumes or pass out, not this close to the dead house. LeBlanc stepped back and put one arm around McDowell's shoulders. *I don't know how the Redhearts managed to dump all that shit in there without goin insane.* Raymond took a deep breath and let his shirt drop so he could use both hands. Then he struck a match, holding it in his left hand with the rest of the book still in his right.

Before Raymond could drop the match, McDowell cried out in misery and pain. Raymond turned. Her hands were pressed to her temples. Blood poured from her eyes.

LeBlanc recoiled.

Jesus fuckin Christ! he said. Ray?

Then, a concussive boom. In retrospect, Raymond would realize he had heard it in his mind, not with his ears.

Something struck his left hand. He screamed as his hand jerked. The match flew from his hand and sputtered out. He stumbled backward, dropping the matchbook and tripping over his own feet, falling hard on his ass, holding his injured hand against his body. It felt like someone had smashed it with a hammer. He held it up. It looked like the gnarled branch of an ancient and misshapen tree. He moaned. What had hit him?

And then he saw. Standing near the corner of the dead house, a pale man held an old-fashioned revolver in one hand as his other arm dangled at his side. His skin and garments were the color of desert hardpan. He wore a neckerchief and an old button-down shirt and torn jeans, tattered boots the mirror image of those lying in the puddle of gas, a low-slung gun belt the twin of the one on the ground. The revolver looked enormous, the bore like a cannon's. And as the sun dipped below the horizon, drenching the grounds in deepening shades of night, the man seemed to waver, as if he were an image on a badly made television.

He swam back into focus. Then he wavered again.

McDowell screamed.

The figure vanished. LeBlanc grabbed McDowell by the wrist and pulled her behind him. He raised his shotgun and panned it, eyes bugging.

Ray, what the fuck? LeBlanc shouted. Where the hell did he go?

Raymond could not answer. His teeth were still clenched in agony. He moaned as fire shot up his arm with every heartbeat, grunting as he pushed himself into a sitting position with his right hand. The left looked lumpy, deep purple.

He swallowed and croaked, You see anything?

Nothin, LeBlanc said. Raymond tried to flex his hand, and fresh contrails of agony pulsed all the way to his jaw. He shrieked and doubled over.

Okay, we're gettin the hell outta here right now, LeBlanc said.

He and McDowell ran to Raymond and grabbed him under the arms, hauling him to his feet. His stomach roiled. *All that jerky's gonna taste like shit the second time.* McDowell smoothed his hair back from his face, pasting it with his own sweat. She had turned a sickly mottled color, like old cheese.

I can stand, Raymond rasped.

Good, said LeBlanc. That sumbitch could be sightin in on us right now.

McDowell stepped away from them and picked up the matches.

Darrell, Raymond said.

Betsy, LeBlanc cried. What are you doin?

He let go of Raymond and raised the shotgun to his shoulder.

Raymond stumbled back a few paces, where he bent to one knee and tried not to pass out.

McDowell held the matchbook between her thumb and forefinger. She ripped a match out and tried to strike it, but her hands shook, and she kept dropping it, picking it up, dropping it again.

Dammit to hell, she muttered.

LeBlanc tried to see everywhere at once.

Not to put any more pressure on you, he said, but you need to hurry.

Shut *up*, Darrell! McDowell barked.

She tore out another match and struck it. This time it flared to life.

The pale figure materialized in front of them. He drew his revolver with blinding speed and fired. McDowell cried out and dropped the match, which extinguished itself as the matchbook flew out of her hands. Pieces of it rained everywhere.

Even though McDowell seemed unharmed, LeBlanc roared in anger and fired at the apparition, which was only five or six feet away.

Nothing happened.

LeBlanc grabbed McDowell's wrist and pulled her away from the boots. Her face, neck, and upper torso were covered in her own blood, all of it pouring from her eyes. Raymond stood, holding his injured hand against his abdomen, and together the three of them ran for the rental car. When Raymond looked back, the pale man was gone, but LeBlanc covered their retreat anyway, ejecting the spent shell and reloading.

They reached their car and jumped in, but before they could pull away, they found themselves boxed in by two Comanche police cars, red-and-blues rotating, sirens they had not even heard blaring in the night.

Bradley arrived just as Austin's streetlamps winked on. He took one look at Raymond's mangled hand and sent him to the emergency room with Deputy Roen. Five minutes later, as Bradley took LeBlanc's statement, C.W. Roark arrived, wearing a coat and tie and looking mad enough to chew glass. He barreled through the onlookers and ducked under the police tape, ignoring the deputies' protests.

Of course, the mayor spat, eyeing LeBlanc as he approached. Brushing past McDowell, he poked LeBlanc's chest with his index finger. I knew it was y'all. Who else would fire weapons inside the city limits and stick around until the police showed up? Even the goddam meth heads got more sense than that.

LeBlanc scowled. Stop pokin me, you dick, or I'll rip that finger off and feed it to you.

McDowell stepped between them as Roark said, You heard him threaten me, Bob. I want this half-assed Sam Spade arrested.

Yeah, Bradley said. And I saw you poke him, which is technically assault. I don't think we should bring charges against each other. We got bigger problems.

Roark glared at Bradley. You wanna be careful which side you pick.

What sides? Seems like we're all fryin in the same skillet. Listen to what the man has to say.

Roark stared a hole in Bradley, but the chief did not back down. Finally, the mayor turned to LeBlanc and said, Get on with it.

LeBlanc gritted his teeth. *Don't punch him. Don't punch him.*

He told Roark the story, sparing no detail, but might as well have saved his breath. The mayor's face filled with contempt, as if he were listening to a lunatic recount a fever dream.

So let me get this straight, he said. You don't think we're dealin with a psychopath or mass hysteria. You really believe you saw a ghost. And that it shot Raymond.

LeBlanc sighed and tried to stay calm. I don't know what I believe right now. I just can't explain what I saw. Ray's hand is proof somebody was here. And I shot the sumbitch at close range. With a shotgun. Ask your boys if they found any blood. I'm bettin they won't, unless it's Betsy's.

Uh-huh. Don't sound nuts in the least.

The chief's men kept well away from the boots and gun belt. LeBlanc pointed in the direction of the Dead House, which was how he had come to think of it—a proper noun, never just a storage building again.

Head over yonder, and look at the matches scattered everywhere. He shot the book right outta Betsy's hand.

You could have tore it up yourself.

LeBlanc spat. Fine. Maybe if you keep your head up your ass, nothin can put a bullet in your brain. You done with us, Chief?

Bradley nodded. Y'all go on and see about Raymond. I know where to find you if I need anything else.

LeBlanc and McDowell walked to the rental. They got in the car and pulled away. LeBlanc looked up the hospital on the GPS. Another of this hole-in-the-road town's many inconveniences—the hospital was five miles down Highway 16 toward De Leon. Someone had told him that, just a few years back, it had stood right across the street, but that would have been far too convenient for their particular brand of luck.

McDowell sat in silence, looking straight ahead, still pale. With all the blood drying on her face and neck, she looked like she had lost a fistfight. Hopefully she would be okay. They would need all their resources if they chose to stay after all this. Darrell LeBlanc felt like a man driving headlong toward an unseen cliff. He hoped he could brake in time.

The ER doctor nearly choked when he saw Raymond's X-rays. The metacarpals of the middle and ring fingers were shattered. Shards lay against intact bones. The trapezium, capitates, and hamates were dislodged. The injured fingers' proximal phalanges were unstable at best. It looked as if Raymond had been precisely struck a hundred times with a ball-peen hammer—or shot with a large-caliber bullet. Even the uninjured digits had swollen like overstuffed sausages. His ring finger puffed around his thick wedding band. The upper digit had turned deep purple.

We're gonna have to cut this ring off, the doctor said.

No, said Raymond.

If we don't, you're liable to lose the finger.

I don't give a shit.

Mr. Turner—

You try to cut it off and I'll rip out your balls by the roots. One-handed or not.

The doctor looked at LeBlanc, who frowned and held up one fin-ger—*Give us a minute or two here.* The doctor backed away.

Ray, said LeBlanc. Losin a finger over that ring is dumb.

Piss on you, Raymond croaked. He had turned pallid.

If I have to hold you down, I will. It ain't Marie. It's just a piece of metal.

No.

Please, said McDowell. She laid a hand on his shoulder. You can have the ring melted down and fixed.

Raymond locked eyes with her. They can't fix the engravin.

You really need that to feel what she wanted you to feel?

He held her gaze for several moments. The doctor stood back, saying nothing. Finally, Raymond turned away, tears in his eyes.

Get it over with, he said. The doctor moved forward.

As they drove back to the hotel, Raymond held the broken ring in his good hand. He had refused to let it go ever since they handed it to him.

Back at the hospital, the doctor had said, You'll need more than one surgery to repair all this damage, and probably some plates and screws. We should schedule you right away.

No thanks, Raymond said. I don't live here. Just make me a copy of the records and X-rays and whatnot. I'll take care of it in New Orleans.

The doctor protested, but he could not make Raymond check him-self in. They set the bones as best they could, gave Raymond a cast and some kind of pain reliever and a prescription for Percocet, and sent him on his way. At the hotel, Raymond tucked the misshapen ring in a pocket of his suitcase, refusing all help.

LeBlanc stood with his arms crossed. They had dropped Raymond's prescription off at a local pharmacy, barely making it before the place closed for the night. How long could Raymond focus with his bones shattered? What would happen if he used the painkillers? *I don't want to see him suffer, but I don't want to find him layin half dead under a tree again either. Hellfire.*

CHAPTER TWENTY-ONE

September 14, 2016—Comanche, Texas

When the pharmacy called, LeBlanc drove over and picked up the Percocet. Back in the room, he handed the bag to McDowell. She read the instructions and shook out a pill. Miserable and exhausted, Raymond watched her like the chicken watches the fox prowling about the coop, looking for an entryway.

McDowell held out the pill, but as Raymond reached for it, her hand closed over it. She put a hand on his shoulder and looked him in the eye.

You can't take more than the recommended dose, she said. And you gotta stop as soon as the pain does, no matter how hard it is.

Raymond's eyes watered. His voice low and quivering, he said, I know. Believe me. I don't wanna start in the first place.

You could always fly home. Get your surgery. We'll handle things from here.

He shook his head. We're already stretched thin. And I ain't leavin my sister.

So have the surgery in Texas. You can work through the pain after it's fixed.

No time. Somebody else could die any day. If I get hooked, you'll have to sober me up when this is over. Sorry, Darrell.

McDowell opened her hand. Raymond took the pill and looked at it for a long time. Then he turned to LeBlanc, trembling. *He's not just miserable. He's scared. He knows takin that pill could mean hittin the same rock bottom that nearly broke him before.* He sat beside Raymond and put an arm around him.

I know what I said when you were drinkin. But this is different. Your hand is wrecked. You can't sleep. You can barely think. I'll respect whatever decision you make, and we won't walk away if you take that thing.

A tear fell down Raymond's cheek. He nodded. Then he took the pill, chasing it with a plastic cup of water McDowell brought him. When it was done, he closed his eyes for a bit.

When he opened them again, McDowell said, You okay?

He tried to smile but couldn't quite pull it off. Good enough. I think it's time to call Frost. His ideas ain't theoretical anymore. Can y'all do it?

Sure, LeBlanc said. Get some rest.

Raymond lay back. Soon his breathing evened out. McDowell left to shower and change. When she returned, Raymond was snoring, the sound so buzz saw–loud that LeBlanc had to roll him over onto his side just to hear himself think.

LeBlanc and McDowell headed through the lobby to their car. She carried the pills in her pocket, just in case. LeBlanc drove them to Sonic, where they bought a few double cheeseburgers and brought them back to the room. LeBlanc put a burger in the mini-fridge for Raymond and laid out their own repast on the desk. They ate in silence, McDowell's face pale and drawn. LeBlanc finished his first burger before she had eaten half of hers. He took her hand.

Are we gonna talk about what happened? she asked.

LeBlanc wrapped up his second burger and stuffed it back in the sack. Sure.

Ray's left hand got blown to hell by a real live ghost.

Well, if it's a ghost, it ain't alive. But I take your meanin.

McDowell tried the burger again. She swallowed a couple of bites. LeBlanc took that cue and reopened his sandwich. He was chewing when McDowell said, What's worse is how mad it was. I felt like I'd stuck my head in a beehive. Just this angry buzz. No compassion, no love, no regret. No guilt. Nothin but pure rage.

LeBlanc had nothing to say. They did not need to parse the Kid's anger. They only had to look at Raymond's cast.

Someone rapped on the door. McDowell got up and looked out the peephole and then opened the door. Bradley entered, took off his hat, and said, He looks down for the count.

Percocet, LeBlanc said.

Bradley sat at the foot of Raymond's bed and said, Well, we're in a fine mess now.

McDowell turned her chair to face Bradley as LeBlanc asked, When were we ever in good shape?

Bradley ran his fingers through his thinning hair. When C.W. figured out what you were doin, he ordered one of the boys to confiscate the boots. He plans on displayin 'em in the diner durin the Pow Wow. You know what that is?

LeBlanc groaned. Ray told me. I didn't know C.W. was such a goddam fool. Don't he know he's puttin everybody at risk?

He don't believe in ghosts. Come to that, I don't either. But I don't aim to take any chances. If tryin to burn that shit flushed our man once, maybe it could happen again.

LeBlanc sat up straighter. You think you can get the boots outta evidence?

I'm the chief of police. If I can't do it, nobody can. The real question is how we're gonna live long enough to burn 'em.

We've got some ideas about that. We might have more if our folklore expert ever answers his phone. Say, how'd you explain the shotgun? Or us havin Roen's truck?

Bradley winked. Your shotgun found its way back into the Ranger, which was blocked off with squad cars by the time the mayor arrived. Far as I know, C.W. never noticed either of 'em.

McDowell shook her head. You boys, she said.

LeBlanc laid a hand on Bradley's shoulder. Know anybody with a reloadin press?

Later, a filled-to-bursting Walmart sack in one hand, LeBlanc knocked at the address Bradley had given him. A grizzled old man opened the door. This fellow had not shaved in at least three days, his graying stubble like a thin coating of frost. His gossamer white hair stood up in corkscrews.

Who the hell are you, and what the hell you want? he asked.

Name's Darrell LeBlanc. You Tidewater?

I ain't sayin shit until you tell me what you're doin here.

LeBlanc reached into the sack and pulled out a box of rock salt. If you're Ollie Tidewater, I want you to load this into some shotgun shells.

The old man scratched his head with long, yellowed fingernails. He looked LeBlanc up and down and shook his head.

You want to put rock salt into shotgun shells, he said. What are you, a nut?

Yeah. The kind that'll pay you.

The old man scratched his head again. Then he moved to the side, motioning LeBlanc into the house. LeBlanc stepped in, the old man's body odor curdling in his nostrils. He wiped his watering eyes and prayed Ollie Tidewater loaded a shell better than he groomed.

Back in Comanche, LeBlanc phoned Frost. The call went straight to voicemail. He tried three more times with the same result. *Hell and damnation.* LeBlanc showered, brushed his teeth, and crawled into bed. Drifting off to sleep, he thought, *Well, with the CPD combin over the diner, at least I don't have to spend all night in that nasty-ass Ranger.*

Raymond woke that afternoon feeling as if he had set his hand on fire and then stuck it in an industrial press. He pushed himself out of bed with his right hand, moaning. LeBlanc was eating a Sonic cheeseburger. It smelled fantastic. Raymond's stomach gurgled and cramped. He felt like vomiting from the pain, and yet he could not remember being this hungry since the agency's earliest days, before LeBlanc's time, when he sometimes sat alone for sixteen hours in a stakeout car.

Afternoon, sleepyhead, LeBlanc said. He put his sandwich on the side table and grabbed Raymond's pills, popping the top and shaking one out.

Raymond dry-swallowed it. Thanks, he said.

What did you do that for? We got Cokes, coffee, and a quart of orange juice.

I'd appreciate a glass of water. I think that pill stuck halfway down.

LeBlanc got up and grabbed a plastic cup from the dresser. He stepped around the corner into the bathroom. Water gurgled from the sink. LeBlanc returned and handed the water to Raymond, who drank it in one gulp.

I got you a couple burgers in the fridge, LeBlanc said. I can microwave 'em if you're hungry.

Raymond rubbed his eyes. Yeah. Just give me a minute to let this water settle. I only wanna taste it once.

LeBlanc poured Raymond some coffee from the little two-cup pot and set it on the side table. Then he plopped down on the bed and resumed eating. Light spilled from a crack in the curtains. Piles of dirty clothes lay in the corners. Soon someone would have to hit the laundromat on the other side of town. McDowell had gone once but had let them know she had not flown all the way to Texas to mother anybody. The coffee, strong and bitter, made Raymond's stomach roil. If only LeBlanc had bought some half-and-half. The injured hand sung, hitting the high notes with shattering volume. *Lord, let me get through this without losin the use of it. And help me keep a handle on the drugs.* On television, one of the *SportsCenter* anchors joked about a football player's contract holdout. Raymond had not thought about the Saints in days. Had the season started?

His head swam, so he leaned against the headboard. LeBlanc finished his sandwich and got up, taking Raymond's out of the fridge and sticking them in the microwave. *I probably should have eaten before takin the meds, but my hand's killin me. And if we're gonna make any real progress, I can't be stumblin about, high as a kite. I'm gonna have to tough it out till bedtime. I just hope I can be useful one-handed.*

The microwave dinged. LeBlanc reached into a drawer and pulled out a paper plate. He set the sandwiches on it and took them to the desk and pulled up the chair. Raymond got up, LeBlanc supporting him, and eased into it. He unwrapped the first burger, picked it up, and bit in, groaning with pleasure.

McDowell knocked on the connecting door. When LeBlanc opened their side of it, she stepped inside, looking bright and radiant, her freshly washed hair cascading over her shoulders. She wore a blue T-shirt and cutoff jeans. LeBlanc whistled. She grinned and hit him on the shoulder before hugging Raymond's neck.

How's the patient? she asked.

Raymond held up his injured hand. At least he missed the one I jack off with.

McDowell burst into laughter. LeBlanc sputtered, dribbling coffee onto the carpet.

She grabbed LeBlanc by the arm and pulled him toward the bathroom. They stood close, whispering. Raymond let this go on for a minute or so. Then he said, Okay, boys and girls. What's goin on?

They rejoined him.

It's Frost, LeBlanc said. Been tryin to call him. He ain't answerin.

Raymond swallowed the food and drank the last of his water.

That could mean anything, he said. Maybe he got laid and turned off his phone. It happens, even to English professors. Just then, Raymond's phone rang, making them all jump. Raymond banged his hand on the desk and cried, Fuck! He doubled over, cradling it.

LeBlanc grabbed the phone and looked at the readout. Speak of the devil, he said. He answered and listened for a moment. Then he laughed. Yeah, that's the road. No, just stay on it until you hit town. Okay, talk to you then.

The big man hung up and winked at McDowell. Guess what? The professor's passin through Stephenville. He should be here in forty minutes or so.

McDowell smiled, but Raymond could only look up, his eyes leaking tears. Great, he croaked.

Frost arrived drenched in sweat, his face nearly as red as his T-shirt. He wore blue jeans that clung to his crotch in ways that looked both uncomfortable and unnecessary. He wore sandals, no socks.

Dragging his suitcase inside, he said, This isn't a state. It's a brick kiln. He shook hands with Raymond and LeBlanc and started to hug McDowell but then backed off, indicating his clothes.

What about our messages? LeBlanc asked. Did you drop your phone down the airplane toilet?

I called as soon as I got them, Frost said. I turned the phone off before I left New Orleans. Just grabbed it and the charger and threw them in my bag. I remembered to turn it on in Stephenville. What's with your hand, Ray?

I got shot by a ghost.

Frost laughed. When no one else did, his eyes narrowed. You're shitting me.

I shit you not. Go get a shower, and put on some clothes that don't smell like a stray dog wiped its ass on 'em, and we'll tell you about it.

One shower later, McDowell gave Frost the hug he had postponed. He had changed into a pair of khaki shorts and a white T-shirt bearing the slogan *Caution: Absent-Minded Professor at Large*. He still wore the sandals, which Raymond would not have recommended, given the hellish nature of the Texas sun. Burnt feet made for poor concentration.

Everyone got comfortable. It took Raymond twenty minutes to tell the story. Frost pulled a small notepad and pen out of his back pocket and scribbled away the whole time.

When Raymond finished, he asked to Frost, What made you decide to light out for the territories anyway?

Once I told my chair about this case, Frost said, she helped arrange guest lecturers for a couple of weeks. It's not every day one of us gets to work on a murder case. Or a ghost sighting.

Raymond scowled as if someone had farted. Great. Now everybody thinks we're some half-ass Ghostbusters tribute band.

The department doesn't care about you, Frost said. There's probably a book in this for me, which means another line for their recruiting materials. Everybody wins.

Except our reputation. Now we're gonna field calls from every old lady who hears a noise in her attic and all the tinfoil-hat-wearin loonies who think Martians are beamin death rays into their brains.

Frost frowned. You want me to go back home?

McDowell touched his arm. No. Ray's just grumpy because he got shot.

Raymond sighed. McDowell was right. Having Frost with them was better than spending half the day on the phone with him, assuming you could find a spot in Comanche with decent service. Thus far, he could discern no logical pattern to when or where he could get a signal.

I can tell you this much, Raymond said. That sumbitch was holdin a gun, and he did somethin to my hand, but nothin broke the skin— just like the murder victims. Tore my muscles and bones all to hell. We gotta be real careful. I mean red-alert, two-minutes-to-midnight careful.

Frost looked more excited than cautious. Did you tell them about my ideas for fighting a ghost? Raymond started to speak, but Frost went on. Apparently, those old boots and that gun belt anchor the spirit. It must have felt threatened when you tried to torch them. It acted in self-defense.

Raymond held up his mangled hand. Surgeries. Pins and plates and God knows what else. Now you're sayin it was my fault for provokin him?

No, no. I'm just explaining how this stuff works. The lore I've read confirms spirits can be awfully protective of the objects tethering them to the mortal plane.

LeBlanc laughed. Tetherin 'em to the mortal plane. Where do you get this shit?

Literature. History. Folklore. It's all there. I suggest using the boots as bait to draw him out. Maybe we can even make contact and find out what he wants.

That's already crossed our minds, LeBlanc said.

Besides, we know what he wants, McDowell said. He wants to kill the descendants of the men who butchered him.

Sure, right, said Frost. But perhaps we can find a solution that doesn't involve further trauma to Ray's extremities. Besides, we've got an opportunity that may well be unprecedented—the chance to contact a spirit and document the experience. Once I've seen the locations, I think I can requisition a couple of high-def video cameras from the film department—

We ain't interested in palaverin or startin a goddam sewin circle, Raymond said. We just want him caught or gone.

But—

Now LeBlanc leaned forward and interrupted. Ray's right. This idea of talkin to that thing—look, you didn't see him. He ain't gonna talk. He's more like to shoot us all between the eyes. Hell, what am I sayin? He ain't even a *he*. It's an *it*.

But I think we'd be safe if we didn't threaten the boots, Frost insisted. Until you tried to burn them, he hadn't gone after anyone but the descendants.

We're not takin chances, Raymond said. Besides, there's another problem.

LeBlanc told Frost about the mayor's confiscating the boots and belt, how he wanted to haul them out for the Pow Wow, and how Bradley planned to liberate the items from lockup.

So we can't do anything unless this Bradley comes through with the boots, Frost said. Bloody hell.

Someone pounded on the door, uptempo, like the bass drum in a speed metal song. Frost started. McDowell looked at the men. She got up and walked over to the door and looked through the peephole.

Aw, shit, she said.

Before anyone could ask a question, the pounding began again, and they heard a gruff, angry voice—C.W. Roark's.

We know you're in there, the mayor boomed. Open this goddam door.

What do I do? McDowell asked.

Let him in, Raymond said. It's that or jump out the window.

McDowell opened the door, and Roark pushed past her, nearly knocking her into the wall. Chief Bradley followed close behind, his expression unreadable. LeBlanc stood and started forward, looking like he might knock the mayor's teeth through the back of his skull. Frost saw it and tried to get between the two men before LeBlanc did something they would all regret. Raymond stood.

But before anyone could say anything, Rennie Roark forced her way into the crowded room, her hair and lipstick as red as ever, her alley-cat-in-heat voice rising as she cried, C.W. Roark, you behave yourself. Don't make me cut a switch.

Roark turned on her. Dammit, you're my wife, not my momma. Quit talkin at me like I'm a twelve-year-old.

Rennie did not flinch. Well, then stop actin like one. I swear, I never seen such a man.

Roark turned away from her, his face red, and glared at Raymond.

I knew you'd make things worse. We should have run you outta town the first night.

C.W., Rennie called.

Raymond tugged on LeBlanc with his good hand. Frost continued to push on the big man's chest. With only one hand and a skinny professor to help him, Raymond never could have moved LeBlanc unless he wanted to be moved, but by that time, McDowell had joined in, climbing over the bed around Roark and grasping LeBlanc's hand. She whispered something in his ear, and he backed away a step, nudging Raymond to the side, still staring a hole in Roark.

The expression would have frightened any man with a sense of self-preservation, but Roark was focused on Raymond.

I left you alone long enough to get your hand doctored and leave, but here you are, after firin a gun within the city limits. What would you have done if you'd killed somebody?

Nobody was there but us and the killer, Raymond said. I reckon you'd be fine if he'd shot more than my hand.

I want you all outta my town by sundown. You understand me?

Raymond said nothing. He held Roark's stare so long that Frost transferred his hand from LeBlanc's chest to Raymond's.

He's my brother, Rennie said. You can't just make him leave.

Yes, I can, Roark said. If you wanna visit, make him give you the name of his next hotel. If he's got any sense, it'll be in Dallas, near the airport.

C.W. Roark, you come outta this room, she said.

She dragged Roark back toward the door, detouring around Bradley, who had said nothing. The chief turned sideways so they could pass, his thumbs hooked into his belt, his expression passive and disinterested.

As the Roarks headed out the door, the mayor said, See 'em gone, Bob, or I'll have your badge as a paperweight. Then he turned back to Raymond. We're gonna reopen the diner tomorrow. I plan to be there myself, and I better not see any of y'all. You get me, Ray? If I so much as hear a rumor you're still in town, you'll be countin our jail's ceilin tiles till your arraignment.

The Roarks bickered all the way out of the hotel.

Bradley turned to the rest of them, shaking his head. Frost looked stunned. Raymond sat in his desk chair and said, Well, that sure was fun. Maybe next time he'll bring a game of Twister with him.

This ain't a joke, said Bradley. Then someone knocked on the still open door. Officer Roen stood in the hall. Come on in, the chief said.

Roen entered.

What the hell's this? Raymond asked.

Roen puffed out his chest and hooked his thumbs in his belt, just like Bradley. We're takin you outta town.

Shut up, Bradley said.

Roen blushed, his expression hangdog, as if Bradley had just stuffed him in a locker in front of the prettiest girl in school. Frost looked from Raymond to the chief as if he were watching a tennis match.

Ray, what's going on? Frost asked.

Before Raymond could reply, Bradley said, What's goin on, mister, is y'all are gonna get dressed, and then we're gonna escort you outta town. Pack up.

McDowell stood up and put her hand on the chief's shoulder. Mister Bradley, be reasonable. We—

Bradley's expression was cold. Don't try none of that with me, ma'am. Looking taken aback, McDowell took her hand away. LeBlanc glared at Bradley. And don't you mean-mug me, boy. I got my orders from the man who signs my paychecks. I aim to follow 'em. Y'all hurry up now.

He and Roen left, closing the door behind them. Raymond's hand throbbed. McDowell got up and began gathering their things.

Frost paced about, fuming. This is fucking bullshit. I just got here. Now I'm supposed to turn around and go home? Don't these idiots care about the killings?

Let's get outta here before they come back, said Raymond.

LeBlanc and Frost helped McDowell gather up the dirty clothes and personal items in the room and stuff them into suitcases. A piece of red shirtsleeve hung out of LeBlanc's bag like a hound dog's tongue. Frost kept grousing until LeBlanc finally threatened to stuff a wet towel down his throat. McDowell left to gather her things. Frost followed suit. LeBlanc went to gas up the car. Raymond sat alone in the room, all his things packed, his hand aching. He got up to piss and stared at the water for several moments, lost in his thoughts, the swirling diluted-mustard patterns of his urine lazing through the water. He put on the pants and pullover T-shirt McDowell had laid out for him, easing his bad hand through the armhole. Then he sat on the bed and turned on the television.

You good to go? LeBlanc asked when he returned. He still looked ready to cave in someone's skull.

Raymond stood and followed LeBlanc into the hall. They left the room disheveled, covers rumpled in piles like relief maps of mountain ranges. LeBlanc pulled two suitcases behind him. Raymond hauled one with his good hand. McDowell came out of her room with her arms loaded down. Both she and Raymond would have to make more than one trip. When they got to the stairs, Frost was already there. He had not even had time to unpack. He took a couple of McDowell's bags without a word and stomped down the staircase.

Jake, this ain't over, Raymond said. They told us we had to leave town. They didn't say we couldn't ever come back. Frost did not reply.

They reached the lobby and found Bradley and Roen waiting for them. Raymond approached the chief. Look, we—

Bradley held up his hand. Save it, Ray. Nothin we can do. Y'all ready?

Me and Ray got some more stuff to fetch, McDowell said.

Bradley nodded at the little deputy. Officer Roen can grab those. When he gets back, we're gonna make a nice little caravan. I'll lead. The rest of you follow me. Officer Roen will bring up the rear and make sure none of you make a wrong turn. Get goin.

LeBlanc looked as if he wanted to punch a hole in Bradley's chest, but he gritted his teeth and said nothing. Frost's face had turned nearly purple with rage, but somehow he held his tongue as well. They walked to the cars, Bradley not offering to help with anybody's luggage. They loaded the bags.

Then, after watching Roen disappear into the hotel, Bradley glanced around. No one stood nearby.

Once me and Roen turn back to town, he said, wait ten minutes. Then head back to Red Thornapple's. He's got plenty of room and some cars you can borrow. Park your rentals out back of his place so nobody sees 'em.

Raymond and the others looked at each other, surprised. For a moment, no one seemed to know how to respond.

Why are you doing this? asked Frost.

Bradley glanced at him. I ain't got time to explain. If y'all got a plan, we need to make it happen yesterday. Got me?

Raymond nodded. We're workin on somethin. But no guarantees.

Bradley shook his head. Ain't that always the way?

When the meal began, Raymond promised to reimburse Thornapple, but the newspaperman waved him off.

Bullshit, he said. My family's been loaded ever since we built this ranch back in the 1880s. My ancestor, the one that worked at the depot and got me into this mess—he died there, too, not long after the Kid—he was dirt poor. But his brother Nat, my great-great-grandfather, made a killin on cattle. We've been doin pretty well ever since.

So why the newspaper? LeBlanc asked.

Because I believe in the First Amendment, Thornapple said. And I hate starin at cow pies all day. Point is, I can afford a little barbecue now and then. Besides, keepin you in town's gonna drive C.W. up the wall.

Joyce Johnstone ate more brisket than Frost and McDowell put together and then excused herself, explaining she had to work in the morning and had never been much of a night owl anyway. They bid her good evening and gathered in the den, where the night devolved into a session of grown-ups telling campfire stories. Raymond gave them an abridged version of the Myrtle's Ghost legend and the story of

Caroline, the helpful spirit of Le Petit Theatre du Vieux Carre. All the while, he winced and grunted whenever he jolted his hand. Around 11 p.m., LeBlanc gave him a Percocet. He washed it down with iced tea and sat back, praying he truly sought relief and not the dulling of his heartache that came with the high.

McDowell told a tale about a bayou medium who could predict locals' deaths by casting the entrails of stray cats.

LeBlanc described a certain house in north New Orleans that was allegedly haunted and how he once went inside on a dare.

And, finally, Red Thornapple narrated how his own grandfather claimed to have seen a ghost at the depot one night in the 1940s.

LeBlanc leaned forward and said, Now wait a minute. Your grand-daddy saw somethin out there nearly *eighty years ago*? Why didn't you tell us this before?

Thornapple laughed. Pappaw spun a lot of tall tales. I reckon it's part of why I wanted to be a writer myself. He told me the depot story when I was maybe eight, a week or so after the one about this old witch who used to live in the woods outside Granbury, and a month before he swore his old sergeant saved his life by fightin a Panzer one-on-one outside a little French village. What I'm sayin is, he was prone to exaggeration.

Raymond understood. His own father had been fond of fish stories, folklore, legends, lies, and half-truths. The old man had prefaced every tale by swearing he had seen it with his own eyes, and even though everyone in the family had known he was full of shit, he had always taken pride in his knowledge of local arcana. Raymond had first heard about some of New Orleans's haunted houses and restless spirits from men like his father, in the dim and often dingy bars dotting the city, places locals tried to keep secret from the tourists who populated the

Quarter's taverns like termites. The truth mattered less than how the tale made you feel in your gut.

He asked Thornapple to tell them the depot story.

Ain't much to tell, I'm afraid, Thornapple said. Pappaw was ridin home on his bicycle around dusk. Claimed he had been playin baseball across town, but they lived way out here, and I doubt his daddy would have let him ride that far on his own, even back then, when you didn't have to worry about some pervert yankin you into a van and carryin you God knows where to do God knows what. Plus, he didn't mention nothin about a bat or a glove. He was probably sparkin some girl. That, or he never came at all. Wouldn't be the first time one of his true stories never happened.

Thornapple took a long swig of Shiner Bock and belched. Good one, said LeBlanc as he raised his own bottle in tribute and drank. Raymond licked his lips. Frost was taking notes on a legal pad, his beer sitting on the coffee table, barely touched. McDowell sat beside LeBlanc.

Anyway, Thornapple said. He passed by the depot, and his bike chain broke. Just busted open. He managed not to fall over and break his neck, and while he tried to fix it, the sun went down. The moon was full, though, so he had enough light to work. He cobbled the chain together and was tryin to work it back on the bike when he looked up and saw this pale man standin ten or twelve feet away, watchin. Pappaw was sittin by the road, not on the depot grounds, and when he saw that fella just standin there like that, he got scared and dove into the ditch. He crawled through the mud—it had rained just the day before, he said—and ran like hell once he got past the depot. Swore he didn't know why. His daddy brought him back for the bike the next day, but it was gone. Said the ghost he seen was the only one in the world that moonlighted as a bike thief. I never figured there was much to it.

Raymond, McDowell, and LeBlanc exchanged nervous, interested glances. Frost kept writing.

That's some story, Raymond said.

I've never believed in ghosts, Thornapple said. But what y'all saw matches my Pappaw's yarn. Maybe it's coincidence. But if it ain't, that means my line could have ended in the forties if not for that ditch. It's literally a soberin thought. He drank, his Adam's apple bobbing. When he finished, he set the bottle on the table and stared at his shoes.

Frost cleared his throat. In my research, I came across the name P.D. Thornapple. He was on duty at the depot when the posse brought in the Kid.

Thornapple nodded. Yeah. Like I was sayin earlier, I'm descended through P.D.'s brother, Nat.

Given the parameters of this story, I assume Nat must have avoided the depot, Frost said.

From what I've heard and read about him, he avoided most everything. Hardly ever left this property, and when he did, it was usually for church or a quick trip to the general store. He liked God and cows and not much else. But I reckon his wife charmed him well enough because they had kids, and those kids had kids, and so on, each eldest child passin the estate to their eldest. I'm the last. Ain't got no kids. Probably never will.

He looked toward his bedroom, to which Johnstone had retired earlier that evening. McDowell sipped her iced tea and said, Not everybody needs 'em to make a full life.

Now that I think of it, everybody descended from that posse was pretty lucky just to be born. Some of our ancestors died not long after the Kid, and if they hadn't already started their own families, we wouldn't be here.

Who died? Raymond asked.

Noseless McCorkle passed away on the depot grounds a couple years after they brung in the Kid.

Noseless, said LeBlanc.

Yeah. Somebody found him layin against that storage buildin, blood runnin from his mouth and eyes and the hole where his nose used to be. Then old Beeve Roark died on the tracks, right behind the main buildin. Train run over him, though nobody ever found out what he was doin there in the first place.

A heavy pall settled in the room. McDowell stirred the cold food on her plate.

Raymond thought about his hand. The man, or spirit, had pointed a gun at him and pulled the trigger. They had all heard the report in their minds, not with their ears like you would with any self-respecting gunshot. And then his hand had exploded from the inside. Add to all that McDowell's bleeding eyes, and now this, the possibility the Kid had been appearing for decades whenever some descendant of that long-ago posse wandered onto the depot grounds and turned him on like someone flipping a light switch. Or maybe it was more like a battery. Maybe the psychic energy had to build. Perhaps Thornapple's grandfather had brought the Kid back to the world gradually, the charge growing a little stronger each time he biked past the grounds. Cut to the present—several descendants ate at the diner multiple times. One of them owned the place. They all met for an evening of interviews, which is when the ghost appeared again, and this time it had remained.

I got a theory, if anybody cares to hear it, Raymond said. He recounted his ideas for them and finished by saying, It all sounds batshit to me, but at this point, I'm about ready to believe anything.

No one stepped forward to say that his idea made perfect sense, but nobody broke out the chains and butterfly nets either, so it turned out better than he had hoped.

Frost cleared his throat. I think your reasoning follows. If ghosts can be connected to certain locations or objects, why couldn't they be tied to people, too?

LeBlanc snorted. Are we really talkin about this?

Frost smiled without humor and drank some beer. If you read different cultures' folklore, you find variations on the basic ghost story. Spirit of the departed can't cross over. Unfinished business, overwhelming anger or sadness, violent death, poor burial, whatever. All of that is true here, according to you guys.

Raymond held up his ruined hand. This is all I know, he said. And that Darrell shot him point-blank without producin a body, or even any blood.

I want to see these grounds, Frost said. What we're doing right now will become part of the future's folklore, even if the Kid kills us all.

No one said anything for a long time. They drank. McDowell got up to pee.

Finally, his expression sour, LeBlanc said, Shit, Doc, you sure do know how to make a body feel good and confident.

Raymond knew how LeBlanc felt. Here's what I don't get. If the Kid's a ghost, how the hell is he shootin people? It ain't like he could hold a real gun or run to wherever you buy ammunition around here.

Frost shook his head. No, but if he's an angry spirit, a manifestation of the living man's psychic or spiritual energy, then it logically follows— and I admit I'm using the term *logic* loosely—it follows that the ghost has to focus that energy somehow. The guns and bullets might just be a symbol of the spirit's memory echoes.

LeBlanc looked confused. Huh?

I mean its energy is lashing out in a form that would have been familiar to the Kid. If we were dealing with his Native American companion's ghost, it might be skewering people with a phantom spear.

Phantom spear? Now you're just makin shit up.

Wait, said Raymond. That's a good point. That same posse killed the Kid's Comanche runnin buddy. Where's his ghost?

The posse didn't dismember the Comanche's body, said Frost. At least nothing I've read suggests they did. Maybe they were so used to Native Americans and white people killing each other they didn't see any need for extra brutality. Or maybe they just used up all their time and effort on the Kid.

So if the ghost uses its energy like the Kid used his guns, why ain't it ever pistol-whipped anybody? asked LeBlanc as McDowell returned and sat next to him.

It probably could, said Frost. I'd wager it controls how its energy manifests, which might also explain why its so-called bullets can pass through skin or muscle but blow apart internal organs and matchbooks. He shoots only what he wants to hit. If he had been more famous for barroom brawls than gunfights, we might see death from blunt-force trauma.

Maybe we should stop lookin for more crazy bullshit to deal with, McDowell said.

The deep throbbing in Raymond's hand had eased. It now felt like a second fevered heartbeat, painful but bearable. I think we gotta move on this tomorrow, he said.

What's the plan? asked Thornapple. You ain't got the boots or the gun belt, and C.W. will call the goddam National Guard if he sees any of you inside the city limits.

Raymond stood and stretched. Bradley will get the boots. I'll call him before I turn in and let him know he's gotta move. As for C.W., I can think of only one thing, short of kidnappin him or blowin up his car. Betsy, you feel up to a little errand tomorrow?

Sure, she said. Her eyes looked hollow and tired. They had all been on edge since they first set foot in the Dead House, McDowell most of all.

Good. Since you've offended C.W. the least, I'd like you to sit with Rennie and help her keep him at home. Me and Darrell will go to the diner in case he gets past you. Jake and Bradley can torch the boots, and the hell with usin 'em as bait—sorry, Jake, but my hand says we ain't got that luxury.

LeBlanc drained his beer and set the bottle on the coffee table, which bore the weight of over a dozen empties. Sounds like a plan, he said. But we're gonna need those salt rounds. If Tidewater delivers when he promised, they'll be ready in the mornin.

Raymond smiled. He felt as if he were floating.

The good feeling did not last long. As they walked down the hall, Raymond took LeBlanc by the elbow and said, Listen, I could use another pill tonight. That last one took the edge off, but I'm still hurtin.

LeBlanc looked hard at Raymond, his eyes cold, his face expressionless. No, he said.

Raymond furrowed his brow. That prescription says every four to six hours as needed. Well, I need some good sleep before I ruin my relationship with my brother-in-law once and for all.

Right, said LeBlanc. Just like you used to need all that whiskey. Just like you needed them beers you stared at all evenin.

Anger flared in Raymond's belly. That ain't fair. I never asked for a drink. And I don't want a pill to get high. I'm thinkin about tomorrow. I can't sleep with an elephant steppin on my hand.

McDowell clutched his shoulder. We said we'd keep an eye on you. That's what Darrell is doin.

It was my idea to stretch out the doses, remember?

And now you're askin to increase 'em, said LeBlanc. With all this shit goin on, we need you sober.

Tomorrow, I'll be as sober as a nun.

Those people out there, McDowell said. Their lives are in our hands.

I know that, goddam it.

Would Marie wanna see you like this? Beggin for a fix?

All the blood drained from Raymond's face. He pushed McDowell's hand away. How fuckin dare you? he croaked. You don't know a damn thing about her.

Don't talk to her like that, LeBlanc said. She's just tryin—

I'm goin to bed, Raymond said, backing into his room. He slammed the door and fell onto the bed, his head swimming, his mouth dry. Water would feel so good—beer, even better. And as that thought crossed his mind, he knew they were probably right. It was best not to strain his tenuous sobriety, even for good reasons. If only he had the energy to get up, go find them, and apologize. But then, he had been right, too. He just wanted sleep, needed it. That was all.

Soon Raymond fell into a fitful slumber, still fully dressed, his hand aching. If he dreamed, he did not remember.

McDowell stared at the ceiling for a long time, her mind running a hundred miles an hour. Raymond had never spoken to her that way before, but it had come from an honest place. She had felt the pain and the worry radiating off him like fever. McDowell worried, too—about Raymond, about going back to the diner and how she would handle whatever happened there, about the people they were trying to protect. So much stress, so little peace of mind—how did Raymond and LeBlanc do it every day?

All those ghost stories, especially Red Thornapple's, seemed to show their lives depended so much on chance—this person meeting that one, accident A avoided, relationship B consummated. If one variable were changed, whole existences might never be. What did that mean for the decisions they were making here? What world were they ensuring? What lives were they devastating without even realizing it?

CHAPTER TWENTY-TWO

September 15, 2016—Comanche, Texas

Raymond awoke the next morning and—seeing the deer head mounted on the wall, plus the window treatments—had no idea where he was. Not in the hotel, and not at home, where nothing hung on the windows but the plain, deep-bruise-colored sheets he had tacked up after Marie died. The old curtains had been hers. She had sewn them herself, working at night while Raymond watched the news and the talk shows or slept in his recliner. After she died, just looking at them hurt, so he took them down and folded them up and shoved them deep in his linen closet.

These curtains, blue with an arabesque pattern, looked like nothing he would pick out. A cedar dresser stood against the far wall, a forty-two-inch television on top of it. It came to him—Red Thornapple's house. Still, he felt like all those times when he would awaken in a strange place, sometimes among people he could not recall meeting, more often alone, his mouth tasting like a rotting whale's anus and his head pounding fit to burst.

He sat up and scratched his cheek, feeling his palm rasp against two days' growth of beard. Yesterday had been exhausting—Roark's visit, their drive to Thornapple's, the strategy session, the pain in his hand, the argument with McDowell and LeBlanc.

When Raymond emerged, the others were already up, and Thornapple had left. Everyone took long, hot showers and drank coffee. Raymond and McDowell muttered apologies to each other and then said little else. He swallowed two BC Powders he found in Thornapple's bathroom and kept the rest of the box close.

The living room's clutter did not extend to the rest of the house, which seemed tidy in places, almost Spartan in others. When LeBlanc mentioned the dissimilarity last night, Thornapple shrugged and said, A lot of the shit in the den was here when my daddy was a boy. The rest of it I've brought in from hither and yon. I mostly just lay it somewhere and then never get around to storin it. My housekeeper fixes up the rest of the place once a week, whether it needs it or not.

Raymond liked the newspaperman. Their houses had much in common.

Thornapple had left a note on the kitchen's granite countertop— Johnstone had gone to work, and they should make themselves at home. Wielding a spatula in his good hand, Raymond helped McDowell cook an enormous breakfast of eggs with hot sauce, bacon strips, sausage patties, and hash browns.

Everyone ate and washed the food down with more coffee until they felt awake, alert, on edge. Frost and LeBlanc washed dishes. Raymond found a screening of *The Quiet Man* on American Movie Classics. They all gathered around and watched it. Despite their stress and anticipation, the caffeine wore off, and everyone but Raymond fell asleep before the movie ended, so he was the only one who heard the truck in the driveway just before 1 p.m.

A moment later, Thornapple walked in, looking tired and sleepy. He saw everyone curled up on his furniture, nodded at Raymond, and said, I got your ammo in the truck. You ought to be able to gun down a whole regiment of ghosts.

Raymond gave him a thumbs-up. Thornapple headed for the kitchen, where he proceeded to bang pots and pans until everyone woke up. Soon the smell of frying meat filled the air. As if he knew what the racket had wrought, Thornapple poked his head around the corner and called, I'm fryin up some steaks and steamin broccoli. Hope y'all are hungry.

They looked at each other, yawning. Raymond found he could eat again. Perhaps the idea of battling a ghost for the lives of a passel of strangers worked up an appetite. His hand was starting to throb, so he downed another BC. In fifteen minutes or so, Thornapple called them to the table. McDowell and Frost ate small pieces of steak and some of the broccoli. Raymond ate a decent helping of both, though Frost had to cut the meat. LeBlanc ate two steaks and a pile of broccoli big enough to choke a tiger.

No wonder Darrell shits three or four times a day.

As they finished, Thornapple asked, So when do we leave?

Raymond pushed his plate away. You don't leave. In an hour or so, Betsy will go to the mayor's place, and Jake will meet Bradley. Me and Darrell will head to the diner around four, in case C.W.'s too stubborn to listen.

Thornapple tapped his fingers on the tabletop. I don't much like other folks doin my fightin for me.

Right now, we can do our jobs better if we know you're safe. If we need your help, I got every confidence you can more than pull your weight.

I don't know how long I can keep your brother-in-law at home, McDowell said. He ain't exactly a sensitive man.

Raymond reached over and patted her hand. If you can delay him even five minutes, you'll be a big help. Jake, you still game to help Bradley?

Yes, said Frost. If you won't let me try to make contact, then performing a ritual to sever a ghost from the earthly plane is a pretty good second choice.

How does Bob plan to get the boots out of the station? Thornapple asked.

He's the chief, said Raymond. I reckon he can check somethin out if he wants to.

And if somethin stops him?

No one had an answer to that.

Johnstone returned around 2:30, just as McDowell and Frost were leaving. McDowell drove Thornapple's old work truck toward the mayor's house, a set of directions complete with hand-drawn map sitting on the seat next to her in case she lost her phone signal. Frost took Thornapple's new Chevy, a candy-apple red extended cab with GPS. In the back seat, Thornapple had stashed a shotgun and a box of salt rounds. Frost had never fired a gun in his life, but he felt confident even he could hit something with a shotgun. He only hoped it would not be Bob Bradley or his own foot. McDowell left first, the truck kicking up a plume of dust that hung in the air. Frost followed until the GPS told him to turn. He waved, even though McDowell probably did not notice. It seemed like the right thing to do.

Bob Bradley entered the station after a late lunch. He carried his old duffel bag. Grooming his skinny black mustache with a pair of scissors and a handheld mirror, Sergeant Gomez greeted Bradley at the desk. The chief headed for his office, thankful for his small force. Every other officer on duty was patrolling the town, and Gomez would not leave the desk unless he had to piss, which would carry him away from where Bradley intended to be—the evidence locker. Once everything had happened and the dust had settled, the chief would likely lose his job, but that could not be helped. He got paid to protect the town, and with all the weird events of the last few weeks, it seemed possible that torching those boots might be the only way to do it. That theory sounded crazy in daylight, but it felt real after dark, when you lay in bed with the covers pulled up and a tree branch scraped against your window screen like talons. Another thing he had never told anyone—he always felt a chill when passing the depot, even with gray in his hair and a gun on his hip. Plus, he still had no explanation for the kinds of injuries the victims had suffered. The county coroner had determined Lorena Harveston and John Wayne died because their internal organs had been churned into soup, but no one had determined any weapon or object or illness capable of that kind of damage. And so, in the absence of other possibilities, Bradley had to accept the notion—privately, at least—that the ghost of the Piney Woods Kid had killed them. He would burn the boots and gun belt and deal with C.W. Roark later. No matter what happened, he would be able to sleep at night.

He reached his office door, opened it, and then closed it hard enough for Gomez to hear. A moment later, the phone at the front desk rang. Gomez answered it. Good.

Bradley slipped down the hall, moving past the break area and the two interrogation rooms, easing by records and the armory. At evidence, he took out his keys, taking care not to jingle them, and let himself in.

Walking up and down the rows, peering into the dimness at taped cardboard boxes stacked on top of each other like a child's building blocks, the chief soon reached the back of the room, where the boots and gun belt had been piled on a middle shelf. *I'm glad they ain't real evidence. Otherwise, I'd be crawlin around with a flashlight, readin labels and hurtin my back.* He grabbed the Kid's gear and stuffed it in his duffel.

He exited and locked the door. So far, so good. Odd to feel grateful that the city had not ponied up for new security cameras inside the station. Creeping back down the hall to his office, Bradley was about to turn the corner when he heard C.W. Roark's voice booming down the hallway, asking after Gomez's wife and two-year-old daughter. Cursing under his breath, the chief dashed into his office and sat behind his desk, cramming the duffel underneath it. He took some papers from his inbox and pretended to examine them.

Heavy footfalls in the hallway and then a sharp rap on the door.

Yeah, he called.

Roark walked in. Hey, Bob. We need to go over the security schedule for the Pow Wow.

Shit. Bradley tried to keep his expression neutral. Okay, he said.

The mayor pulled up a chair and sat down. Outside, the wind picked up, the sun riding high in the sky.

McDowell pulled into the Roarks' driveway at 2:45 p.m. Rennie's car was parked near the house, but the mayor's was gone. Overhead, a long line of thick, white clouds bordered the blue sky to the west. The wind had risen, blowing grit across the yard. Weather reports that morning predicted a late-afternoon storm and, by evening, hard rains and high winds that would lash Comanche for most of the night. Hopefully, Bradley could burn the boots long before then, but if Hurricane Katrina and what happened afterward had proved anything, it was that no plan was ever executed perfectly. Back in '05, McDowell had gotten out of town just ahead of contraflow, planning to spend the night in Baton Rouge, but the only available hotels, mostly cheap places catering to out-of-town construction crews and the like, had jacked up prices far beyond a fortune-teller's budget. She had traveled well into central Arkansas before she found a place to stay. McDowell had spent nearly a week in that cruddy motel, eating lousy food and watching the news, before heading back to make more stable arrangements.

Who knew what would go wrong today?

After she parked, she rapped on the door, the painted wood grainy against her knuckles. She had always enjoyed texture—the roughness of pilled sheets, the minuscule roadways in wood's grain. Despite the heat and the goat-head sticker she had stepped on the one time she had gone barefoot, she enjoyed Texas for the textures alone.

Rennie opened the door, a telephone held to one ear.

Yeah, Rennie said, nodding to McDowell. She just got here. Right. Right. We'll do our best. Y'all be careful. She ended her call and stuck the phone in her pants pocket. Hey, hon. That was Raymond. Come on in.

McDowell entered. Where's Mr. Roark?

Rennie shut the door and led her into the house. At the police station. You might wanna call your teacher friend. He's likely got a long wait ahead.

She took McDowell into the kitchen and poured tall glasses of sweet iced tea. Then she took some lemon slices out of the refrigerator and stuck a wedge in each glass as McDowell dug her phone out of her purse and dialed Jacob Frost. Rennie carried the glasses out of the room, giving McDowell her privacy.

Frost answered after three rings. Hello?

Hey. I'm here. The mayor's at the police station, so I reckon the chief's gonna be late. Try not to boil alive out there.

Shit. Thanks for the heads-up. Be careful.

You, too.

In the den, Rennie sat on the couch. McDowell joined her and took a glass of tea.

Rennie sipped hers. Raymond told me everything, she said. I thought he'd been drinkin again. A ghost—Lord above.

After what we saw out there and what happened to Ray's hand, we can't deny it anymore. If there's a logical explanation, we ain't smart enough to figure it out.

What if that thing shows up here? Rennie said. I doubt you can stop it with your good looks.

McDowell laughed. You're right, I expect. But if it really is a ghost, we got an edge. Jake says there's rules. A ghost would be bound to a certain place or a certain item.

I like you. You got no bullshit about you. But you didn't answer me. What do we do?

Get in the car and drive as fast as we can, McDowell said.

And what if it's a man after all?

I reckon you got guns around here somewhere.

Rennie raised one eyebrow, as if McDowell had proposed they break the laws of physics. Honey, this is Texas.

Then get a couple. If trouble comes, and we can't get away, we shoot.

Rennie reached behind the couch cushion and pulled out a .38

snub-nosed revolver.

There's a .45 on top of that curio cabinet yonder, she said. If it comes to that.

McDowell glanced at the cabinet and said, When's your boy get outta school?

He always comes straight home from football practice and gets a shower, so probably around five thiry or six.

McDowell drank her tea and looked at her watch. 3:20 p.m. She hoped the mayor would arrive first. He would be easier to corral if he had to wait on his son.

Frost followed the GPS to the gravel road Bradley had indicated and parked with the passenger-side tires in the sloping ditch. The rocks on the road looked dull, like tarnished metal. On the other side, another grassy ditch led to a barbed-wire fence, beyond which lay a field that rolled over hills like cresting waves. In the distance, a handful of cows stood in ankle-high grass. They stared at each other, not moving except for the occasional swish of their tails. What did cows think about all day—being milked or finding the best clover in Texas or a world in which they dined on peopleburgers? *God, I must be bored out of my mind. All these trees and fields, all this open space—it's too damn quiet to hear yourself think.*

Jacob Frost had been born in Connecticut and completed his undergraduate degree at UConn before earning his MA and PhD from SUNY–Buffalo. His first postdoctoral instructorship took him to the University of Chicago, where he stayed until the job in New Orleans brought him south for the first time in his life. Whenever he drove through sleepy small towns, he knew that, should he ever find himself living in such a place, he would blow his brains out. He loved New Orleans, even after Katrina and everything that happened—the dirty politics and the gentrification and the shattered culture that stubbornly refused to die no matter who tried to kill it, president or nature or the steady and unforgiving march of history. He loved walking the Quarter and stumbling over street musicians, finding the little-known dives where real jazz ripped itself from the bones of old men and assaulted you with its urgency. He loved sniffing the air at lunchtime when the po' boys were hot, and spices drifted through the air like fog. Nature scenes had their appeal, certainly, but in the end, Frost wanted a city that would reveal not the unchanging grandeur of a pastoral scene but the mutability of humans in close contact.

One of the cows mooed. A fly settled on the truck's windshield. Soon enough, Frost would have to turn off the engine, after which he would start to broil. Plus, he had to pee, and he did not relish the thought of tramping into the woods, hoping to find a tree big enough to hide behind.

Would I even recognize poison ivy?

Frost looked at his watch. He had studied folklore all his life, including some intense ghost stories and fairy tales. Vengeful spirits, creatures of fang and claw and bristling fur, human deviancy in all its forms. Now, just such a tale unfolded right here, but so far he had missed it all. The desire to experience whatever might happen next ached in his bones. Even if this errand with Bradley came to nothing, which it probably would, he could tell the story to his children, should he ever get around to having any.

2:55 p.m. The gas tank was full, but Frost could not leave the truck running while it pumped carbon into the air and fueled this furnace of a state even more. Twenty minutes more, and if Bradley had not arrived, Frost would shut off the engine.

A black bull joined the cows. It mounted a spotted one and humped away, careless of who might be watching. At least somebody was having fun. The fly buzzed away, leaving Frost alone with his thoughts.

At 4:15, Raymond and LeBlanc parked on the perimeter of the diner's lot. Despite another BC, the deep, throbbing ache in Raymond's hand was cycling up. LeBlanc cranked down the window and shut off the engine, letting in the hot summer air. The lot was half full already, the sky still blue for the most part, though some clouds were rolling in from the west—tall white structures like cotton ball buildings sculpted by children. Farther out, they darkened, light grays giving way to near black. The agency needed fair weather. If the Kid showed up, they might not see him in the rain.

LeBlanc looked to the west. What the hell do we do if it comes a turd floater in the middle of a gunfight?

Raymond watched the front doors. Get wet, I reckon. Think I can slip up yonder every now and then and get us somethin to drink?

If you don't, we're gonna turn to dust and blow away.

If only they had a case of beer. It would have quenched Raymond's thirst even as it took the edge off his pain. *If wishes were horses. Don't dwell on the heat. Or beer. Or whiskey on the rocks.*

They watched the incoming vehicles. Roark would likely appear later in the evening, but in a situation like this, you could never be too careful.

All this ghost shit, LeBlanc said. You ever think about Marie?

Whether you could see her again this side of heaven?

It was the kind of question you seemed to hear on half the TV shows or movies you ever watched: What would you do, what would you give up, for one last moment with your dead father, sister, daughter, wife? What would it be like to see Marie, to tell her all the things he had never gotten around to saying? If anyone had asked him before the Piney Woods Kid materialized out of nowhere and shot his hand to hell—well, Raymond probably would not have invited them to fuck off. But if he had answered, he would have said he would brave any danger, make any sacrifice.

Things were different now. He had seen a real spirit, and it was no glowing-around-the-edges angel come to comfort and speak kind words. It was an angry, hateful thing. The Kid had died hard, but so had Marie—her body smashed, her brain jostled enough to put her into a coma. She had lingered in that godforsaken hospital for weeks, a ventilator forcing oxygen into her lungs and deflating them again, her body creating and excreting waste, pumping blood. She had lain that way until the insurance ran out and then some, until Raymond sobered up long enough to see what she had become, and then he had signed the papers. The doctors had unplugged her machines, and she had slipped away. He held her hand until she passed, and then the orderlies came in and pulled him away, prying his fingers from hers. Tears spilled out of him as if his body hid aquifers as bottomless as grief. He had been drunk at her funeral and, for months afterward, had soiled her house with his carelessness, had not visited her grave for nearly a year, afraid the very sight of her tombstone would blind him, drive him insane—or worse, that it would do nothing at all. That, in his own way, he would be as comatose as Marie had been. When LeBlanc forced him to go, the wracking, chest-bursting sobs erupting from him felt like the kind of relief that could kill.

Now, he shook his head. Marie was the sweetest woman I ever knew, he said. Gentle. Kind. I wouldn't wanna see her like this. It would be blasphemy.

LeBlanc watched him for a second and then nodded. They both turned toward the diner and fanned themselves with their hands. Again, Raymond wished for a beer, a Percocet. Outside, a dry wind blew dust off the bare patches in the courtyard, the graying, hard-packed earth as tough and solid as iron. What would a hard rain do to the ground? He did not want to find out while a ghost stalked them. He closed his eyes and breathed, trying and failing to will the heat and clouds away, to ignore the pain.

Roark left Bradley's office after 5 p.m. The chief had tried to sneak away three times, but whenever he managed to get out of his office, Roark found him, even following him to the bathroom and talking while he took a shit. Once the clock hit 3, and the mayor kept bird-dogging him, it seemed Roark was keeping him in pocket on purpose.

When the mayor finally left, Bradley thought about calling Frost but feared any delay might give Roark an opportunity to come back. Walking out of the station with the duffel on his shoulder, Bradley opened the door to his cruiser, tossed the bag into the passenger seat, and got in. Shadows of buildings and trees lengthened as the day limped onward. Dusk was still a couple of hours away, but it felt later, as if time itself were against them. The chief backed out of his parking space and pulled onto the road.

Minutes later, Bradley turned onto the back road down which Frost had traveled hours ago. He hoped the professor would still be there. He did not want to conduct this business alone.

The cracked and pot-holed pavement gave way to gravel that pinged against the undercarriage like thick hail on a tin roof. Bradley did not slow down. A sense of urgency built inside him until his chest felt tight, as if the buttons might pop off his shirt. He half expected to see the Kid on the road, leveling those legendary pistols.

Red Thornapple's truck was parked across from a barbed-wire fence. In the field beyond, a bull and eight or nine cows stood motionless. They seemed like a good omen. Bradley had always found cattle soothing—their peacefulness, their stoicism in the face of bad weather and stupid high-school kids with pellet guns and summer days that threatened to cook them alive. Bradley pulled up behind the truck and parked, taking several deep breaths, eyes closed, the shotgun beside him, his sidearm heavy against his hip. Frost waited in the truck, one arm crooked out the window. *Things will be fine. Two grown men can burn a pair of boots in broad daylight.* They would do it in the road so old Trip Allen's meadows and hills would not burn to a crisp. He turned off the car and got out, hauling the duffel. He shut his door and walked up to the truck's driver's-side window.

Frost turned to him, his red face dripping sweat, and said, That bull has fucked half a dozen cows since I got here. I was beginning to think I was delirious.

Bradley laughed. Sorry about that. C.W. showed up and stayed all afternoon.

Bradley stood back while Frost got out. The professor stretched and grunted.

I've pissed three times, Frost said. Probably got poison oak on my balls. Next time, I'm bringing a porta potty.

Ain't gonna be a next time.

Frost regarded him. Do you believe in the ghost?

I believe in coverin my backside. Come on. Let's get this done.

Together, they knelt in the hot gravel and opened the bag. Bradley pulled out the boots and the gun belt and dumped them in the center of the road. Frost dug out the lighter fluid and the matches.

CHAPTER TWENTY-THREE

September 15, 2016, Concurrent—Comanche, Texas

McDowell spent the afternoon drinking Rennie Roark's iced tea and watching the windows. The clock on the wall read 5:10 when a vehicle pulled into the driveway. McDowell looked at Rennie, eyebrows raised. Rennie got up and went to the window, peering between the curtains.

It's Will, she said. He's early.

Rennie came back and stood by the couch. McDowell kept her seat. A moment later, the boy walked in. Taller than his mother but shorter than the mayor, around 180 pounds, he wore a Dallas Cowboys number 82 jersey. He grinned when he saw McDowell and then looked away. His hair was wet with sweat.

Hey, he said.

Hay is for horses, said Rennie. Say a proper hello to our guest. This is Miss Betsy McDowell.

His face reddened. He looked at the floor. Hello, Ms. McDowell.

Betsy, said McDowell. Pleased to meet you.

How was school? asked Rennie.

Fine, he said. I gotta shower.

He stole another glance at McDowell and scurried from the room.

Rennie watched him go, her brow furrowed. It was nearing suppertime for people like the Roarks, small-town conservatives who probably went to bed by 10 and would likely die of shock on a Bourbon Street Saturday night. The mayor could arrive at any time.

Some minutes passed, and then another vehicle pulled up. Rennie turned, her hand covering her mouth for a second.

It's C.W., she said.

McDowell stood. Okay. Here we go.

The door creaked open. Roark's heavy tread thudded through the foyer. McDowell's half-full glass of tea jiggled on the coffee table, like that scene in *Jurassic Park* where the lawyer got trapped in the shitter. And when Roark walked into the den, he looked about as friendly as Spielberg's T-Rex. He saw McDowell and glanced around the room, as if expecting random New Orleans natives dripping with Mardi Gras beads to tackle him.

McDowell put on her best disarming smile. Evenin. I've been enjoyin Ms. Rennie's company. She makes a mean pitcher of tea.

Roark's jaw clenched as his hands balled into fists. He turned on Rennie.

Where's Raymond and his pet gorilla?

McDowell's smile never faltered. It's just me. Nothin to get upset about.

Like hell! I can't even get away from you people in my own house.

Rennie faced him, hands on her hips, her stoplight-red hair piled high on her head. There was no trace of her brief trepidation.

C.W., be civil, or I will personally stick my shoe heel through your left nut.

Roark glowered. Sweat ran down his face in thin rivulets. Then he turned to McDowell and jabbed a finger at her. I'm callin Bob Bradley.

If you're still in Comanche County when he finds you, you can't say
you weren't warned. He turned and stomped down the hall, shouting,
Will! Let's go!

Rennie chased Roark down the hall, berating him like a squirrel
barking at a black bear. McDowell winced as waves of fear and anger
swept over her, a red-orange ball of fire that threatened to cook her
brain. She put her hands to her temples and rubbed counterclockwise,
which always soothed her and helped her focus.

Soon, Will Roark wandered back into the room in fresh clothes, his
hair dripping. He stared at McDowell's breasts for a moment before his
parents realized he had left and followed him down the hall, still grousing.

You can stay if you want, the mayor was saying, but I won't be a
prisoner in my own house, and I won't have the town thinkin I'm scared
to take the same chances they are. I'm eatin chicken fried steak and
gravy at our diner tonight, and my son's comin with me.

You ain't takin the same chances they are, you damn fool, Rennie
said. You're takin more. Nobody's after them.

Will watched his parents' row with some interest.

Come on, son, the mayor said. I'll buy you a cheeseburger and
some steak fries.

Will did not have to be asked twice. He followed his father toward
the front door, awash in the bulletproof aura of teenagers and fools.
Rennie chased them, demanding that Will stop, that C.W. leave the
boy out of this.

Will hissed protests like, Chill out, Mom. Geez.

McDowell considered intervening, but the vibes she had gotten
from Roark felt dangerous. He was wound tighter than a guitar string.
If she plucked him the wrong way, he would snap, and woe to anyone
in his way.

The front door slammed. McDowell took out her phone and called Raymond.

They're on the way, she said. Sorry.

We'll be ready, said Raymond. You heard from Bradley or Jake?

Not since I called about the chief bein late.

Okay. We'll be in touch soon, one way or the other.

McDowell hung up as Rennie stormed back through the room and down the hall. A moment later, McDowell heard things being tossed about, the musical tinkle of metal on metal, the muffled whump of fabric billowing in the air. She followed the sounds and turned into the Roarks' bedroom. A king-size bed took up most of the space. It was piled high with clothes and shoes and cardboard boxes. As McDowell watched, another shoebox flew out of a walk-in closet and landed on the growing pile.

A moment later, Rennie stepped out, holding what appeared to be a bulletproof vest. She held it out to McDowell, who took it, unsure of what else to do.

I knew this goddam thing was in there somewhere, Rennie muttered. She brushed past McDowell and back toward the living room.

McDowell set the vest on the floor. That won't help, Ms. Rennie.

Rennie picked up the .38 and started for the door.

McDowell reached her and laid a hand on her shoulder, sending out all the calm and peace she could muster.

Rennie took a deep breath and exhaled. Her shoulders slumped. She turned to look at McDowell, tears in her eyes. He's my only son, she whispered.

I know, said McDowell. But you can't go after him, or you're liable to get yourself killed. That boy needs his mother.

A single tear slipped down Rennie's cheek. We can't just sit here.

McDowell squeezed her shoulder. I'll go. And remember your brother and Darrell are already there. Give me your keys. I can't be worryin you'll change your mind.

Rennie nodded and crossed the room, picking up her purse and digging inside it. McDowell looked at her watch. It was 5:25 p.m.

LeBlanc returned from the diner, where he had gone for a piss and a to-go cup of sweet tea. Raymond climbed out of the truck.

C.W.'s on the way, Raymond said. You ready?

LeBlanc drank some tea and set the cup on the car's roof. Yep. How long you think they'll give us for assaultin the mayor?

If C.W. has his way, they'll hang us. Twice.

They leaned against the car and watched the road. Several vehicles turned into the lot—the dinner crowd. Raymond frowned. The killer would likely show no compunctions about gunning down whoever stood between him and the Roarks. Raymond's own hand served as evidence of that. Yet they had no authority to shut the place down.

As if LeBlanc could read his mind, the big man said, How's the hand?

Hurts like a son of a bitch.

You need to sit this out?

I'll manage.

Soon enough, the mayor's Chevy turned onto Austin Street. Raymond elbowed LeBlanc. The two of them trotted to the parking lot entrance and stood a few feet apart, blocking the path. They left their guns behind, knowing that if they threatened Roark with weapons, nothing would keep them out of jail.

The mayor slowed down, fuming over the steering wheel. Will sat beside him, wearing earbuds and plinking away on his phone. He didn't even look up when his father stopped the Chevy in the driveway's mouth and waved Raymond and LeBlanc aside. Raymond shook his head and gestured for the mayor to turn back. More cars pulled up behind the Chevy, the head of a traffic line that would snake all the way down Austin and back to Central if the mayor held ground. Annoyed drivers glared at Raymond and LeBlanc. Someone honked.

The mayor rolled down his window and stuck his head out. Get the hell outta the way before I run you both down!

No, said Raymond. We ain't about to let my nephew die just because you're a stubborn son of a bitch.

Roark threw the Chevy into park and got out. Will looked up, alarmed, as his father strode the ten feet or so between the Chevy and Raymond, fists clenched. Raymond spread his feet shoulder-width apart and prepared to get punched in the nose. He would not fight back, but he could distract C.W. long enough for LeBlanc to grab him and wrestle him off the property.

The boy started to get out.

Will, no! Raymond yelled. You stay put!

Will jumped back into the Chevy and closed the door.

You're gonna wish you had left, Ray, C.W. said. He took out his phone and dialed, waiting while Raymond and LeBlanc watched. Then he sputtered, Goddam it, Bob, I don't know where the hell you are, but this is the second message I've left in the last fifteen minutes. Get your ass to the diner, and arrest these gator-eatin sons of bitches, or so help me God, I'll have your badge. He hung up and stuck the phone back in his pocket.

Raymond shook his head. You're a fool, C.W. You're gonna get that boy killed.

Roark stepped forward. LeBlanc put a hand on the mayor's chest. Roark ignored him, pointing at Raymond and growling, Don't tell me how to raise my son. Get off my property. And while you're at it, one of you get David Roen's piece-of-shit truck away from here before it draws flies.

Raymond stared down the mayor, his eyes cold, his voice even. Every second y'all stay here makes it more likely somethin real bad's gonna happen.

You threatenin me?

No, you hardheaded jackass, LeBlanc said. He's tryin to help you.

Roark seemed to see LeBlanc for the first time and pushed his hand away. But he also backed off, his eyes closed for a moment. When he opened them again, he seemed calmer.

Look, Roark said. You got no right to stop folks from comin here. And you're trespassin. If you're still here when Bob Bradley shows up, Rennie won't be able to help you.

Raymond crossed his arms over his chest. You sound like a broken record. We ain't goin nowhere.

Someone honked again. Roark glanced over his shoulder. More cars had arrived. Sure enough, they stretched all the way to Central. A couple more waited to turn onto Austin, their signals blinking.

Roark looked at Raymond. And what if I get back in and floor it? You gonna stand there and get run down?

If you run over one of us, you better get us both, LeBlanc said, because if you don't, the one still standin will be a hell of a lot less civil.

Roark watched them for another moment and then spat. He got back in his truck and reversed. Then he pulled forward and down past the drive, parking halfway in the ditch. Raymond and LeBlanc stood aside and let the other cars enter, the drivers favoring them with dark looks.

What do we do now? LeBlanc asked. They're just gonna get out and walk.

We tackle 'em. Will ain't dyin on my watch.

Frost doused the boots and gun belt with lighter fluid. Bradley held a box of matches. They looked at each other. Bradley swallowed hard. Frost stepped back ten feet and nodded.

The chief took out a match.

Then the air shifted behind him. Frost turned pale, as if someone had cut his throat. He dropped the can of lighter fluid. Bradley looked back, and the match snapped in his fingers, the ends flying in opposite directions.

A gray figure stood five yards away, clad in the kind of gear you might expect to see on a wandering gunfighter in an old Western. Cannonlike six-guns rested in their holsters, slung low on the man's hips. His arms hung limp, the long fingers tapering to dirty, ragged nails. A hat concealed his eyes. Still holding the matches, Bradley turned to face him, circling around the boots. The man did not move.

Frost started forward.

No. Stay put, Bradley said.

Frost stopped. The cowboy stood still, as if carved from marble. Slowly, Bradley raised his free hand.

Where the fuck did he come from? Frost whispered.

Where do you think? Bradley hissed.

The chief touched the matchbox with his right hand, never taking his eyes from the cowboy. He eased one of the matches out. His lungs burned; he had been holding his breath. Exhaling, Bradley struck the match.

The cowboy's arms blurred into motion. A deafening bang, and then something struck the chief's face, knocking him backward. As he fell into darkness, he was not even aware he could not think.

Frost believed he had accepted the possibility of a ghost's existence, but when the gunfighter materialized, he nearly shat his pants and knew that, deep down, he had been as skeptical as the mayor. Then Bradley struck the second match, and the gray figure drew its pistols. No one had ever moved so fast. A boom, as much a force as a sound, seemed to pulse behind Frost's eyes, and Bradley flew backward as if he had been shoved. He rolled in the dust, landing face up, where his open eyes stared at the gathering storm clouds overhead. His forehead looked sunken, as if something heavy and blunt had struck it with great force. Hematomas grew like rising dough. His face turned dark purple as blood pooled underneath the skin. Frost ran to him and knelt at his side, knowing he was dead. The professor felt for a pulse anyway. Nothing. The chief looked confused, as if he were trying to work out a difficult math theorem. The box of matches had fallen from his hand and lay on the ground a few feet away.

Don't vomit, Frost told himself. *Don't run.*

The man—the ghost—had not moved. His arms dangled at his sides, the guns reholstered.

Frost leaned forward, ready to sprint. *Get the box. Then evasive action.*

Another boom, and the matchbox flew into the air. Frost cried out and fell on his ass, hands held out to ward off the kill shot that never came. The matchbox lay in ruins, splinters scattered everywhere. The cardboard burst into flame, well away from the boots and gun belt. Thunder echoed through the sky, and the first fat raindrops pattered the gravel, the cows, Jacob Frost, Bradley's corpse.

When the rain began in earnest, the Kid faded away, as if the water had evaporated him. When he was gone, Frost turned to the heavens and screamed.

McDowell pulled up to the diner, parking next to a Suburban. The mayor's Chevy sat halfway in the ditch. Perhaps the Roarks might still be inside. But no, there they stood at the lot entrance, Raymond Turner nose-to-nose with the mayor. At least nobody had been shot, and the Roarks were still within spitting distance of the street. McDowell got out and ran to the men. A crowd had gathered in a loose semicircle. Some people took pictures and videos on their phones.

Lord, the internet's gonna have a field day.

Will meandered a few feet from the men, his face red. He kept glancing at the crowd and looking as if he wished the earth would swallow him. McDowell gave him a sympathetic look. The boy, who had earlier seemed horny enough to squirt in his shorts if she so much as looked his way, hung his head. He was well built and handsome in a way his father was not, and yet he seemed to know that what happened here might define the next several years of his life more than anything he himself might do. He shifted from foot to foot, as if unsure of whether to help his father or duck into the truck and curl up in the seat where no one could see him.

As she sensed the boy's emotional torment and the men's anger and frustration, McDowell's own rage boiled over. She marched over and stepped between the two men, planted both hands on Raymond's chest, and pushed him backward with all her might. He cried out in surprise and went down, trying to cradle his bad hand. Then she turned and shoved Roark, who, having seen Raymond's fate, managed to stay on his feet, though he stumbled two steps backward.

Mister, she said to Roark, I don't know if you even give a shit, but your son's watchin you act like a second grader, and so is half your town. If you want 'em to remember you lookin like a spoiled brat who didn't get a cookie before supper, then keep on actin like one. Then she turned to Raymond, her voice kinder. Sorry, Ray. I didn't have time to be diplomatic.

LeBlanc pulled Raymond to his feet.

Hell, Betsy, I wish you had shown up five minutes ago, Raymond said. Might have saved us some time.

You heard from Jake or the chief?

No.

They should have called in by now. Somethin's wrong.

Raymond looked at his watch and frowned. To Roark, he said, Get your boy off this property. Now! Then his phone rang.

Roark put one arm around his son. Let's go, Will.

He pulled the boy toward the road as Raymond answered the phone.

Jake? Raymond said.

Bradley's dead, Frost said, sounding as if he might be hyperventilating.

That thing shot him and destroyed the matches, and now it's raining. Do you understand what I'm saying? Ray, we couldn't burn the boots.

Raymond dropped his phone. Light rain splotched the concrete and the patches where the hardpan had beaten back the grass. He turned toward the Roarks, eyes widening.

McDowell saw his face. What is it?

Too late, he whispered.

Then he ran at the Roarks as fast as he could go. Images of Marie's shattered body flashed through his mind, how her limp hand felt as he clutched it, the helplessness, the despair. Not again. Not Will. No matter the consequences. Footfalls behind him, too light to be LeBlanc's. McDowell was chasing him.

Where are you, Darrell?

Then the Kid appeared between the Roarks and the road. His hands hung near the holstered guns. The crowd shrieked. C.W. and Will froze. They all stared at each other as if they stood on the main street of an old frontier town, waiting on the clock to strike noon.

CHAPTER TWENTY-FOUR

September 15, 2016, Evening—Comanche, Texas

Raymond almost reached the Roarks, but the Kid's arm blurred into motion. *Too late too late too late.* The guns boomed. Roark threw himself in front of Will. Something seemed to strike him, and he tumbled backward onto his son.

As they went down, Will screamed, Dad!

Raymond skidded to a halt near them. The mayor's tall, thick body covered Will's. The boy struggled to push his father off as the mayor spat blood. The Kid floated toward them, arms dangling.

McDowell appeared beside them, her voice calm and smooth. Will, stop fightin. That thing's after you now.

Will's eyes widened. Help us, he whispered.

Hang on, Raymond said, grasping Roark, ready to pull him away.

Roark moaned and coughed, spraying blood into McDowell's face and hair and upper torso. She turned aside and vomited. The Kid hovered in front of Raymond. The specter's clothes were wrinkled and stained. Three days' stubble covered his cheeks. His hat was torn at the seam. His guns looked cartoonishly enormous. *It's your mind playin tricks. Don't think about how you're about to see the business ends.* But he did, imagining the barrels yawning like the maw of some deep and uncrossable gulf.

Another gun fired nearby. Raymond jumped and cried out. His ears rang, but in his mind, the Kid roared like a wounded lion. The apparition disappeared, winking out like one of those science-fiction movie holograms. People in the crowd covered their ears and held their heads as if in great pain.

Raymond turned. LeBlanc stood behind them, holding a shotgun. *Salt rounds. We brought only salt rounds, and they hurt that thing.* The other shotgun lay at LeBlanc's feet. *He must have got 'em from the car when I was helpin with C.W. and Will.* LeBlanc tossed his gun to Raymond, who caught it with his good hand. His heart kept trying to pound through his chest and go hopping down the road like a frog. LeBlanc picked up the second shotgun.

Raymond stood on one side of the Roarks. LeBlanc turned around and scanned the other direction. The crowd had dispersed in panic. Somehow no one had been trampled.

Somebody call 911! Raymond shouted. Your mayor's hurt!

Uncle Ray—Will said, still underneath his father.

Help's comin, Raymond said. Roark gurgled.

Now the rain started to pound them, fat drops like globs of birdshit. It diluted the blood on McDowell, though it looked as if her eyes were bleeding again, and the trickles and chunks falling from Roark's mouth. The mayor's eyes were closed, his face as gray as the Kid.

Movement to Raymond's left. He wheeled about as the Kid materialized five yards away. Raymond raised the shotgun to his shoulder, balancing it on his left forearm, and fired into the Kid's torso. Again, that lionlike roaring as the ghost dissipated, plus the hail-on-a-tin-roof sound of salt striking parked cars. In the distance, the whine of sirens. Perhaps an ambulance. Raymond glanced at C.W. He had slipped sideways, exposing Will's head and upper torso.

Betsy, Raymond said, you gotta get Will off the property. We'll cover you.

Tucking the gun under his injured arm, Raymond bent and pushed the mayor sideways, his hand slipping in the blood and rainwater, as McDowell pulled. Roark groaned while LeBlanc wheeled about, trying to see everywhere at once. The crowd pushed its way back into the diner. Some decided to forego the line and dashed around the building, running for Central.

Raymond helped Will up. You okay?

The boy was as pale as his father. How's Daddy?

LeBlanc fired again and shouted, Hurry up! I can't keep him off you forever!

Get outta here, Raymond said to Will.

McDowell tugged on the boy's arm. He looked at his father. I can't. Not without Daddy.

Raymond grabbed him by the back of the neck and shoved him toward the road. I said get.

Will stumbled past McDowell, who ran after him and pushed him along, saying, Move. They'll bring your daddy.

She and Will reached the mayor's Chevy and leaped in, slamming the doors. McDowell fired up the engine, but before she could change gears, it sputtered out.

The Kid appeared in the ditch beside them.

McDowell and Will screamed. She yanked the boy down into the seat and ducked as the Kid drew and fired both guns. Nothing happened to the truck, but if they had not moved, their brains would have splattered inside their skulls.

Up at the intersection, an ambulance turned toward the diner, three police cruisers behind it. Roen drove one. Nearby, LeBlanc fired. That animalistic roar filled Raymond's skull again. McDowell tried to start the Chevy, its whirrs and chugs almost rhythmic amid the screams and the rain driving onto the pavement. Raymond waved the ambulance into the drive. It turned in and parked near the mayor. Roark's eyes were closed.

The cops pulled over on the far side of the road and exited with guns drawn. One blond-haired kid who looked about twelve years old leveled his service weapon at Raymond and said, Drop your weapon and get on your knees. Hands laced behind your head.

Lower your weapon, you goddam idiot! Roen snapped.

The deputy seemed not to hear. Drop the gun, or I'll blow your head off.

Roen shoved the kid's weapon toward the ground, screaming in his face as the other three officers converged on LeBlanc, who raised his hands but did not drop the shotgun.

Will opened his car door and yelled, Leave 'em alone! They're helpin my dad!

McDowell clawed at him, pulling him back in.

To the men covering LeBlanc, Roen bellowed, Stand down! He's with us! Then he sprinted to Raymond and the mayor.

The paramedics had disembarked and knelt next to Roark.

Gunshot to the torso, Raymond said. I think it's his lung.

No evidence of a wound, muttered one medic.

You'll have to take my word for it. Get him outta here.

We can't move him until we know what's wrong.

Raymond seized the man by his shirt. If you don't move him, he's gonna die. The assailant's still here. He shoved the paramedic away.

Roen watched them work, eyes bugging. What can we do?

Help 'em get C.W. outta here, Raymond said. We'll do our best to hold off the Kid.

Wait, the *who*?

The Kid appeared nearby, flickering in and out of focus, the rain passing through him. The officers' mouths fell open. One dropped his weapon in a puddle near his feet and swayed as if he were going to pass out. Jesus *Christ*, said another.

What the hell is that? Roen cried.

Raymond whirled, still balancing the shotgun barrel on his left forearm. He fired at the Kid, who disappeared with another howl of pain. Roen covered his ears, grimacing. The Kid reappeared fifteen feet away, next to an officer who screamed and fired his service weapon at him. The bullets passed through the apparition's head and smashed through the window of a truck. Its alarm blatted as someone screamed in surprise and terror.

Cease fire! Raymond shouted. Your guns won't hurt him!

The paramedics had stopped working on Roark. They stared at the spot where the Kid had vanished. Raymond nudged the nearest one with his foot. The man shook his head and slapped his partner in the chest, saying, Get him on the goddam gurney right now.

They loaded the mayor while Raymond covered them. LeBlanc stood near Roark's car. A bit of McDowell's hair was visible through the windows. *Probably still layin on Will. It's gonna get her killed if we can't get 'em outta here soon.* Behind him, the paramedics leaped into the ambulance, one in the driver's seat, the other in back with Roark. When the driver tried to start the engine, it chugged and chugged but would not turn over.

Raymond beckoned to some of the bystanders and the cops. We gotta get 'em past the property line, he said.

For once, no one questioned the sanity of what Raymond said. All the officers ran over and started pushing the ambulance, Raymond walking behind them and scanning the property. Three men dashed from behind cars in the lot and joined the effort.

Raymond spotted the Kid to his right and fired. The apparition vanished again.

Who's shootin? one of the civilians asked, scared out of his mind.

Just push, Raymond said. I got you. But he was trying to reload with one hand.

LeBlanc ran over. Take my gun, he said. I'll reload.

What the hell are you doin here? Protect Betsy and Will.

I told 'em to get out and haul ass and not stop until they couldn't hear shots anymore. If that thing's really bound to the property, they're safe.

That's just a theory. It got far enough away from here to kill Bradley.

Fuck, LeBlanc spat.

Go after 'em.

I don't even know where they went.

Did you just say the chief's dead? asked Roen as he pushed the ambulance.

Raymond looked at Roen but said nothing. LeBlanc shook his head. Roen's face screwed up as if he were going to cry, but then he clenched his jaw and looked straight ahead, still pushing. A moment later, LeBlanc's shotgun crashed. More almost-musical sounds of salt striking metal and glass. They had nearly reached the road when two of Red Thornapple's trucks turned onto Austin. Frost drove one. Thornapple himself piloted the second, with Joyce Johnstone sitting beside him.

Aw, shit, LeBlanc said. What else can happen?

He dashed toward the vehicles. They pulled over as he flagged them down. Frost got out of the truck, holding the boots and gun belt.

Jake! Raymond called. Get that shit onto the property!

Frost ran across the street and onto the parking lot. LeBlanc headed off Johnstone and Thornapple, gesticulating and pointing toward Central. They jumped back in their vehicle and backed away as the men managed to shove the ambulance onto the road under Raymond's protection. *No help if this thing don't start.* But the engine turned over, and the driver took off, siren blasting. Raymond, LeBlanc, and the men from the diner stood on the street and watched it go, the rain driving down hard enough to sting.

Someone near the diner called, Hey, y'all, it's back.

Raymond turned and saw Jacob Frost holding the boots in the middle of the lot. He had stopped to watch the ambulance, too. In the meantime, the Piney Woods Kid had appeared behind him, staring at him with those merciless gray eyes.

The ghost stood between Frost and the Dead House, hovering six inches above the ground. Frost tried to swallow, but the spit lodged in his throat like a chicken bone. Thunder rumbled. Lightning strobed behind the clouds. He gripped the boots and gun belt harder, afraid of what might happen if he dropped them, afraid of what might happen if he did not.

The Kid made no move.

No, Raymond said. No guns. He'll kill Jake.

To whom was he talking? Too dangerous to turn around and find out. And was what Raymond said true? The Kid had dispatched Bradley when the chief threatened to set the boots on fire. Then the Kid destroyed the matches, not Frost. The boots and gun belt must have comprised the key to the Kid's existence. If so, he would protect them with a ferocity that Frost could barely imagine.

Back on the road, LeBlanc called, Just throw the goddam things down and run.

But Frost thought that a supremely bad idea. Any sudden move might be misinterpreted as aggression, in which case he would not stand a chance. He had to move slowly and with purpose, despite his triphammering heart, his knocking knees, his shaking hands, his rubbery legs and spine.

Raymond and the others had found the old boots in the Dead House. That might be the best chance. Moving an inch or two at a time, Frost took the gun belt in his left hand and kept the boots in his right. Then he held them out to the Kid.

The ghost's mouth turned up in what might have been a snarl.

No, no, Frost said. Nobody's going to hurt them. I'm putting them back where they belong. Do you understand?

The Kid said nothing, did not move.

Frost edged toward the Dead House in an irregular parabola. He shuffled his feet side to side, crablike, watching the Kid, who rotated as Frost moved around him. The rain fell even harder, water flowing into Frost's eyes, obscuring his vision, and he dared not even shake his head or pass a forearm across his eyes. Around him, everyone had hushed. The only sounds were his feet sloshing through puddles and cruddy runoff from the hardpan, the intermittent thunder, and the rain striking surfaces of all kinds—pavement, flesh, bare ground, shingled roof, cars. He kept shuffling until he reached the Dead House. Then he inched to the door. When he arrived, the Kid disappeared. Frost exhaled.

He turned. The Kid hung in the air beside him.

Now he could smell the ghost, a scent like a wet dog that had rolled in rotten meat. Frost had to bite his tongue to keep from screaming, tasting blood, hoping he could still talk when this was over. If he lived.

He draped the gun belt over his shoulder and used his free hand to open the door. Then he stepped inside.

According to Raymond, the boots had originally rested on one of the back shelves. Several shapes hugged the wall back there, obscured in the shadows. Frost stepped inside and picked his way around the junk on the floor, praying not to trip, knowing if he did, the rattles and thumps of falling diner detritus might be the last sounds he would ever hear. The Kid's presence felt like a twenty-pound weight in his mind. He reached the shelves. The boots' and gun belt's irregular shapes were outlined in the dust. He set the boots back and then bunched up the belt and put it beside them. When Frost turned, the Kid stood in the center of the room, a man shape, gray even in the dark, the outlines of the crates on the floor visible through him. Frost held his hands up again and circled back to the door, watching the Kid, who rotated in the air, watching back.

Frost reached the door and backed out. The Kid floated in the center of the room. The professor pulled the door shut. Then he walked to the end of the building and sat down near the corner, unmindful of the rainwater soaking into his pants and undershorts. He ran his hands through his hair and sighed, his breath wavering, his pulse pounding. Spots danced in front of his eyes. *Don't faint. Just don't.* Moments later, Raymond and LeBlanc approached, people from the diner a few feet behind them, others emerging from behind cars.

Raymond went to the window and peered inside.

What's he up to in there? Frost asked.

Nothin, Raymond said. He's gone.

Half an hour later, the rain subsided, and the police had cleared out the customers. Raymond's rental car and Roen's weathered Ford Ranger were parked end to end on the west side of Austin. Frost's truck sat amid police cars lining the east side. Raymond had called Rennie, who hung up on him. Then, thirty seconds later, she remembered McDowell had taken her keys, and she called back, asking Raymond to send Will to pick her up. Red Thornapple and Joyce Johnstone had disappeared. And Frost had conferred with Roen about Chief Bradley, after which Roen called for a second ambulance over his radio and then left. He had peeled out in reverse, burning rubber on the faded asphalt, narrowly missing the side mirrors of every vehicle, nearly T-boning an SUV on Central. Its driver swerved and honked.

While the remaining deputies sealed off the diner with their inexhaustible supply of yellow tape, Raymond stood alone in agony, eyes watering. God, he needed a pill, a fifth of whiskey, something. He called LeBlanc and Frost over, out of the officers' earshot.

I say we burn 'em right now, Raymond said through clenched teeth. We can torch the whole goddam building if we have to.

LeBlanc's expression was savage and sharklike. We'll need a combustible. Where's the nearest gas station?

Frost shook his head. No. We can't do a damn thing right now, and if you think about it logically, you know why.

I don't give a shit about logic, Raymond said. You saw what happened to Bradley. C.W.'s hangin by a thread, if he ain't dead already, and Will would have died like a dog if we hadn't been here. Now you wanna wait?

Frost sighed. He looked ten years older. No, I don't want to wait.

When that thing showed up there—well, I've never been so scared. I wouldn't be surprised to learn I've shit my pants. But we can't act emotionally. That will only get us or somebody else killed.

Killed, hell. We got enough salt rounds to keep the bastard off us till we can burn that godforsaken shed.

It isn't just a shed, Frost hissed. Raymond recoiled. It's a Dead House, and it served both this depot and the town cemetery. Would you care to speculate on how many bodies that place held over the years? I'd say it would number in the hundreds, the way so many people died young back then. What if we start to burn the place down and find we've got more than one angry spirit to deal with? What if you or Darrell moves a bit too slowly, and one of us dies? You want that on your conscience?

Raymond said nothing. He couldn't stop picturing C.W. lying in the mud, Will underneath him, sobbing and choking on rainwater. Imagination furnished Raymond with other unwanted pictures—Bob Bradley sprawled on a muddy road, eyes open and glassy, flies flitting about his mouth.

I'd trade my house for a belt of Jack Daniel's.

You've been awful quiet, Darrell, Raymond said. A little participation might be in order, since it's your ass on the line, too.

LeBlanc had been staring at the Dead House. I wanna see that fuckin place burn to the ground, but I think Jake's right. We could have died fifty different times just now. Ain't no tellin what would have happened if that thing had been after us. We don't wanna stick our necks in a noose.

Raymond spat. All right, goddam it. But whatever we're gonna do, we gotta do it soon. Casper's shot his last person.

Frost looked relieved. You're doing the right thing, Ray.

Right, my ass. It's your idea, so you're takin the lead. What's first?

Well, said Frost, I think we should go to the hospital. I know you want to check on your sister, and Betsy needs to have her say. I'll tell you more about Bradley on the way.

They walked across the lot toward their vehicles, through the rainwater and blood and silty gunk. Raymond's injured hand ached like a bitch.

McDowell stepped out to get coffee. Rennie sat bolt upright in her chair in the Operating Room waiting area, Will beside her with his elbows on his knees. He had said nothing since Raymond and LeBlanc arrived. Rennie wore a sensible black dress, midcalf length, dark red lipstick, hair coiffed as if by a professional. But the makeup on her cheeks had streaked. She was removing mascara smudges with a wipe and a compact mirror. Soon, she started reapplying, filling in the holes, smoothing out the glops. Raymond and LeBlanc had taken seats in the stiff chairs across from the Roarks. Neither had said much. Frost had stepped away to phone some of his university colleagues.

They had not heard from Roen. Raymond kept imagining the little man stepping out of his car on that gravel road and taking an invisible bullet to the forehead, falling on the rocks beside the chief.

McDowell came back with four cups balanced in her hands. Her clothes were still wet, her hair darkened and dripping. She never wore much makeup, but what she had applied that morning had washed away. Rennie took a cup, her expression unchanging. McDowell handed two other cups to Raymond and LeBlanc.

Sorry, she said. I'm too wet to carry sugar packets. She sat beside

Rennie and leaned forward. The surgeon caught me in the hall and asked me to tell y'all. They're givin the mayor blood and tryin to stop the internal bleedin. Doc said his left lung is pretty much gone.

Raymond looked at his clublike hand. Jesus, he muttered.

Well, at least it missed his heart, said LeBlanc.

They drank more coffee. And they waited. Frost returned and sat next to Raymond, who turned to him, eyebrows raised. Frost glanced at Rennie.

Maybe I should tell you later, he said.

Rennie regarded him. Her eyes were moist, but no tears fell.

My husband's layin on a table gettin his chest cut open. My son almost got killed. Anything you got to say, you say it in front of us.

Frost cleared his throat. Raymond looked at him with sympathy. McDowell took Rennie's hand and squeezed.

Well. Um, yes, Frost said. I've consulted with a colleague at the University of Southeast Arkansas. He specializes in occult legends of the American Southwest. He's never read anything about the Piney Woods Kid in connection with ghost sightings, but he did confirm some things I already knew.

Such as? Rennie asked.

Um. Well. I've been through this with Ray, but for the rest of you: Salt and cold iron repel ghosts. And spirits of those who died violently or whose bodies weren't respected—both of which seem to apply here—tie themselves to a certain locale or an object. Our ghost seems connected to the diner grounds, particularly the Dead House, but mostly to those old boots. The stains on them must really be the Kid's blood, like that old article claimed.

Rennie's eyes were almost as cold as the Kid's. How do we kill it?

Well, the legends suggest that if you destroy the focal object or consecrate the ground, the spirit's links to this plane will break. Burning the bones also works, but we have no idea where they are.

Sounds like you ain't sure anything will work at all, Rennie said.

I have no way of knowing. If at least some of the legends are true, there's a good chance. If not... Frost trailed off and shrugged.

Raymond sipped coffee and wiped his mouth on his shirtsleeve. His hands shook, the ruined one on fire. He needed a pill or a half dozen BCs, and soon.

We find a way to burn the storage shed with the boots inside and stay alive, Raymond said. Two birds, one stone. But if he's tied to the property itself and not just that building, I don't know what we'll do. Call a priest, I reckon.

If we could get our hands on some holy water, some hosts, and a whole bunch more salt, we could try it ourselves, Frost mused.

Raymond stared at him. You mean literally salt the earth?

Just to keep it away from us. But I'm no priest. I'd probably fuck up the Latin and get us killed. So that leaves burning.

Deputy Roen arrived, soaked to the bone. Water dripped from his hat brim. Seeing Rennie and Will, he blushed, and his bottom lip quivered. His eyes moistened. Rennie stood and went to him. She put her hands on his shoulders and squeezed. Roen could not look her in the eye. Rennie hugged the little man, knocking his hat askew, not caring that he soaked her clothes. He laid his head on her shoulder and sobbed.

Now, now, she whispered. It ain't your fault. She pushed him away, not unkindly. This town needs you. You're the chief, at least until the town council finds somebody permanent.

Roen looked at her as if she were crazy. Me? In charge? I ain't sure that's such a good idea.

Rennie patted his cheek. Nobody's expectin you to be Bob. Just do the job you've been trained for.

Roen sat. He stared into space, as if he had been bopped on the head with a sledgehammer. Rennie had no authority to make appointments, but it seemed unlikely anybody would argue with her for at least another day.

The council's gonna run the city until C.W.'s up and about, Raymond said.

She turned to him. Two members are outta town. Another one's in this very hospital with her ulcer. The other two can't get a quorum until one of the others gets back. And we ain't got a deputy mayor.

How much time do we have before they stick their noses in?

No tellin.

Raymond squeezed her hand and looked at everyone in the room, one at a time. We need to talk about what's next, he said. Right now.

An hour later, they had concocted a plan that, Raymond hoped, was too simple to screw up. But they needed supplies, so they could not implement it for at least a day. LeBlanc and Frost had already left, bound for the Walmart Supercenter in Stephenville, with instructions to head on to Granbury or even Fort Worth, if necessary.

Raymond and McDowell stayed behind with Rennie, who had begun a de facto mayoral administration from the waiting room. She made phone calls, sent texts, and took more calls on the waiting room landline. Her husband was fighting for his life on an operating table, and here she was, barking out orders and taking notes on the backs of old magazines and shedding nary a tear, as if she had allowed herself one cry and would not indulge in another until she had squared away the town. *She's stronger than me. It ain't even close.*

Roen had left to secure the diner, having promised to assign at least one car to sit on the place until the agency arrived.

Rennie had given Raymond some aspirin. They dulled the pain a bit, but it was still with him, festering and boiling.

Raymond turned to Will. Walk with me?

Will got up. Raymond led him into the hall. They walked side by side down the corridor, the chirpings of monitors emanating from every room with an open door. Raymond followed the signs until they found the cafeteria and went inside, where Raymond bought them coffee. They sat at a round table with four ratty chairs. Raymond's was unbalanced. Every time he shifted his weight, the chair's off leg struck the floor, jarring his hand. He grimaced.

Will blew steam from the top of the cup and nodded at the hand. How is it?

Only hurts when I'm conscious. Raymond drank the scalding coffee, wincing as it outraged his tongue and soft palate. Maybe it would take his mind off the hand.

The kid looked like he had done two or three hypodermics' worth of bad heroin, all saucer eyes with bruised-looking bags under them, his hair corkscrewed and dirty.

You think Daddy's gonna be okay?

I think he's tougher than hell and too stubborn not to walk outta here.

Will looked Raymond in the eye. The guy that shot him—

Raymond held his gaze. Wasn't no guy. But I guess you figured that out.

I just wanted somebody to say it. I thought maybe I was goin crazy.

Not unless we all are. I wonder if psych hospitals give group discounts.

Will laughed, but it sounded hollow and brittle. So. Did you know?

Did I know what? That y'all was bein haunted? Or that a ghost could shoot you?

Will shrugged. Either. Both.

Not until it did this, Raymond said, holding up his cast. I mean, we knew what folks was sayin, but we didn't believe it. Who would?

The boy's jaw tightened. But you did know. Before it shot Daddy.

Raymond sighed. He felt a hundred years old. I reckon I did. Look, son, we thought we had a plan. But ain't none of us ever done this kind of thing before. And we tried to get your daddy to stay away from the diner.

So it's his fault?

No. But you know how he is. Especially with me.

Will looked away and nodded. I guess I do. I want to be mad at you, but you didn't shoot him.

Be mad at me if that's what you need. I'll still love you.

Will drank his coffee. I wanna help kill that thing.

No, sir.

It's my daddy in there.

I know. But it's your momma in the waitin room. She needs you. And if I'm watchin you, I can't do my job.

You don't gotta watch me. I'm almost a grown-up, legally.

It don't work that way. I'll worry about you when you're fifty. That's family.

Will laughed again. Shit. So I just sit around. What if you get killed while I do nothin?

You're takin care of your momma. That's the most important job of all. It's the one your daddy would want you to do.

A tear formed in the boy's eye, but he wiped it away. He sniffled. This *sucks*.

It surely does. After they finished their coffee, they went back to the others.

Another hour passed. Raymond managed not to drive to the nearest liquor store and stockpile whiskey and bourbon, even though it would have been easier to face the coming hours drunk. Instead, he ran to Dairy Queen, catching them just before they closed, and pissed off the manager and teenage staff by ordering enough food for a dozen people. He swung by the hotel and grabbed his Percocet. When he returned, Rennie ate two burgers and a fistful of fries. Raymond took his pill. McDowell wolfed down her food, but Will barely touched his. He sprawled on the floor, using his mother's purse as a pillow, and fell asleep.

At some point, someone started a ruckus down the hall. Raymond and Rennie investigated, leaving McDowell in case the boy woke up or the surgeon returned with news. At the end of the corridor, Police Chief Bob Bradley's body had arrived. His uniform was soiled. His eyes were closed, his face pale, his forehead sunken in places and lumpy in others and deep purple. Comanche's off-duty officers stood around the gurney, heads bowed, holding their hats. Some of them prayed. Raymond and Rennie joined them. The mud caked on his own pants and shoes shamed Raymond. You ought to mourn when you're clean. Somewhere a woman wept, her wracking sobs reverberating through the corridors like thunder in a canyon. Probably Bradley's wife, whom Raymond had not met. What might the woman look like? Did she have children? What kind of house did she live in? Raymond had worked beside Bradley for days and days, had conspired with him and argued with him, but had never bothered to find out who he was or what his life was like. That kind of self-centered behavior had been common when he was drinking. What was his excuse now?

Percocet dulled only a certain kind of pain.

He walked down the hall and leaned against a doorjamb. His hand throbbed in time with his heartbeat. Another hospital, another corridor, another death. Nothing about it ever changed. The nurses' sympathetic looks. The doctors' voices and movements, as brisk and efficient as automatons. Once he had stood in an ER waiting room as a short man in light blue scrubs approached, a surgical mask dangling from his neck. This doctor wore an expression akin to sympathy, but his eyes remained alert, detached. *Mister Turner, we did everything we could. We've stabilized her, but I'm afraid your wife has slipped into a vegetative state. Yes, sir, I understand. Time will tell us a lot more, but we're reading only minimal brain activity. Most people with this kind of damage never wake up. Yes, sir. You should inform your family.* Later, a second neurologist stood over Marie's smashed and withering body and said much the same. That woman's eyes seemed softer than the first doctor's, her sympathy more genuine, but it made no difference. There is no nice, polite, conciliatory way to tell someone his wife is brain dead, that the most he can hope for is a future of suppurating bedsores and bags full to bursting with piss and shit. Then came the orderlies, who had pulled Raymond out of Marie's room after she died, big men with strong arms and powerful thighs who had nevertheless found it nearly impossible to drag him away. The prick high on his upper arm as someone shot him full of sedative. The droning voice of the priest someone called in, spouting his useless words.

Raymond had hated hospitals ever since. He had not even gone to see Dwayne Hirsch, his old NOPD partner, after he got shot breaking up a domestic disturbance. The bullet had passed through Hirsch's outer abdomen, missing every major organ. The hospital kept him for only two days, mostly monitoring the wound for infection, but

Raymond could not bring himself to cross the building's threshold.

Now it was Mrs. Bradley's turn to fall down grief's bottomless hole. Her turn to wake in the night, blissfully unaware, just for a moment, of the absence beside her. And she would live through that nightmare because Raymond had failed again. He had not been with Marie when she crashed, and who knew how he might have altered things? Now he had let Frost and Bradley out of his sight, and the chief lay as dead and cold as ancient stone.

An orderly arrived and muttered his condolences to the men and women gathered there. Everyone stepped back so he could push the gurney to the morgue. A crying woman came in through another door. She was five and a half feet tall and probably 180, with shoulder-length brunette hair and a small white scar across the bridge of her nose. Mrs. Bradley, Raymond presumed. He wanted to kick himself for noticing details at such a time. The woman was not a suspect. She was a widow. A nurse walked with her, arm around her waist.

Rennie hugged Mrs. Bradley. Helen. I'm so sorry.

Helen Bradley tried to speak but only sobbed harder, the words lost in grunts and expostulations. The nurse nodded at Rennie and pulled Mrs. Bradley through the doors. Roen followed. Were they going to make that poor woman identify the body when everybody in town knew the chief? Or perhaps the chapel lay in that direction.

Rennie returned to Raymond's side.

They got two girls, she said, one of 'em in junior high. Bob just bought a bass boat, too. They loved their fishin. Poor woman.

Yeah, Raymond said. But she ain't the only one whose husband got shot. How are you?

Mine's alive, so I'm feelin pretty good, all things considered. We better get on back before Will wakes up. Together, they turned and walked back down the hallway. But when they reached the waiting area, Rennie stopped him.

I know you did your best. You and yours risked your lives, and I love you all for it. But this can't happen to Will. It just can't. I need you to be your best self now. The brother I grew up with. The one who was willin to drive to Austin and kick C.W.'s ass after we had our first fight in college. The one who dug himself out from under his grief and got his life back. I need the fighter. And I need him right now. If the council decides to shut you down, I won't have a say in it.

Raymond nodded. For the first time, they had a hard deadline. He rubbed his temples and sighed, knowing the coming night would be long and stressful, that he could not risk taking any pills past a certain point.

He walked outside to call Red Thornapple and was only mildly surprised to find the man interviewing the two medics from the diner. Raymond waited until Thornapple shook hands with the men and started toward the hospital doors.

A word? Raymond said.

Yeah. Off the record, I reckon.

That's right. We need equipment.

Thornapple looked weary. Like what? A tank?

No, Raymond said. More shotguns. 20-gauges. One for you, your lady friend, and Adam Garner.

So we're all gonna fight.

I hope not. But if you have to, you'll need guns that fit our salt rounds. Can you do that?

Thornapple laughed, a hollow, exhausted sound. If I can't scare up a few shotguns, I'm a jackrabbit.

At 2 a.m., Roark's surgeon entered the waiting room. Rennie sat still, composed. Will lay on a cot someone had brought in. LeBlanc and Frost had not returned. They were likely still waiting on Ollie Tidewater to reload more rounds with rock salt. Raymond stood up with Rennie and McDowell, who put one hand on Rennie's shoulder.

Yes? Rennie said.

The surgeon, whose name Raymond never heard, crossed his arms and said, Mr. Roark was rolled out of surgery twenty minutes ago. He's critical, but we're optimistic.

Rennie's lips quivered, but her voice was steady. What's the damage?

He lost most of a lung, and his system's had quite the shock, but he's stable. In the short term, he's going to hurt, and I doubt he'll ever run a marathon or deep-water free dive. But unless something unexpected happens—and you have to realize it's always a possibility—his long-term prognosis looks good.

The doctor left the room. McDowell hugged Rennie, who looked at Raymond.

You want us to wake up Will? he asked.

I'll do it. Just give me a minute.

She walked past them and down the corridor, as if she were pursuing the surgeon. Raymond and McDowell looked at each other. Raymond raised his eyebrows and nodded in Rennie's direction. McDowell shook her head. Raymond deferred. When it came to emotions, she always knew best. Just then, deep, throaty sobs echoed along the hall, the sounds of someone either falling through chasms of sadness or finding a nearly bottomless relief, perhaps both. A nurse passed by. She did not look in the waiting room and did not seem alarmed at the noise. In hospitals, people lost control all the time, the sounds as familiar as the beeps of machines and the low-frequency mutter of the PA system and the whispers of relatives making plans for events they probably expected but never sought.

CHAPTER TWENTY-FIVE

September 16, 2016, Early Morning—Comanche, Texas

The group sat around Red Thornapple's dining table, drinking strong coffee and eating cinnamon rolls Joyce Johnstone had whipped up from scratch. Raymond, McDowell, Frost, and LeBlanc tried to rub the weariness from their eyes. No one had slept.

Doing his best to ignore his hand as it screamed bloody murder, Raymond had called Rennie, saying, We just can't get there any faster, not if we all wanna keep our body parts sittin where they grew.

The council's supposed to meet this afternoon, Rennie said.

Can you stall 'em?

The hell with 'em. I don't care if they vote to bring in the National Guard. Finish what we started.

Damn right.

He sounded more optimistic than he felt. How much support would David Roen provide? If the council appointed him acting chief and ordered him to cordon off the diner, he might do it. He would not like it, and he would probably cuss, but the little fellow had spent his career following orders. The fact that Bradley himself had bucked authority to do what was right might make a difference, but it might not. Better to plan for Roen's absence, even his hostility. Raymond reached for another roll and sipped his coffee, watching Frost try to stay awake.

Thornapple brought in another pot of coffee and set it on the table. LeBlanc helped himself to a cup as someone knocked on the door. Everyone stiffened. Frost looked alarmed. Johnstone swallowed hard, the gulping sound almost comical.

Be right back, Thornapple said.

If it looks like trouble, give us a head start, Raymond called.

Thornapple did not reply, but Raymond meant it. If the Comanche Police Department raided Thornapple's house to drive them out of town or hold Frost for questioning in the chief's death, they would have to postpone the plan for God only knew how long, and then the Kid might kill again.

But Thornapple returned, followed by a thick slab of a man in a tight white T-shirt and faded, stained jeans.

Thornapple put a hand on the new arrival's back. Everybody, this is Adam Garner.

Damn if y'all don't look like the world's boringest family reunion, Garner said, his voice booming. Now what's this bullshit I hear about a ghost?

Raymond stood and shook Garner's hand. We thought you weren't interested in joinin our party. What changed your mind?

Garner looked grim. I've been to see Pat Wayne a couple times. She's a mess. Plus Bob Bradley gettin killed. If this asshole's willin to gun down the chief of police, it's gotten too crazy around here to sit on my ass. And by the way, who are you?

During the story, Garner drank two cups of coffee and ate the last of the rolls. Now Johnstone hauled pan after pan of homemade biscuits into the room, along with slabs of butter and saucers for everyone. If she ever tired of the small-town life with Thornapple, she could make a killing as a New Orleans baker. *And if anybody can fatten up Ichabod Thornapple, she can.*

Garner poured another cup of coffee. Sounds crazy to me, he said. But I'm outnumbered and surrounded, so I'll go along. What the hell do we do?

Rennie and Will ain't about to leave that hospital, Raymond said, so they should be safe. Jake's got a plan, but we need all of you if it's gonna have half a chance. If you ain't willin, tell us now. We can't get there and watch you all run like hell while the Kid blows holes in our vital organs.

Raymond would not have blamed the civilians for taking a long fishing trip or telling him to go to hell. But they held his gaze, the fear in their eyes mixed with determination and more than a little anger. This thing had risen out of the past and slaughtered Lorena Harveston, John Wayne, their chief of police. It had obliterated their mayor's lung and turned Raymond's left hand into a plaster-wrapped maul. It would have killed them all if they had ventured onto the diner's lot at the wrong time. Yet their expressions told him they would see everything through. He admired that.

All right, he said. I'm gonna turn this over to Jake. We're gonna go over the plan until we all know it backward and forward. And then, if there's any time left, we're gonna get some rest. We want everybody's head clear. Jake?

Raymond poured himself the last of the coffee and sat back. Jacob Frost stood as if he were behind a podium at a conference, not hunting ghosts in Texas. *If he lives through this, nothin in the academic world will ever scare him again.*

Okay, said the professor. We've got to destroy the gun belt and the boots, along with whatever blood and tissue might still cling to them. We've tried that before, but we've got to accomplish it. If the lore is anywhere close to accurate, we'll never be rid of the ghost until we do one of two things: help it with its unfinished business or destroy its connection to our world.

Adam Garner scratched his nose with a dirty fingernail. Doc, I understood only about half of what you just said, but I'm gonna go out on a limb and say its unfinished business is killin everybody in this room.

Well, not everybody, said Frost. Just you, Joyce, Red, the mayor, and Will Roark. The McCorkle woman, too. If all the descendants were dead, it might just fade away, but obviously, we can't allow that.

Thornapple snorted. I think we're all on board with that idea.

That leaves us with severing its connection. I still think fire is the best method. The problem, as we've seen, is staying alive long enough to burn something.

Raymond held up his left hand, the cast bulky and milky white. Or in one piece.

Frost gestured to Raymond. Right. So. We've tested a couple of the legends and found they're true. Salt repels it, and it's scared of fire getting anywhere near the boots. Here's what I propose. Ray, Darrell, Betsy, and I go to the diner. Raymond and Darrell cover Betsy and me as we ring the Dead House with salt and douse it with gasoline. Then we toss a match on it and run like hell. That should take care of everything connecting the Kid to our world.

And what keeps that thing from killin y'all? Red asked.

Frost cleared his throat. Well, when I was on that back road with Chief Bradley, it didn't come after us until we struck a match. I'm theorizing it understands the threat of fire but not the accelerant. Or that it knows the accelerant is useless without the flame. If we use the gas first, then lay the salt ring, we should be able to set the fire from just outside the circle.

Joyce Johnstone, who had been sipping a cup of coffee, said, What do Red, Adam, and me do? Cuss at it?

No. You stay here. Eat something. Watch a movie. Anything but come near the diner.

And if we find it's trapped outside the salt circle with us? asked LeBlanc.

Frost looked grim. Then I suppose you and Ray will have to be very good shots.

Johnstone got up and walked to a window. She pushed aside the curtains and let in the light. The sky peeked around the trees in the yard. It was overcast, the clouds dark gray and backlit. She looked over her shoulder.

Forecast is for showers, she said. What happens if it rains?

Then we'll go to plan B, Frost said.

No one replied. They waited on him to explain as if they were a group of college freshmen. He took a deep breath and detailed their backup plan, a much more dangerous gambit for the surviving descendants, one he hoped to avoid.

Raymond, LeBlanc, Frost, and McDowell packed the guns into the rental while Garner, Johnstone, and Thornapple watched from the porch. A gumbo of hope, fear, anticipation, guilt, and shame radiated from them, straight into Elizabeth McDowell. Johnstone projected love and concern, probably for Thornapple, who projected the shame. He probably felt like less of a man for staying behind, not pulling his weight. Such archaic ideas were silly, but Red Thornapple was a traditional man living in a conservative town. He had very specific ideas of what a man should do, and hiding out while others, including a woman, risked their lives would not make the list. Adam Garner betrayed no such conflicts. He seemed content to let the so-called professionals handle the Kid. If he knew them better—that McDowell spent most of her time reading palms and tarot cards and dispensing advice on love; that Frost practically lived in the classrooms, libraries, and offices of his university; and that Raymond and LeBlanc had never faced a ghost until one shot Raymond's hand to pieces—then he might change his mind, but they had revealed little about themselves to these people. For all the descendants knew, even McDowell was a hardened detective who might shoot you before lunch and order her steak bloody.

She could not feel Raymond's physical agony, but she read the heavy weight of his responsibility as if it were written in the dust on a pickup's rear window.

Once the guns were secured, Raymond turned to her.

You and Jake ain't full-time professionals, he said. If you want out, we'll understand.

She smiled and patted Raymond's cheek. Hush. I'm goin.

Raymond tried to smile back, but he was frightened half to death, his eyes as haunted as the diner grounds. Trembling, he embraced her. When he pulled away, he said, Okay. Let's get this show on the road.

He got behind the wheel. She climbed into the passenger seat. In front of them, LeBlanc and Frost piled into their own vehicle. Thornapple, Johnstone, and Garner watched from the porch, shoulder to shoulder, as if the proximity could shield them from whatever might come. Thornapple raised his right hand and waved as his left arm snaked around Johnstone's waist. McDowell waved back. Raymond started the car. They circled Thornapple's driveway and headed for the Depot Diner.

Half a mile down the road, the first raindrops struck the windshield. The trees by the roadside swayed. Dark clouds inched in front of the sun.

A skinny deputy with a pencil mustache slept in his radio car beside the diner's entrance, cap pulled over his face, dripping sweat. He had cranked down all his windows to take advantage of whatever breeze might blow, but now, everything was still, the clouds hovering low. Strobe lightning flashed like cameras at a press conference. The guy had pluck, if not professionalism. Not everyone could rest easy at the scene of two murders while a storm rolled in. LeBlanc and Frost parked across from the deputy and started unloading salt rounds from the back seat and trunk.

Let's try not to wake up yonder cop, LeBlanc said. We don't know his orders, so the longer he's asleep, the less we gotta worry about him.

Frost glanced at the radio car but said nothing. The professor seemed to be feeling the weight of what they were about to do—take on a murderous being, defy local authorities, commit arson, and hope for the best. LeBlanc and Raymond had done some questionable things in their time—had bent laws nearly in half, had broken some—but that came with the territory. Frost, on the other hand, taught folklore and wrote dry articles nobody except other folklore scholars read. He designed lectures, directed studies, helped set policies. He was a kind of authority, a stable, safe man today's events were likely to change, if he survived them. He would forever after be the kind of person who set fire to buildings, who subverted the edicts of mayors, who loaded shotguns, and who put himself in harm's way. Such a sea change had to be traumatic.

The professor unloaded boxes of ammo, stacking them in the center of the blue tarp LeBlanc had bought. Together, they lifted the tarp's ends and folded them over the shells. Then they hefted their load and set it in the trunk amid dozens of boxes of rock salt. If anyone saw this cargo, they would probably believe Frost and LeBlanc were headed to the world's biggest redneck ice-cream social, where shooting contests would comprise the entertainment.

Rain began to fall. LeBlanc shut the trunk, and they got back in the car. Across the street, the deputy stirred when a fat raindrop hit his elbow, which hung out the window. He muttered and pulled the arm back in, and then he moved no more.

Raymond and McDowell parked behind LeBlanc and Frost as light rain began to fall.

Be right back, Raymond said. He got out and ran to LeBlanc's door.

LeBlanc rolled down the window. Lovely goddam weather we're havin, ain't it?

Yeah. Maybe we should wait till it blows over.

You heard Joyce. Forecast calls for showers. Frankly, that sky looks more like it's gonna thunderstorm.

Raymond spat. He motioned for McDowell to get out.

LeBlanc watched her trot through the rain. I wish we'd thought to buy slickers, he said. At least we could have stayed dry while we're gettin killed.

Let's get this done before it gets worse.

Frost got out. LeBlanc popped the trunk and followed, carrying his shotgun. Raymond went to retrieve his own shotgun as McDowell and Frost unloaded the garden sprayers LeBlanc had bought at Walmart, backpack models with a pump for maintaining pressure. Raymond wanted battery-operated models, but the store had none in stock. LeBlanc leaned his gun against the car and pulled out two red plastic gas cans, both full. He took the cap from one and fixed the nozzle. Then he poured the gas into the sprayers while McDowell and Frost held them steady. Once the sprayers were full, LeBlanc helped Frost and McDowell strap the units onto their backs. He showed them how to use the pumps and wands. The professor and the medium looked like Ghostbusters, which they were.

Don't cross the streams, Raymond muttered.

McDowell looked up. Huh?

Nothin.

By the time Raymond and LeBlanc loaded their guns and pulled out the tarp-covered boxes, Raymond toting one end with his good hand while struggling to keep the shotgun tucked under his other arm, the rain was falling harder. The group walked past the snoring deputy and across the lot. They would have little margin for error if the Kid pressed them hard.

We better not drop our ammo in a mud puddle.

They reached the Dead House without incident. Raymond and LeBlanc unfolded the tarp, leaving one layer over the boxes. Then they flanked Frost and McDowell, who took two boxes of rock salt apiece and started pouring a line on the ground, Frost going first, circling the building. Raymond and LeBlanc took care not to step in the salt as they panned their shotguns, back-to-back, LeBlanc walking backward, Raymond calling out whenever a slippery patch of ground presented itself. When Frost's boxes ran out, McDowell took up where he left off, skirting the edges of the gathering puddles.

The plan worked fine until they reached the halfway point when the rain intensified again, spattering them in great plops. In half a minute, they stood and watched as their neat barrier blossomed into off-white puddles and dissipated. At first, McDowell and Frost ran to and fro, trying to replenish the line. But after they had exhausted half a dozen boxes, the line was still barely visible in some places, obliterated in most.

Screw it, Raymond said. Come on, Darrell.

He and LeBlanc trotted over and laid their guns on the diner's porch. Then they returned to the tarp and grabbed more salt.

What are we doin? asked LeBlanc as water streamed down his face.

Let's set up around the building. Me in the back, you in the front, Betsy and Jake on the sides.

They tried it that way—first walking toward each other, meeting, then turning back. Then they started at equidistant points and chased each other around the Dead House. They tried walking one behind the other and replenishing the line as they went. Nothing worked. The driving rain turned the courtyard into a swamp, and their salt line lumped up, floated away, dissolved. They had more supplies back at Thornapple's, having emptied every grocery store for miles around, but they had exhausted most of what they had brought with them.

Raymond turned to Frost and said, What do you think?

Frost looked disgusted. If the line's broken anywhere, and I mean by like a millimeter, the Kid can cross it. And so can his bullets. There's no way we can keep it solid in these conditions.

Frost was right. It was like writing your name in the sand at high tide. Raymond waved them back toward the cars. Frost and LeBlanc rewrapped the remaining boxes in the tarp and carried it between them. They splashed through the parking lot, Raymond and McDowell trotting behind them with the guns. When they reached the cars, LeBlanc opened the trunk, and he and Frost tossed the ammunition-filled tarp into it. Then they stood back while Raymond and McDowell unloaded and packed in the guns. Finally, LeBlanc helped McDowell and Frost out of the sprayer units and stored them. They shut the lid and got in the car, Frost and McDowell climbing in the back.

McDowell wrung out her hair onto the floorboard. What now? she asked. Plan B?

I reckon so, Raymond said.

LeBlanc wiped water from his face. Well, we could gas up and haul ass back to New Orleans.

He seemed to have meant it as a joke, but nobody laughed. They all sat there, dripping rainwater onto the seats and floorboards, watching the Dead House, only its outline visible through the pouring rain. Lightning flashed, illuminating the gray landscape. Even the sleeping deputy had awakened at some point and rolled up his windows. If he had noticed the trespassers, he had left them alone. Perhaps he saw little point in getting wet for people who were running away from the property he was supposed to guard. In any case, the rain showed no signs of letting up.

Eventually, Raymond sighed. Well, the day ain't gettin no younger. Or drier. We better head on. Jake, you and Betsy take the other car. Me and Darrell need to talk.

Frost and McDowell got out of the car and sprinted to the other vehicle. Raymond started the rental. After a moment, he asked, You think we can get through this without gettin somebody killed?

Too quickly, as if he had no doubt, LeBlanc said, No. I don't.

Back at Thornapple's house, the four of them dashed for the front door, splashing through more puddles, cursing.

Thornapple met them in the den, his face grim. Well, we're in trouble now.

Rennie sat on Thornapple's couch. Thornapple must have picked her up from the hospital. She stood as they came in and said, Y'all look like you just swam across from Mexico. Her eyes were puffy and red. The end of her nose glowed pink.

Raymond tried to wring out his shirt with one hand. The rain caught us. We couldn't make the salt line.

Both Rennie and Thornapple looked as if they had expected this. A moment later, Joyce Johnstone and Adam Garner carried in a platter of sandwiches, a pitcher of iced tea, and glasses. They set their trays on the coffee table and joined the others, Garner standing with his hands in his pockets, Johnstone sidling up to Thornapple and taking his hand.

For if you're hungry, she said.

LeBlanc made a beeline for the tray, tracking mud and water across Thornapple's floor. The rest of them pulled off their muddy shoes and stood near the entryway.

Speaking mostly to Raymond, Rennie said, The council's gonna meet this evenin, tomorrow at the latest. I talked to Fred Deese. He expects they'll honor C.W.'s wishes and let the police handle the case.

Who's Fred Deese? Raymond asked.

Councilman. He usually knows which way the wind's blowin.

Hell.

Yep.

Raymond looked at the others. They seemed grim, though his own people had expected no less. Ever since they hit town, the local authorities had tried everything short of tar and feathers and an old rail to make them leave. But they had stayed because Raymond's family was in danger, and because people were dying, and because Raymond knew that, if he left, he would never be able to look at his wife's picture without remembering his own cowardice. Now he would have to lead them all back to the Dead House—for Rennie and for himself and for Bob Bradley, who lay cold and alone in the morgue. Some of them were likely to die. For what seemed like the thousandth time, he wished he had a drink, or fifty.

It's on to plan B, he said.

What about yonder flood? Garner asked. He nodded at the window. Rain streamed down the glass, obscuring the outside world. Lightning flashed.

Raymond shrugged. We'll try to wait it out. But Rennie says the council's meetin, maybe as soon as tonight. If it don't blow over, we take our shot anyway. In the meantime, I suggest we try to get some sleep.

Thornapple scoffed. Yeah. Right. I'm sure we'll sleep like babies, knowin what's comin.

I'll stay up and watch the weather, Garner said. I'm used to pullin long hours.

Thanks, Raymond said. Last chance—anybody wanna walk away?

For a moment, no one said anything. Then Red Thornapple cleared his throat.

I'm in, he said. But I don't want Joyce out there. Me and Adam should be enough.

Johnstone laughed without humor. That's real sweet, hon. But you don't speak for me. I'm goin.

Red turned to her and held her by both shoulders, looking at her with as much intensity as he could muster.

That goddam thing's already killed three people. And look at Ray's hand.

She shook loose from his grip. I've seen it, darlin. But I'm no kid, and if you're in to all that helpless-woman's-gotta-be-protected-by-a-big-strong-man bullshit, I ain't for you. I'm goin.

Red hit the wall with the side of his fist. Goddam it, can't you do what I tell you just once?

She took his fist and uncurled it, roping her fingers into his. Nope. I might do what you ask, but I won't ever do what you tell me. Especially not now.

Then I'm askin.

Good. But I'm still sayin no.

He glared at her for a moment. Then he snatched his hand away and stalked off.

Raymond, raising his voice so Thornapple could hear even in full retreat, said, Since my underwear's stickin to the crack of my ass, I'm gonna make the futile gesture of puttin on some dry clothes before we go get soaked and muddy again.

He hugged Rennie. She hugged him back, expressionless. If she minded getting wet, she said nothing about it. Raymond had already told her to stay at the hospital with Will or go back to their house or leave for Australia—be anywhere but the Depot Diner. Hopefully she would listen. He released her and headed for his room. Behind him, the others moved toward their respective parts of the house.

Red's a good man, Johnstone said to no one in particular, but sometimes I think he wants to bop me over the head with a club and drag me back to the cave by my hair.

Alone in his room, Raymond's meager confidence slipped away. He stripped and dried himself with yesterday's shirt. Then he sat on the bed and rubbed his forehead, feeling old and tired and incompetent and afraid and alone. Soon it would be time to saddle up and lead a pack of amateurs into battle against something he did not understand. It all seemed so absurd and surreal. He kept expecting to wake up years in the past, Marie beside him, the sheets sweated through, her hand on his shoulder as she shook him awake. Then he would look into her emerald eyes until his breathing and heart rate slowed, take her in his arms, brush her auburn hair away from her face, play his fingertips over her lips and the little scar on her chin and the beginnings of crow's-feet around her eyes. Then he would kiss her and hold her until the day's responsibilities drove them from bed.

But no such thing could happen. Marie was gone, and he would wake every day of his life alone, her side of the bed empty, her pillow still cool.

He looked at the ceiling and said, I ain't spoke to God since he took you away. I ain't said much to you either. Reckon I've been a mite pissed you left me here. But if you're up there, and you've got the Lord's ear, do me a favor and ask him to let me do good. Let me make the right decisions when the time comes. I ain't askin for my life. But if he listens to you, maybe ask him to turn his face toward us long enough to get this done. And if I see you tonight, well, that's probably the best thing I could ask for. You take care, darlin.

Raymond lay back on the bed and closed his eyes, not dozing, not thinking, just listening to his own breath and the sounds of the house until it was time to get up and do what he was afraid to do.

McDowell had just finished putting on dry clothes, knowing, given the conditions outside, how futile it likely was, but it made her feel better anyway. She knelt in front of the bed, rested her elbows on it, folded her hands, closed her eyes. And then, for five straight minutes, for the first time since discovering her empathic abilities, she prayed. She had been raised Catholic and had observed every ritual, every custom, until she turned thirteen. Then, at Mass one day, emotions burst forth from the congregation and battered her senseless—deep faith and the concurrent happiness and peace. Sadness and loss, hypocrisy, guilt. As if she became everyone in the room at their most vulnerable. She had thrown up on Mr. Breedlove in the next pew up, and then she had run from the chapel screaming. Her parents forced her to go back, Mass after Mass after agonizing Mass, where she sat bent over, hands pressed to her temples, concentrating on the hymnal, the floor, anything but what she felt. After turning eighteen, she had never stepped foot inside a church again, had avoided crowds whenever possible, had never been to a concert or a ball game, had never again gone to Carnival. She lived in the city because she loved it so much, but she stayed home as much as possible.

Still, she had always associated her abilities with God. Perhaps he had cursed her. Perhaps her human mind could not comprehend the nature of his blessing. That ambiguity had haunted her, kept her off her knees and away from her rosaries. Now she pleaded for her friends' safety, for a good end to these terrible events, for the mayor's health, for Rennie's peace of mind. She prayed for them all, and when she said her amen and opened her eyes, Elizabeth McDowell wept. Part of her felt relieved. Until the prayers spilled from her, she had never realized how much she missed that feeling of intimacy with the Mysteries. The rest of her was terrified. But she could not stay inside, safe from the emotions and how they flayed her mind, not when people were dying. She stood up, wiped away the tears, and looked around for her dry pair of shoes.

Then a light knock, as if someone had dragged their knuckles across the wood. She opened the door. LeBlanc stood there, his hair wet and slicked back, his clothes dry except around his neck and shoulders.

He entered. She closed the door and leaned against it, hands clasped behind her. No more than three feet separated them. They looked at each other, neither speaking, the sound of the rain falling outside the window somehow soothing, the intermittent thunder like voices speaking in the next room.

Finally, LeBlanc said, Look. I just wanted to say. Um. Look.

I'm lookin.

LeBlanc swallowed hard. If he had not been radiating desperation, she might have laughed.

It's okay, Darrell. Just spit it out.

He inhaled. Look, I ain't very good with words, but it's no secret how I feel about you and I wish I could talk you into sittin this one out, but I also know you ain't gonna, so before we go get killed, I just wanna make sure you know how I really feel deep down.

He exhaled.

McDowell moved closer and put one hand on his bicep, feeling his tension, his strength.

We already talked, she said. On the street in New Orleans. In the hotel. Don't torture yourself into sayin what I already know.

She grabbed him by the back of his neck and pulled him down. She pressed her lips to his, their tongues flicking out, finding each other, flicking back. It lasted almost a full minute. When it ended, they both trembled. LeBlanc put both arms around her and pulled her close.

She laid her head on his chest.

They sat on the bed together, their bodies touching, his right arm around her, his left hand in hers. He kissed the top of her head, and they lay down together, still holding hands. It was still raining when they fell asleep.

CHAPTER TWENTY-SIX

September 16, 2016, Dusk—Comanche, Texas

The rain fell all day, flooding Thornapple's driveway. Twice, it had nearly stopped. Garner had awakened them all both times, but by the time they had gathered, it was pouring again. On TV, a flash flood warning cautioned against trying to cross standing water on roads, especially in low-lying areas.

It was still raining when everyone gathered in the den just before 7 p.m., Raymond and LeBlanc in the center of their half circle. That was the price of having your name on the agency letterhead—or would have been if the agency had any letterhead. Thornapple, Johnstone, and Garner had procured shotguns of their own. The weapons lay on the table, pointed toward a wall. *It's like they grow on trees around here.*

LeBlanc nudged Raymond. He had been woolgathering.

All right, Raymond said. Let's go over it one more time. I'm real sorry it's come to this, but we're outta time.

Ain't nobody blamin you, Turner, Garner said. Just get on with it.

The others nodded.

Okay, said Raymond. The plan's divide and conquer. Me and Mr. Garner here—

Adam, said Garner.

Raymond took a deep breath, trying to maintain his composure. If Garner kept interrupting him, he might lose his nerve and run for New Orleans as fast as he could go.

Me and Adam here will flank Jacob and Betsy. Since we can't ring the place with salt, they'll douse it with gas. Once that's done, they'll light it up, and we should be able to watch the place burn down. As for the rest of you, we're gonna make the Kid choose between killin his targets and protectin himself. You'll be on the far side of the property, actin as decoys. Darrell will run things on your end. Your job's to stay alive. If the Kid keeps hittin us and only us, come a-runnin and help. If not, stay where you are, and keep him distracted. Just don't shoot each other. And don't shoot us.

Thornapple raised his hand. How come y'all only got two, guns and we got three?

Because we're hopin the Kid will come after us, LeBlanc said. If we can keep him busy, the others can set the fire quicker and safer.

Garner nodded. Sounds okay so far. But what happens if we manage to set the buildin on fire and this ghost keeps comin at us?

Raymond frowned. Then we get off the diner property and stay off. Jake will look for another solution, but I don't know that we'll get to try it. This is our best shot, and it's all we know to do with the time we got. Any more questions?

There were none.

Raymond smiled, trying to be reassuring, but it felt false. Okay. Let's saddle up. And if any of you are prayin folks, send up a few on the way. We need all the help we can get.

The motorcade arrived at the Depot Diner with Raymond and LeBlanc leading, McDowell and Frost riding with Adam Garner in the middle, and Thornapple and Johnstone bringing up the rear. They had stopped by Brookshire's, where LeBlanc bought cheap slickers for everyone except Thornapple and Johnstone, who had honest-to-God raincoats at the house. Then they drove straight for the depot.

As they turned onto Austin and parked on the side of the road, they all saw exactly what they had hoped not to see—three CPD cruisers parked in the diner's driveway, blockading the entrance. Raymond assessed the landscape. The ditch on either side of the drive was too deep for the rental car and Thornapple's truck. Either one would likely bottom out before the front tires could make the other side. Garner's extended cab had a chance, but if it got stuck, they would be completely at the Kid's mercy, and he seemed to have none. Acting Chief Roen stood in front of two taller, beefier officers, one white and one Latinx, all three of them wearing slickers, their arms folded across their chests. They looked like men intent on guarding the entrance with their lives. Raymond sighed. He had never seen a town so intent on allowing its citizens to die.

Raymond and company piled out of their vehicles, leaving their weapons behind. The cops stood between Raymond's group and the squad cars, and for a moment, they sized each other up, Raymond calculating the distance and the logistics and the likely consequences of jumping the three of them right there in the street.

Roen nodded at him. Mr. Turner.

Raymond said, Chief Roen.

Roen grimaced. I'd appreciate you not usin that title with Bob not even cold yet. The council's meetin again tomorrow. They'll probably give it to somebody else, and that's damn fine with me.

My apologies. So what now?

Roen's officers said nothing, their faces expressionless, their eyes hooded in the rain and fading evening light.

I reckon you know what the council wants, Roen said.

We heard. Don't seem like the smartest play.

The rain spattered on them and puddled in the street. Thunder grumbled like a sleeping god in the grip of a nightmare.

Red Thornapple stepped forward and said, The best way to honor Bob's memory is to finish what he started.

One of the deputies began to speak, but Roen shook his head. *That fella could break your arm off and tie it in a bow around your neck,* Raymond thought. Yet the deputy closed his mouth. Roen still held Raymond's gaze.

I don't need you or nobody else tellin me about Bob, he said to Thornapple.

To his credit, the newspaperman said nothing. Adam Garner cleared his throat. LeBlanc tensed. If Raymond gestured, at least one of the cops would be unconscious before hitting the ground. But it should not come to that. At best, it would lead to their arrest. At worst, they might all shoot each other and save the Kid's ammunition.

We just wanna help, Raymond said. It's all we ever wanted.

Roen rubbed the bridge of his nose and squinted, as if his head were pounding. I know it is, he said. And I got no idea how to arrest a ghost. So me and my boys here, we're just gonna drive our cruisers up the road a piece and block off this street at both ends. Last thing we need is some lookie-lou gettin his ass shot off. You folks need anything, you just holler.

Shit, Garner muttered. I reckon we'll holler even if we don't need nothin.

One of the deputies leaned in and said, The council's gonna have our heads if any of these townsfolk get killed.

Roen looked about and shrugged. Then let 'em come down here and deal with this shit their own selves. If you boys wanna leave, go on, but block the road first and walk.

The Latinx deputy, whose badge read *Gomez*, said, We'll stay. We seen what happens when our chief goes off by hisself.

Officer Roen, Raymond said, if we don't make it, stoppin this thing will fall to you. Use salt rounds to drive it off. Then burn that storage buildin. Make sure them old boots and gun belt go up with the rest.

Roen stuck out his hand. Raymond shook it. Good luck, Roen said.

The three officers turned and walked to their cars. Roen opened his trunk. He took out half a dozen long flares and fired up three of them, placing them across the road ten yards north of the diner's driveway. The deputies set up a redundant roadblock at Austin and Central, their lights flashing. One man stood on Central's shoulder with a flashlight, waving the sporadic southbound traffic toward the east. Then Roen got back in his car and pulled out of the drive, turning south on Austin. He stopped after ten or twelve yards and got out, setting three more flares across the road. Then he drove to the intersection, where he maneuvered the vehicle to block access. He got out and stood with his back to the diner, ready to redirect any northbound traffic.

The Depot Diner had been cut off.

Raymond's group fell back to their own vehicles.

Did that really just happen? Frost asked.

Johnstone grinned. That little fella probably don't weigh more than a hundred pounds soakin wet, but eighty of it is guts and nuts.

Raymond burst out laughing. They looked at him as if he had lost his mind.

I'm glad you're gettin a kick outta this, LeBlanc said.

Once his laughter tapered off, Raymond said, Okay. Red, you and Ms. Johnstone park way over there by the east fence. Darrell will ride shotgun and call the shots. Once they're in position, Adam, back your truck close to the building. Remember you're carryin all the combustibles. I'll park about halfway between Adam and Red. Everybody be ready for anything. If you see the Kid, shoot him. That means we'll have to watch each other, too. All that salt's gotta go someplace, and it would just as soon bury itself in our asses. Let's don't get killed.

They helped McDowell and Frost into the sprayers. Getting in and out of the vehicles while wearing them would be a pain in the ass, but it could not be helped. Who knew when the Kid would appear? After McDowell and Frost struggled into the truck, everyone else embarked. The drivers started the engines and waved to each other. Then they drove across Austin and onto the Depot Diner grounds.

Thornapple zipped across the lot, past the diner and the Dead House, all the way to the chain-link fence separating the lot from the feed mill. His tires splashed through puddles in the parking area and made shallow imprints in the soaked caliche. The water spilling back into them looked like gravy. He parked the truck with its grille inches from the fence and jumped out, a salt-loaded shotgun in hand. LeBlanc and Johnstone piled out of the other side. LeBlanc yanked down the tailgate, their half of the ammunition sitting on top of one blue tarp and covered by another. They readied their guns. Dusk was falling like a curtain, the air almost as gray as the clouds overhead.

Huddling with the others against the rain, LeBlanc said, Remember, we can't all shoot at once. I'm first. Red, you go next. Joyce, cover us. If all three of us run outta ammo at once, we're dead, so don't panic, you hear?

I got it, Johnstone said. Her eyes were wide and alert, her jaw clenched.

Yeah, said Thornapple, his gaze roving everywhere.

Driving alone, Adam Garner pulled into the parking lot and headed straight for the Dead House, leaving Raymond to U-turn so he could back in. The building loomed out of the rain, its windows like a skull's blank eyes. Garner's 20-gauge sat in the gun rack behind his head, its barrel pointed toward the passenger door. The five-gallon cans of gasoline and the tarps with all the extra ammo and salt shifted in the bed as he bounced over the uneven ground. Near the fence, LeBlanc and the others leaped out of Thornapple's truck and fanned out, their guns readied like soldiers walking behind enemy lines. When Garner got close enough to the Dead House to see the individual chips in its paint through the driving rain, he braked and maneuvered through the grassy parts of the yard, making a half-turn and then backing up until his tailgate pointed at the Dead House's front door. Then he put the truck in drive and moved it away another five yards or so. Too close and the truck would go up when the building did. Too far and they were all likely to die trying to reload. He clambered out, the rain beating down so hard his slicker's hood fell over his face. He grabbed the shotgun's stock and yanked, wondering if he would feel slugs slamming into his abdomen, his jaw, his temple, if he would find himself falling down a long dark hole with nothing at the bottom but Lorena Harveston and John Wayne and maybe even the Kid himself. But when he got the shotgun free and pulled the hood off his head, nothing was there.

Holding the shotgun in his right hand, Garner trotted to the tailgate, his heavy tread splashing water and mud as high as his waist. He let the tailgate down and listened to Turner and the others slogging through the yard. Hopefully, they would make it across the open field of fire without incident.

McDowell winced as the sprayer dug in to her back. Raymond threw the car into reverse and eased toward the Dead House. The rental had not been built to mud-hog in a goddam monsoon. If he lost control, he might run Garner down or, even worse, careen into the truck. If that happened to start a fire that ignited the ammo in the trunk, the four of them would be blown to the moon, and even with salt rounds, LeBlanc and the others would get torn to shreds. The rental slid, the caliche as solid as steel underneath an inch or two of mud.

Any sign of the Kid? Raymond asked.

No, said Frost and McDowell.

Raymond rolled up beside Garner's truck, the vehicles five feet apart and ten yards from the Dead House. He popped the trunk, and they stepped into the driving rain. Dark seemed to be coming faster than it should have in late summer, as if the storm had appeared just to blind them.

Raymond retrieved his shotgun. Frost stood beside Garner. McDowell pushed the trunk lid down without shutting it, to provide easy access to the ammo and salt. Raymond joined her, still watching the grounds.

When the other group bunched up near the Dead House, LeBlanc cursed. *Y'all watch your interval*, he was about to shout, but before he could, the air in front of him shimmered, and the Kid appeared, those long stick arms hanging at his sides as if attached without muscle and sinew. Somewhere to his left, Johnstone cried out in a strangled voice. *It's one thing to hear about this. It's another to see it.* The Kid's eyes ran and shrank and vanished, leaving only the baleful glare of empty sockets.

Thornapple fired, and the Kid winked out, his scream filling LeBlanc's head. Thornapple's mouth hung open, and he was looking at his gun as if he had never seen one before.

I told you to let me shoot first, LeBlanc said.

Thornapple looked embarrassed. Sorry. It was instinct.

From somewhere behind LeBlanc, over the steady rain and the grumbling thunder, Johnstone called, Get off his back. It ain't like we fight ghosts every other weekend.

LeBlanc ignored her. He scanned the property, hoping to see the Kid close by or not at all. The rain intensified, pounding as if it had something against them, nearly obscuring the Dead House. He could make out Thornapple's shape but not his features, could not even tell which way the man faced. Gooseflesh broke out all over LeBlanc's body. He did not know if the Kid were close, or if he were just scared shitless, or both.

Raymond's group had nearly reached the Dead House when a shotgun boomed near the fence line. Garner wheeled around. McDowell and

Frost paused, looking toward the sound.

Ignore that, Raymond said. Do your jobs.

McDowell turned to him, her face a mask of anguish and fear. But they could ill afford to pause.

She got moving, and the rain intensified, obscuring their view of LeBlanc's crew. They tramped through puddles and slid through muck and slipped over the steel-hard ground beneath it, trying to cover those last few yards before anything else happened.

And then the Kid floated in front of them, blocking their path. McDowell and Frost stopped in their tracks, Frost's feet flying out from under him. He splooshed into the standing water and mud like a child falling backward into a shallow pool, landing with his spine arced across the sprayer unit, grimacing in pain. He moaned and tried to stand. Garner helped him up, both goggling at the Kid.

McDowell's eyes were bleeding again, her jaw clenched in pain as she tried to ease around the apparition. He floated like a Halloween dec-oration. Raymond's scrotum tightened. He gripped the gun so hard he might well have left impressions in the metal. Watching the Kid for any sign of movement, he still barely registered when the Kid whirled, drew his gun, and fired at McDowell, the sound of the report thundering in Raymond's mind. Frost winced, one hand at his temple. McDowell skidded in the mud just before the shot. The bullet did not strike her in the head or the heart or wherever the Kid might have aimed, but it hit her nonetheless. She screamed and spun, falling into the water.

Raymond cried her name, aimed, and pulled the trigger. The Kid vanished. Salt smacked into the Dead House, knocking loose three or four boards. Raymond and Garner splashed toward McDowell.

Oh, hell, Frost said from somewhere near the building.

Garner turned and said, Aw shit.

The trucker tried to run back the way they had come, his feet slipping and sliding under him in ways that would have been comical under other circumstances. He held the 20-gauge above his head and yelled, No! Here!

The Kid had reappeared in front of Frost and had drawn both of his Howitzers. Frost raised his hands as if he were being robbed, the sprayer wand swinging at his side, bumping against his leg and twirling about. The Kid fired anyway. Frost held his hands in front of his face. After a moment, he patted his torso, looking for the wound.

Garner reached him and pointed to the wand. The hose had been blown apart. The wand lay in the water at Frost's feet. Frost picked it up, held it out to the Kid, and then tossed it aside. He grabbed the dripping hose and tied it off.

An almost imperceptible movement of his head suggested the Kid had noticed Garner.

Frost stepped in front of the bigger man, hands up.

Move, Doc, hissed Garner.

No, said Frost, his voice shaking. He isn't after me.

You're takin a hell of a chance.

The Kid did not lower the gun, but he also did not shoot. Gently, slowly, Garner pulled the sprayer off Frost, the professor holding his arms back to allow the contraption to slide off.

Shit fuck hell, he whispered.

When it was free, Garner said, I'm backin up to the truck.

Frost nodded, and they walked backward, glancing at the truck every few steps until they reached it. Then Garner dropped the sprayer unit into the bed, and they eased away.

McDowell moaned.

Hell, I forgot all about her, Raymond thought.

Raymond knelt beside her. She had rolled onto her right side and held her left arm, her eyes shut tight, her teeth clenched in agony. Trying to balance his gun in the crook of his own injured arm, he put his good hand on her back.

He got me, she whimpered. Oh shit, it hurts.

Maybe the Kid aimed for her sprayer unit, too, and her slippin in the mud got her shot. Or maybe he knows she can feel him and don't like it. Either way, she's gotta get outta here.

Raymond needed to remove her slicker to examine the arm, but ignoring the Kid that long seemed like a terrible idea. Raymond helped McDowell sit up and eased the sprayer off her back. He put a hand on her good shoulder.

Get to the street, he said. We gotta finish this.

She waved him off. Don't worry about me. Go.

LeBlanc's group shouted at each other, but Raymond had no time to listen. The Kid appeared in front of him, those blank, gray eyes regarding him. Raymond set the sprayer on the ground and moved away from it. The Kid watched. *Huh. He knows what they're for.* Raymond reached out slowly, as if to touch the sprayer again, and would have sworn in a court of law that the Kid's hand twitched. He straightened up and backed away. The Kid vanished.

He's watchin every move we make, Raymond said. Adam, go fetch Darrell and them.

Garner splashed toward the fence while Raymond stood near McDowell in the driving rain. Once Garner disappeared into the darkness, Raymond picked up the unit and ran for the truck. The Kid did not reappear. Raymond set the sprayer in the bed and then waded back to McDowell. The vehicles sat there, lumps in the dark, bright in the intermittent lightning. Frost remained near the truck, looking lost.

They could not get near the Dead House with the units. What the hell were they supposed to do?

When the gunfire at the Dead House began, LeBlanc could make out only vague shapes moving in the downpour. Thunder boomed. Hard rain spattered the standing water. *If it rains any harder, we're gonna see a boat loadin animals two by two.* LeBlanc had no idea what to do. He might as well have been trying to navigate the Mississippi in pea-soup fog with cotton stuffed in his ears.

I can't see a goddam thing, Thornapple said. What now?

First off, get back to your position before we both get shot. Don't do nothin unless I do it first, you hear?

They could be gettin massacred over there. We can't just leave 'em.

Goddam it, you think I don't know that?

Thornapple looked at him for a moment and then backed away. Johnstone was nowhere in sight, but he could not worry about everyone at once. If all three of them moved in, they would be abandoning their strategy and might get somebody killed, yet he could not leave Thornapple and Johnstone alone. He gritted his teeth and cursed, wishing the weather would at least give him a clear line of sight. How was he supposed to decide when he could not even see?

And then, in the thunder's brief cessation, high-pitched and anguished, connoting all the pain he had hoped to spare them from: a woman's scream. The thunder boomed again, cutting off the sound, but he had heard enough.

He cupped his free hand to his mouth. Red! Joyce! Get over here!

They ran to him, their weapons held in both hands and pointed at the ground, as hunters were taught to move through the forests.

We goin in or what? Thornapple asked.

We're goin in, said LeBlanc. Spread out. I'll take point. If the Kid shows himself, know where you're shootin. If either of you hits Betsy, you won't need to worry about that fuckin ghost. And call out so the others know you're comin. Do we understand each other?

Johnstone's eyes widened. She raised her gun to her shoulder. Somethin's comin through.

LeBlanc whirled, raising his gun as Thornapple stepped up and aimed. A human form trotted toward them, splashing water. It carried a shotgun, not pistols. Plus, the shape looked all wrong. The Kid was shortish and gaunt and floated along. This one was taller, beefier, its legs pumping. They could hear it. After another second or two, the clothing and the god-awful slicker became visible.

LeBlanc lowered his weapon. Don't shoot. It's Garner.

The big trucker ran up, huffing great lungfuls of air, and croaked, Y'all, come quick. The Kid keeps cuttin us off. He shot Betsy.

How bad? LeBlanc asked, dreading the answer.

I don't know.

LeBlanc motioned Johnstone and Thornapple forward. They fanned out. Johnstone swung wide to the southwest, circling around the cars. Thornapple headed straight for the buildings. That left the middle, so LeBlanc and Garner moved several feet apart and marched toward the vehicles.

CHAPTER TWENTY-SEVEN

September 16, 2016, Full Dark—Comanche, Texas

The rain would not let up. *I doubt we can set that building on fire in this storm,* Raymond thought. *Unless we get inside.* He glanced toward the fence. The others should be close. His decision to bring them over would likely get someone killed.

The ghost rematerialized in the same spot from which it had disappeared. It watched Raymond, as if waiting for his next move.

After a moment, everyone's voices rang out—Johnstone's low and smoky and somewhere in the lot, Thornapple's close to the Dead House itself, LeBlanc's familiar baritone coming from who knew where. Though it likely did not depend on human senses, even the ghost seemed confused. The water dripping into Raymond's eyes might have played tricks on him, but it seemed the Kid's head turned back and forth, just a little. Had they managed to confuse him, coming from so many directions at once?

Then Thornapple loomed behind the ghost, appearing out of the rain like a specter himself, shouting, *Move!*

As the Kid turned toward Thornapple, Raymond whirled and covered McDowell with his body. He jarred his bad hand and screamed, white-hot agony shooting up his entire arm. He dropped his gun.

Thornapple fired, and the Kid disappeared, salt zipping over Raymond and McDowell's heads. Turner screamed. Had he been hit, despite the warning?

Johnstone slipped up behind Raymond and McDowell, trying, like the rest of them, to see everywhere at once, when the Kid appeared in front of her. She fired from the hip. The Kid dissipated, that agonized yowl echoing in Thornapple's head. The newsman felt weak. If Johnstone had shot just a few degrees to the side, he and Turner would have taken salt rounds to the face.

Johnstone must have realized it, too. We're gonna shoot each other, she called.

Converge on us, but don't bunch up, Turner said, sounding miserable. He rolled over as more gunfire erupted nearby.

The pealing thunder, the guns' roaring, Turner's expostulations, the others' shouting—every sound seemed to come from everywhere. Visibility remained poor. The rain would let up for a moment, and Thornapple would glimpse someone darting toward God only knew what, and then the deluge would intensify again, obscuring everything farther than eight or ten feet away. He moved toward McDowell and Turner, who held his injured hand in agony, his mouth a rictus grin. McDowell tended to him with one arm.

Is he hit? Thornapple asked.

McDowell's bleeding eyes were wide and shocked. No, he landed on his bad hand. You see his gun anywhere?

Thornapple felt his gorge rise. McDowell looked like a victim of some exotic disease. He bent and felt about in the standing water with his free hand.

Gunfire boomed again. Someone groaned, followed by the sound of a large body hitting the water.

Turner managed to sit up. Never mind my gun. Help Darrell and them.

Thornapple stood. *Shit fire and save the matches. We're just runnin all over the place. Please, y'all, don't shoot Joyce.*

When LeBlanc heard the shots, he stopped in his tracks. Everybody sound off! he cried.

Here, Garner said.

Johnstone and Thornapple did not answer. He was about to shout their names when multiple voices erupted from beyond the vehicles he and Garner had not even reached. Thornapple and Johnstone, acting like the goddam amateurs they were, must have practically run over there while he and Garner walked like they were in a minefield. He cursed.

Adam, you got any idea where they are?

Garner opened his mouth to reply, but then the Kid floated before them. LeBlanc raised his shotgun and fired. The specter evaporated before Garner could move.

Shit, that fucker's fast, the trucker said. And then his eyes widened, and he shoved LeBlanc to the side, yelling, *Look out!*

Garner fired. Salt thudded against the Dead House's façade as LeBlanc stumbled five or six feet, skidding in the mud. As he regained his balance, his legs spread nearly to the point of ripping his groin muscles, the Kid appeared behind Garner. LeBlanc raised his shotgun. Garner saw him and dropped, the water splashing as if he had cannonballed off a diving board. LeBlanc fired, and the Kid disappeared again. The shotgun's kick overbalanced LeBlanc. He fell on his back, and the lot almost swallowed him whole. Mud and loose grass and rainwater flowed into his eyes and up his nose, and as he sat up, sputtering, the Kid appeared again. LeBlanc raised his shotgun and fired from the sitting position, obliterating the Kid and one of the Dead House's windows. Garner got to his knees, coughing and hacking, covered in mud.

Who's shootin? Johnstone cried. Where is everybody?

We're just in front of the trucks, LeBlanc called. Where's Ray and Betsy and Jake?

He and Garner struggled to their feet, Garner still coughing. How much damage were they doing to the trucks? Could salt ignite gasoline?

This ain't workin, LeBlanc said. We need a new plan.

Johnstone cursed to their left somewhere. They got moving again.

Thornapple stood guard over Raymond and McDowell as they searched for Raymond's gun. They both looked as if they might puke or pass out at any moment. The others needed to get here soon. Thornapple had only one shell left.

Turner found the gun as Frost arrived, carrying several boxes of shells. McDowell managed to stand and take a box. Her hand shook. She and Raymond reloaded. While Frost gave Thornapple some shells, guns fired from the other side of the trucks. Salt struck metal and glass. Raised voices spoke words they could not make out.

I'm going to try and get the rest of this to the others, Frost said.

Thornapple grasped his shoulder. Stay out from between us, and whoop every now and then so we know where you are.

Frost nodded and ran into the gloom.

Then Thornapple saw movement, a grayness, from the corner of his eye. He turned and fired, not bothering to aim, and the Kid winked out again. But from somewhere in the darkness, Adam Garner cried out. Thornapple went cold all over. He had just shot someone.

Stop shootin, goddam it! LeBlanc yelled. You're hittin us!

Thornapple turned to Raymond and said, Oh, hell.

Thornapple disappeared into the rain, searching for Garner and LeBlanc. McDowell looked pale and wan and scared half to death. Raymond handed her the shotgun and said, My good arm's about wore out. Can you carry it for a second?

She held it in front of her like it was radioactive, the barrel pointed straight up. Raymond pushed it down.

I don't know that I can hit the broad side of a barn, especially with one arm, McDowell said.

Don't even try. Just let me rest a minute.

They set off after Thornapple, Raymond calling out to the others every few feet. They slogged until they found Garner on the ground. Thornapple stood over him, apologizing. The trucker was trying to sit up.

Hey, y'all okay? McDowell asked.

Garner spat out muddy water and winced. Just scratched me. My left side's on fire.

He struggled to his feet. And just then, behind him, the Kid appeared, his empty eyes glaring. The big man must have sensed it, because he started to turn around.

Duck! Raymond cried.

Then he yanked the gun out of McDowell's hand.

Frost located Johnstone, who had swung south of the vehicles. She plodded along, wiping water from her eyes. Frost pulled the boxes of shells from under his slicker.

You seen it yet? Frost asked, breathing hard.

Not since I came over this way. What happened over yonder? Who got hit?

I think it was Garner.

Johnstone glanced in that direction as she reloaded. Frost tried to watch her back. He saw nothing but rain and the outline of the Dead House, looming like a hill made of human bones, radiating eeriness and dread. Full dark had fallen, but the nearby streetlights had never come on. Frost shivered, and not just from the rain's chill. Just then, the downpour slacked off a little. Visibility improved.

Oh, shit, Johnstone said.

Some yards away, Garner stood ankle-deep in muddy water, holding his wounded side. Raymond and McDowell were nearby, the medium carrying Raymond's gun. Red Thornapple stood in front of them, perhaps three feet from Garner.

The Piney Woods Kid ghost floated directly behind them.

Raymond cried out. Garner started to turn. Raymond yanked the shotgun away from McDowell, nearly toppling her as Thornapple looked on, seeming stunned. McDowell skidded about, flapping her good arm for balance, holding the other one close to her body as Raymond crooked his own injured arm and laid the shotgun on top of his cast, aiming at the Kid. Frost had just enough time to think,

He's going to hit Garner. But Raymond never got a chance. The Kid drew, his speed so blinding that he seemed not to move at all, as if his arm had always been cocked at that same angle, the gun unholstered and fired before Garner could even complete his turn. Frost felt that odd sensation of hearing the report with his mind, like the pulse of a migraine. Garner fell to his knees in front of Raymond and McDowell, clutching his gut, grimacing. Then he flopped face down in the mud. Raymond let loose a strangled cry and sighted in. The Kid stared at him and McDowell, those eye sockets now empty like the barren windows of the Dead House itself.

Frost forgot all about Joyce Johnstone standing right beside him with a loaded shotgun. He dropped the rest of his shells and ran straight at the Kid, shouting, Leave them alone! *Look here!*

LeBlanc covered the ten yards separating the buildings and the vehicles as everything happened: the Kid's appearance, Raymond grabbing the gun and nearly knocking McDowell back into the mud, the gut-shot that felled Garner, Frost's suicide run. The Kid rotated toward the professor as if he were standing on the world's axis and the rest of them were part of the scenery. Johnstone pursued Frost, who waved his arms and screamed, Here! Leave them alone! *Look here!*

Raymond made his move, but as he shifted his weight, his feet slipped out from under him. He fired high, skidded backward, and tripped over McDowell. They both crashed into the murk, screaming as they jostled their injured limbs.

The Kid seemed not to notice.

Johnstone tackled Frost from behind. The two of them hit the water on their bellies, Johnstone's gun skittering away and disappearing as they hydroplaned into Garner. A moment later, another gunshot, followed by Thornapple's near-hysterical voice: I got you that time, you bastard.

Raymond and McDowell sat up as Frost and Johnstone scrambled to their knees and searched for her shotgun. LeBlanc slid to a stop nearby. Holy shit, he whispered.

Adam Garner moved. He forced himself to his knees, then stood, both hands still holding his gut, blood dripping from his open mouth.

CHAPTER TWENTY-EIGHT

September 16, 2016, Storm's Apex—Comanche, Texas

Raymond sat up as Adam Garner staggered to his feet like a zombie. The big trucker's lips moved as if he were involved in a conversation only he could hear. Thornapple said something to LeBlanc. Then he went to Frost and Johnstone, who were digging through the mud. What had happened to them? From somewhere behind Raymond, McDowell moaned through chattering teeth, and for the first time, he felt the cold in his bones. He scooted backward, his ruined and outraged hand screaming fire and murder, his teeth grinding. Garner trudged along, staring straight ahead, eyes wide, sockets as hollow and haunted as the Kid's, his shotgun forgotten in the water. LeBlanc followed him as Thornapple helped the apparently unshot Frost to his feet. The professor spat out water and coughed. Thornapple pounded on his back as Johnstone fished out her weapon. *I hope the goddam thing still shoots.*

Betsy, you see my gun? Raymond asked.

No, she rasped. I'll feel around for it.

It's been submerged twice. We might be in big trouble here.

💀

McDowell and Raymond needed help, but LeBlanc had to back Garner. If only he were back in New Orleans, watching the sun set over the river as he enjoyed a glass of red wine whose name he could not spell. All their plans had gone to shit, and now they were scattered from hell to breakfast, no one knowing what to do, because the Kid kept zipping in and out, forcing them to run and dive and shoot in all directions. Everyone was confused and terrified and muddy and cold. Who still carried weapons? Who was defenseless? Only Garner moved with purpose.

LeBlanc fell in beside Garner as he trudged on, step by shuffling step, covering inches at a time. His lips moved.

Adam, LeBlanc said.

Garner did not reply. He did not even turn his head. LeBlanc put his free hand on Garner's shoulder, but Garner shuffled onward. If he noticed LeBlanc, he gave no sign. He seemed headed for his truck. He coughed, and long ropes of blood-thickened saliva spewed from his mouth, but his pace never wavered.

Good, LeBlanc said. Go to the truck. That's right. Maybe the hospital—

But when they reached the vehicle doors, Garner kept walking.

Hurts, he muttered.

LeBlanc turned to the others. Y'all get over here. I think Adam's takin a shot at the Dead House.

Time seemed to stretch out, every one of Garner's steps weighty with hope and dread, everyone's movements furtive and slow, as if the very fact of their motion would bring ruin down upon them. Raymond had found his gun and was struggling to his feet, as was McDowell, who left her sprayer lying in the mud. In the intermittent flashes of lightning, her face still ran pink with blood and rain. They all came together and followed Garner, five feet behind the trucker's steady pace. If their guns were operable, they had a chance. Thornapple dabbed at his shells and hammer with his shirt.

What are we doin? Johnstone asked.

No idea, LeBlanc said.

Johnstone nodded. Then, too fast for him to shout a warning, the Kid appeared behind Thornapple's party and shot her in the back of the head.

Thornapple saw LeBlanc's expression change, his eyes widen, his mouth fall open, and without even turning or hearing the shot or acknowledging the chill running up his back, the newsman knew the Kid had returned. And in the split second before the shot, he knew one of them would die, that he could do nothing to stay the final irrevocability of that fact.

He planted his feet and tried to turn anyway, wanting to look the ghost in whatever passed for its eyes before it happened. But hearing the shot meant he would live at least a little longer, take a few more steps, keep drawing breath, perhaps even make it home again, just as he knew none of it mattered, because the shot, the splash that followed, signaled the end of his life.

Johnstone fell on her face. Thornapple whirled and fired from the hip, screaming without words, his throat burning, his eyes filled with rainwater and tears. Nothing was there. The Kid had vanished again.

Frost was already on his knees, turning Johnstone over. Her eyes were open. Blood trickled from them, from her nose and ears. And as LeBlanc bellowed somewhere near the vehicles, Thornapple turned away and vomited, somehow managing to hold on to his gun, hating himself for it.

Garner trudged on through the gruelish mud, the drizzling rain. Sheet lightning flickered in the clouds. Thornapple moaned and sniffled as he fell in beside the rest of them. He sounded like a wounded cow, lowing and stomping, lowing and stomping. LeBlanc wished he had the words. *I hope somebody covers him. I hope Ray can still shoot with that hand and waterlogged shotgun.* McDowell was hurt, and Frost had no experience with guns. They were running out of people. Yet there was no sign of the Kid, as if the specter understood the gut shot would be enough. And it would. Garner coughed blood, his hands clenching his abdomen. The internal organs would now be so much macabre soup. It was both mystery and miracle that Garner could walk.

They reached the rear of Garner's truck. Thornapple stared straight ahead, his eyes bulging and unblinking even in the misting rain, his jaw clenched. He lowed deep in his throat and gripped his shotgun as if he were strangling it.

Garner grunted as he opened the tailgate and dug under the blue tarp, pulling out a five-gallon gas can with one hand, the other still pressed against his midsection. He opened his mouth and spat out black blood, which splattered on the tarp and rolled into the truck bed like thinned tar. Then Garner turned and marched toward the Dead House.

Jake, LeBlanc yelled. We'll need ammo.

Raymond, Frost, and McDowell had not left Johnstone's body. It seemed cruel, inhuman, to abandon her to the mud. Frost had never seen a gun fired in anger before yesterday, and now four of his compatriots had been shot, two fatally. All the incidents had happened in seconds, but with Johnstone, it seemed even more sudden. He could scarcely credit the inert thing lying in the mud was the same woman he had spoken to only moments ago. Was he in shock? Raymond shivered. McDowell swayed on her feet. Raymond handed her his gun and bent down, taking one of Johnstone's arms in his good hand. He looked up at Frost, who made no move to help.

Come on, Raymond said. We can't just leave her like this.

Ray, McDowell said. Raymond did not look at her. His eyes were fixed on Frost's, his jaw set.

Ray, there's no time, Frost said. The others—

I said we can't fuckin leave her like this!

Frost recoiled. McDowell stared at Raymond. When no one bent to help, Raymond tried to hook his casted arm under Johnstone. He tugged, but the body did not move. He fell to his knees and grabbed her again, dragging her toward the parking lot, inch by inch.

McDowell turned to Frost and nodded.

All right, said Frost. We won't leave her.

Together, Raymond and Frost dragged Johnstone's corpse toward the concrete lot. McDowell followed, carrying Raymond's gun.

Then LeBlanc yelled something about needing ammo. Frost looked up. The others were marching on the Dead House.

Frost glanced at Raymond, who seemed to have noticed none of this. He kept tugging on Johnstone, his eyes far away, his teeth clenched against his own pain and outrage. The lot seemed miles away.

I can't, Frost said.

He dropped Johnstone and took the shotgun from McDowell. It felt alien in his hands. He had seen Johnstone feed shells into the little slot on the side. Could he do that under fire? Frost pumped the gun once. A perfectly good shell ejected and spun off into the mud, but if it worked like he thought it did, another had taken its place. Good.

Raymond looked at him with haunted eyes.

Sorry, Frost said. The others need us more than she does. We have to let her go.

Let her go? Raymond asked.

Frost did not answer. He ran toward the vehicles. When he reached them, he opened the rental's trunk and grabbed three boxes of ammo.

Raymond and McDowell dragged Johnstone's body halfway to the slab before their backs and abused muscles gave out. They had reached the paved walkway, so they laid the body face up in the shallowest of puddles. Together they looked back at the scene—the vehicles, the Dead House, the others following Garner's excruciating pace. Frost had left them behind to provide Johnstone whatever respect they could. He had done it for the best of reasons, but he had still abandoned them. Raymond wanted to smash his teeth in.

Then he looked at Johnstone's face—misshapen, bruised. Nothing had ever looked so dead—not even Marie when the machines stopped pumping, and her chest ceased its shallow rise and fall, rise and fall. He had watched Marie waste away under the harsh fluorescent lights of that awful hospital room, her arms and legs turning to sticks, her hair thinning, her cheeks hollowing until she looked like a skeleton with a sheet thrown over it. Bedsores, catheters, bedclothes full of shit. And it had been his fault. The accident had put her in that bed, but he had let her lie there because of his own cowardice, his fear of being alone. Because he could not let her go.

Now it was happening again. He stood vigil over someone who no longer needed him. Fiercely guarding what might as well have been stone. Here beside him was Betsy McDowell, living flesh and blood and soul, still in danger. Frost had already figured it out: The dead need no help. Now the professor walked beside Darrell LeBlanc, Raymond's partner and best friend, still alive. Red Thornapple, insane with grief, but still alive. Even Garner moved forward, despite every outrage the Kid had visited upon him. Everyone moving but Raymond, everyone clinging to life while he wallowed in death.

No, he whispered. He forced himself to rise and wiped snot from his nose.

Get to the road, he said to McDowell. Not much you can do without a weapon.

I ain't gonna leave y'all, McDowell said.

No. But you're gonna go where the Kid can't follow. If we die, get Roen and his boys. Maybe they can finish this.

He trotted away. She did not even have time to protest.

McDowell watched him go. Her back ached, and her arm throbbed, and he was right. She had no weapon, no energy. But she could not bring herself to leave.

The hell with it. Roen and them know the plan.

She stood and ran after Raymond.

The others stopped long enough to reload. Garner trudged onward, slow and implacable. No one seemed concerned he would reach the Dead House without them. More likely, he would fall over dead first.

LeBlanc looked past Raymond as he arrived, eyes widening. *What's she doin here?*

Raymond glanced over his shoulder and sighed. McDowell was trailing behind him. *Whatever she wants, I reckon.* To Frost, he said, You sure you can handle that?

Frost held the gun as if it might turn of its own volition and shoot him in the face.

No, Frost said. But Betsy and Adam are hurt. There's nobody else, unless you can do it.

Garner shuffled on, the gas can slapping his thigh. The group got moving again. LeBlanc and Thornapple flanked the big trucker. The newsman walked backward, his bulging eyes on the lot. *I hope he keeps it together until we get this done,* Raymond thought. *Especially if—oh, shit. Oh, damn. Nobody's got any salt.* He turned and splashed back to the car. The trunk lid was still partially open. He lifted it and grabbed two five-pound boxes, holding them against his body with his forearm just as someone's gun roared. Raymond stacked another box on top of the first two and ran, not bothering to shut the trunk.

Garner stopped at the door, regarding it as if it were a painting in the Louvre. He swayed, almost tottering over, but Thornapple did not care. The world existed five feet away, seen and heard through a veil.

He floated in his own pocket universe filled with red pain and augurs of loss. The ghost blinked into existence; LeBlanc fired; the ghost vanished; salt struck the Dead House wood, pockmarking it. The sounds were muted, unimportant. Even his thoughts seemed distant, like muttered conversation. The ghost could have snapped its nebulous fingers and sent them all to the red and boiling surface of Mercury for all he cared. It had shot Joyce Johnstone in the back of her skull, executed her like a mob hit man might strike down a stool pigeon in some old movie. She had fallen in the mud. The shitty, flooded lot of a diner had been the last sight she had seen on God's Earth. And now all Red Thornapple wanted to do was shoot the Kid, and then do it again, and again. Somewhere in his mind, a voice reminded him he could shoot from now until Doomsday, and it would solve nothing, but that voice was rational, and he wanted nothing to do with logic. He wanted the Kid's meat and gristle.

In the silence, the Kid appeared in front of him. Thornapple's shotgun boomed, the stock kicking his right shoulder, before he realized he had seen the ghost or raised the gun.

He felt nothing.

Struggling with the salt, Raymond rejoined the others. Red Thornapple looked crazed, the shotgun held against his shoulder. He turned in circles and did not bother to lower the gun when it pointed at someone. Garner swayed in the middle of them, five feet from the building. How he had lasted so long Raymond could not imagine. The trucker stared at the Dead House door as if unsure of what it was or how to get past it. Then his milky, distant eyes locked onto the boxes of salt. He shuffled forward. His lips still moved.

Raymond turned to LeBlanc and said, Keep it off us.

Before LeBlanc could reply or ask any questions, Raymond raced forward, opened the Dead House door, and stepped through, dropping two salt boxes and ripping at the top of the third with his good hand.

Behind him, guns roared.

He set the salt down and kicked over the stacks of diner equipment and shoved it all to the side. Then he hip-checked the stacked tables toward the north wall. The circle needed to be as large as possible. He worked hard and fast, trying to finish before Garner blundered in. And then a gun thundered from inside the Dead House. Raymond cried out, his ears ringing, as that same outraged roar filled his mind.

Thornapple stood in the doorway, already reloading. Wherever the Kid had appeared, he was gone now.

Raymond picked up the open salt box and poured, forming a crude circle extending from the door to the piles of junk. When the box emptied, he bent down and ripped open the second one. Then he stood and poured again. The boots and gun belt were still piled on the shelf where Frost had left them, innocuous-looking lumps among a gaggle of shapes and shadows.

Finally, Raymond completed the circle and stepped inside it.

Somebody bring the gas! he shouted.

LeBlanc ripped the can away from Garner. Then he stepped into the Dead House.

Outside, a gun fired. The others yelled and bickered, their voices commingling like the quacks of frightened ducks. And then LeBlanc leaned inside, holding out the can, looking harried and terrified.

Take it, he said. We're under fire.

More shots. Thornapple shouted something unintelligible. LeBlanc set the can on the floor and disappeared.

Raymond picked it up and unscrewed the cap, the smell hitting him hard in the close quarters, making his eyes water and his head spin. He walked to the circle's farthest edge and splashed gas on everything beyond it, holding the can by the handle, his cast tucked underneath for balance. He pistoned the can from behind his hip to a point near eye level, the accelerant arcing, catching the intermittent moonlight and glittering, dissolving into shadow. The sound of it hitting the floor and walls was like a hand slapping bare flesh, wet and meaty and flat.

Someone bumped Raymond, nearly knocking him out of the circle. He turned.

It was Adam Garner, his eyes wide open and staring straight ahead, his tongue protruding, his chin and neck and torso caked with blood. He must have been hemorrhaging inside. Faster than Raymond would have thought possible for someone in that shape, Garner tore the can from Raymond's hand and shoved him away. Raymond fell outside the salt circle and tripped over the mess on the floor. His bad hand struck something. The world went gray as he shrieked. When he focused again, the smell of gas overwhelmed him. Garner was splashing it everywhere. Raymond's eyes and throat burned. Some had spattered onto his shoes and cuffs. How could Garner make that pistoning motion? The seesaw effect on the hips and abdomen had to be excruciating.

Sure enough, Garner's strength ebbed. The can's upward motion arrested a little more with each toss. Then Garner stopped, spent, gas dribbling onto the salt circle, washing part of it away. Raymond cursed and clambered to his feet. He picked up a salt box to fill the breach, but Garner kept dripping fuel and blood everywhere.

Damn it straight to hell.

Movement in front of them—the Piney Woods Kid floated there, his arms dangling, his empty eye sockets staring at the spot where the circle diluted.

Motherfuck, Raymond said.

He tried to take the can from Garner but only succeeded in sloshing more gas onto the salt, which washed away, leaving a six-inch gap.

Garner turned to Raymond, his eyes as big as moons. He opened his mouth.

Guh, he whispered. Guh. Guh. Go. Now.

Raymond said, *Fuck*, just as the Kid drew his weapon and fired. Garner's head snapped backward. He fell onto his back, eyes open. Dead.

From outside, LeBlanc hollered, Betsy, no!

When Frost saw what Garner intended to do, he turned and ran, slipping and sliding across the grass lot, through puddles on the paved parking area. He reached Austin and ran for the flares Roen had left on the road. He picked one up. The long red cylinder's light cut through the rain and darkness. It felt warm but not scalding. Frost turned and ran back, reaching the parked vehicles just as McDowell sprinted for the building's doorway and LeBlanc screamed for her to stop.

McDowell hurdled the salt line and skidded to a stop beside Garner's body. The Kid watched her. Raymond stood still, wanting to run, afraid it would get him killed. He studied the Kid's blank expression and thin lips and empty eye sockets, trying to think of something, anything, to do.

Get outta here, Ray, McDowell said.

I'm not leavin you, he whispered.

The Kid turned to her. McDowell's brow furrowed in concentration. She did not blink. Her hands balled into fists.

Go, she repeated.

Raymond started to reply, but then it struck him—an emotional force like a cresting wave. It obliterated his senses, his spatial awareness, his ability to think. Fear, anguish, rage, determination, hate, a love so deep it might have been infinite—they smashed him, driving him to his knees. He cried out and burst into tears.

McDowell had not moved. Blood poured from her eyes, her nose. Her teeth were clenched.

The Kid floated backward. His hands covered his ears. His mouth fell open in a silent scream.

That's right, asshole, she hissed. This is what you brought us. How do you like it?

McDowell's assault poleaxed LeBlanc as he tried to enter. He fell to his hands and knees at the threshold, his stomach clenching against a sadness so deep it felt like nausea, a fear as sharp as muscle cramps, pain as wide as the imagination. He vomited, spat, vomited again. The Kid's wailing cannonade—frightened now, and hurt—blasted through

LeBlanc's brain. He forced himself to look up. McDowell stood over Raymond, who wept on the floor. Her feet were set shoulder-width apart, her fists clenched, her chin thrust forward as if daring someone to punch her. The Kid floated back, inches at a time, as if the far wall could shelter him from this storm.

Get up. Help them.

LeBlanc crawled. He reached Raymond and managed to stand. Then he pulled Raymond up, back, past Garner's body. The two of them overbalanced and hit the muddy water on their backs and skidded. Frost sprinted past them, kicking up sludgy water and holding a burning flare.

Betsy, get outta there! Raymond screamed, rolling off LeBlanc.

Thornapple had fallen to his knees. LeBlanc dragged him away and shoved him toward the trucks.

Go, LeBlanc said. Then he turned to the Dead House. Betsy, he cried.

Frost fell to one knee near the door, his free hand clutching his head.

Betsy, get out of there, he said.

LeBlanc pushed past Frost and into the Dead House. The nausea hit him again. He fought through it, a step at a time. The Kid shimmered in and out, grimacing in pain.

I don't know how Darrell's still standin, Raymond thought as LeBlanc took McDowell by the shoulders. He pulled her out of the Dead House, past Frost. She never took her bleeding eyes off the Kid. The air between her and the Dead House shimmered, all that energy made manifest. Her nose gushed blood. Seeing her, Frost wavered and nearly dropped the flare.

Betsy, LeBlanc said. You gotta stop. You're hurtin yourself, and Jake.

She said nothing. Frost had dropped the shotgun somewhere and braced himself with his free hand.

LeBlanc shook her, hard. Her head rattled back and forth. Her eyes unfocused. And that god-awful power lessened, faded, disappeared.

Everybody get back, Raymond said.

In the Dead House, the Kid's pained expression vanished. His gaze bore into McDowell. He snarled.

Now, LeBlanc cried.

Frost tossed the flare toward the doorway. He turned and tried to run, slipping to one knee, even as the flare sailed end over end through the door. Then he regained his feet and sprinted as the fumes immolated, racing the flare to the Dead House and beating it by half a second. Then the building itself caught fire in an enormous *WHUMPH*, the remaining windows blasting outward and raining glass everywhere, flames spewing from the broken panes and out the door and over Frost's head as he dove into the mud, the light searing everyone's eyeballs.

McDowell collapsed. LeBlanc caught her and carried her like a bride to the vehicles. Thornapple jumped into Garner's truck bed as Frost climbed into the cab and started the engine. No one had bothered to worry that the motors might not turn over; either the Kid would be dead or weakened, or no one would be left to turn the keys. Thornapple stood up in the bed and threw one of the sprayer units at the Dead House, hoisting it over his head with both hands and thrusting it forward as he might a large stone. It landed a few feet in front of the building and skidded to the open front door. Then he tossed a gas can just as Frost spun out, tires rooster-tailing mud until they got traction. The vehicle shot forward, and Thornapple fell into the bed as Frost veered around Johnstone's corpse and passed over the parking lot, through the driveway, and onto Austin Street. He parked beyond the driveway.

Raymond had gotten into their rental's passenger seat as LeBlanc laid McDowell in the back. Then the big man got in and drove out of the yard. They parked near Garner's truck. Everyone but McDowell got out. They stood there for a while as the building burned.

And then the fire reached the can near the entrance. It exploded, sending a ball of fire thrusting into the night sky and over the courtyard. Everyone recoiled and covered their ears. The misshapen remains of the can fell onto the concrete slab. Chunks of board and glass dropped like hail. They all ducked inside the vehicles until the debris stopped falling.

Then, without a word, they got back out. LeBlanc and Thornapple walked to Johnstone's body in silence. They picked up the corpse and carried it onto the road, where they laid it next to the truck. Then LeBlanc jogged to the vehicle at the fence line.

As LeBlanc drove back off the lot, Raymond approached the Dead House's gutted, burning hulk, getting as close as he dared. The front wall had caved in. The roof was mostly gone. The explosion's force had turned the assorted junk inside to shrapnel, which had punched holes in the other walls. The yard was full of burning fragments. Some had landed on the diner.

Inside, the Kid floated where they had left him, regarding the flames with no more expression or passion than he had shown when slaughtering Johnstone. The boots and gun belt lay near his feet and blazed like hot coals in a campfire, blackening and curling.

Soon, the others joined Raymond. The Kid flickered like the fire itself, now bright and distinct, now faded.

That's right, you fucker, Thornapple whispered. Burn.

No one else said anything. Frost looked shell-shocked and wet and sick. The rest of the roof collapsed, flaming boards and shingles raining on the Kid and passing through him, the smell of Garner's burning flesh rank and acrid. And then the walls fell in. The fire rose higher, and as it did, the Kid waned. Then he winked out.

Still, they watched until Roen and his men came back and stood beside them, until the fire engines arrived and began the work of saving the diner, until the ambulances came to take away the injured and the dead. The Kid did not come back.

CHAPTER TWENTY-NINE

September 20, 2016—Comanche, Texas

Raymond, LeBlanc, McDowell, and Frost drove from the cemetery in their rental, which was now peppered on one side with pea-sized dents where someone's salt rounds had struck it. Flaming debris had burned and smudged the paint job. The car looked like it had survived a minor skirmish in downtown Baghdad. Raymond had insured it at the airport, but who knew how much the policy would cover? His shattered hand still throbbed. He slept fitfully and took Percocet when he could no longer stand it.

McDowell wore a cast from her shoulder to her wrist. The Kid's phantom bullet had clipped her humerus at the point of the deltoid tuberosity, breaking the bone and causing the deltoid muscle to roll up like a window shade. The ER doctor had put on the cast and advised her to see her own physician, as she would need surgery to reattach the muscle. The emotional toll had been much greater. She slept for two straight days and needed a pint and a half of blood to replace what she lost at the Dead House. Tests showed no lasting neurological damage, a minor miracle considering all she had done.

When they had arrived in the ER, their clothes unrecognizable and every inch of bare skin coated in drying mud, McDowell looking as if she had just worked a shift at a slaughterhouse, the doctor seemed spooked until he saw acting Chief of Police Roen, who accompanied them. Roen answered most of the man's questions. Everyone else could barely speak—too tired, too sad.

Now they had just attended their third funeral in four days. On the eighteenth, Bradley's had hosted the uniformed officers of the Comanche Police Department past and present, members of the Comanche County Sheriff's Office, and officers from the highway patrol. Bradley's wife sat in the front pew, dressed in black and crying into tissue after tissue. The rest of the church filled with civilians Raymond and his group would never know. The agency crew sat in the back pew with Rennie, nodding to Thornapple when their eyes met, speaking to no one and eschewing the graveside service. Raymond did not feel responsible for Bradley's death, and he had seen no indications that the others did either. The man had done his job willingly and well. He had not followed them blindly. But his family might have felt differently, and none of Raymond's party wanted to make a horrible day any worse. They paid their respects by showing up, left while the rest of the congregation filed by the coffin, and drove back to Thornapple's place. They could have gone back to the hotel, but they stayed mostly so McDowell could help Thornapple regulate his emotions. He had been stoic. McDowell worried about what he might do when they left.

Sue McCorkle attended Bradley's funeral. She did not seek them out, did not thank them, would not even look at them, as if their alien presence reminded her of what might have happened had she and her boys stayed in town. Raymond and the others left her alone. What was there to say?

They had also seen Morlon and Silky Redheart. Morlon shook their hands. We appreciate y'all, he said, while Silky stood behind him, silent.

Then they both walked away. The Redhearts had attended the other funerals as well. From across the room, Morlon nodded each time, but they did not speak again.

On the nineteenth, they said goodbye to Adam Garner in church. Almost nothing had been left to bury, just some of Garner's charred and blackened bones and a surgical pin from his right knee. The bones had been gathered and examined and cremated, and though he wondered what would be done with the ashes, Raymond had not asked. Garner had followed them to the Dead House, but he had done so only because none of Raymond's party could think of a better solution. The circumstances with the town council and Roark's injuries had forced their hand that night, and the rain had ruined the plan that might have brought them all through safely. Still, Garner died on Raymond's watch. And as Raymond saw Garner's family and close friends holding each other in the hot and humid Baptist church, he wanted a drink. Afterward, they retreated to the Thornapple ranch again, where they drank iced tea—everyone but the newsman, who put away enough Jack Daniel's and Coke to float a battleship before passing out in his chair. He snored there until LeBlanc carried him down the hall and tucked him into bed.

Raymond could relate.

Today, the twentieth, they saw Joyce Johnstone into the ground. They learned she had two ex-husbands and one stepson, three grown men with tears in their eyes, white faces hovering above their dark and somber clothing. Thornapple talked with them for a long time.

The agency's flight out of Dallas/Fort Worth was scheduled for the twenty-first at 3:20 p.m., and they still had to pack, see Rennie one more time, and say their goodbyes.

McDowell rode in the back with Frost. She had been looking out the window ever since they left the church, watching the trees and stubby-looking houses and scrub oak and mesquite fly by. Now she said, I'm scared for Red. What he'll do without her.

No one replied. They could not babysit Red Thornapple for the rest of his life, nor would he want them to. Raymond remembered Marie's death, the prolonged agony of every solitary night, the sheer bravery it took to crawl out of bed in the morning. He remembered welcoming liquor's fog, the way it rolled in over his mind and his vision until he wept without knowing why, laughed for no reason, broke things and punched men with little provocation. LeBlanc had helped as much as he could, mainly by keeping him out of jail and yelling at him when his misery led to thoughts of eating his own gun. But in the end, you had to decide for yourself whether to live or die. If Thornapple chose death, he would find a way. If he wanted to live, he had other, older friends who could stand with him much better than people he had known only a few weeks. Already the close camaraderie that had formed during their sortie was starting to fade. Raymond had been a guest in enough houses to know when the atmosphere turned, when the host wished you gone. And so they would pack, and they would go.

LeBlanc turned into Thornapple's driveway. They disembarked and entered the unlocked house that already smelled stale and masculine and strangled. Then they went to their separate rooms and packed. LeBlanc and McDowell entered the same room together. Raymond watched them go. He smiled and nodded. And then, because his obligations had been met and his hand ached like hell, he went into his room and took a pill.

Rennie sat beside C.W.'s bed, reading a Larry McMurtry novel. Will was nowhere in sight, but then, it was a school day. A Tuesday, if Raymond were not mistaken. Now that his father had stabilized, Will would be back in class, where he could resume his life as if the ghost of a vicious gunfighter had not tried to murder him. Rennie stood when Raymond, LeBlanc, and McDowell entered. She hugged their necks and kissed Raymond on the cheek. C.W. was awake and watching Raymond as they moved about the room. He looked pale and drawn, dehydrated, malnourished. An oxygen tube was taped to his nose. He locked eyes with Raymond, but there was no anger there, no hatred. Nothing that suggested forgiveness or gratitude either, but it was better than open hostility.

Raymond squeezed his shoulder. Hang in there, he said.

Roark nodded.

Doctors want him to keep his mouth shut, Rennie said. I told 'em good luck.

Roark smiled.

McDowell sat in a chair beside the mayor's bed and talked to him, her voice soothing and somnambulant. LeBlanc squatted on his heels beside her. After a moment, Roark's eyes fluttered.

If I had known her when Marie died, it would have been easier. But Betsy would have paid for it when all my anger—at Marie for dyin, at God for lettin her, at myself for livin—burst out of me like pus.

That was what she did, though. McDowell took on other people's pain. She was one of the strongest people he had ever known. She would want to help them leave the Dead House in the past, and they would probably let her, even if it hurt her. What did that say about them?

Sometimes self-awareness sucked ass.

Raymond and Rennie stood near the door, speaking in whispers.

She nodded at his hand.

You get that taken care of first thing.

I will. How's C.W.?

Rennie looked back at her husband. Better. Especially knowin the Pow Wow's gonna happen. So far, nobody's gone to the press with any crazy stories about a ghost.

What about them folks who saw C.W. get shot? I figured somebody would have filmed it and put it on the Internet.

There's half a dozen videos. I've watched 'em all. They show you and C.W. yellin at each other, and then all hell breaks loose. Lotta nice shots of people runnin around half crazy and cars not startin. But not one trace of a ghost. From the comments I read, most people seem to think you were rehearsin a movie scene. One kid said he thought it would be great once they added in the special effects.

I reckon that's good.

As for the folks who saw what happened to the Harveston girl and John Wayne, nobody believed 'em in the first place.

So the local situation's handled.

Even the *Warrior-Tribune* didn't mention anything weird. Ran Joyce Johnstone's and Adam Garner's obituaries and a story about a burnin storage building. I guess Red didn't have the heart to write the truth, or else he saw the sense in lettin it lie.

Well, you know people. When they don't know the truth, they make up a story that fits what they already think.

I wish I didn't know the truth.

Raymond looked at the floor. I'm sorry we didn't do better. We came here to save folks and lost more than half of 'em.

Rennie made a go-along-with-you gesture. You saved folks, too: C.W. Will. Red Thornapple. Sue McCorkle and her kids. God knows who else that thing might have gone after.

That percentage would be good if we were playin baseball. But we ain't. It's enough to drive a man to drink.

She squeezed his arm. We all did the best we could. Because of you, my boy gets to grow up. C.W.'s gonna see his old age. And Red Thornapple will grieve and get on with his life. If you let this send you back to the bottle, I'll tan your hide.

He smiled. But he felt like crying.

C.W. Roark, McDowell, and LeBlanc sat in a patch of slanted sunlight coming in through the open blinds. McDowell and LeBlanc held hands.

Look at those teenagers, Raymond said.

They're happy, Rennie said. That's good. Too much misery in the world as it is.

Yes, ma'am. There sure is.

I love you, Raymond.

I love you, too.

CHAPTER THIRTY

September 20, 2016, Afternoon—Comanche, Texas

Raymond leaned against Will's truck in the Comanche High parking lot. Kids passed and whispered to each other, grinned in an embarrassed way, snapped photos with their phones in ways they probably thought subtle. They all knew what had happened: Will's drunken P.I. uncle had ridden into town, shot up a diner, and then burned the whole place down. It must have seemed like they had missed an action movie.

Let 'em gawk. I'm just leanin against a truck.

Will approached, walking alone, the fingers of both hands tucked into his front jeans pockets. He wore his football jersey, number seventy-six—a defensive end, if Raymond remembered correctly. It had been so long since he and Rennie had spoken of such things. When the boy saw him, he raised his chin in greeting. Raymond nodded. Will leaned against the chassis near Raymond. Together they watched the other kids drive away, honking at each other, shouting across the lot.

All this shit seems silly, Will said.

Raymond picked at some dried mud caked at hip level. I reckon seein your father shot puts things into perspective.

I guess. What's up?

We're leavin tomorrow. I know you're busy, what with school and the hospital, so I thought I'd swing by. In case we don't get another chance.

Chance for what?

To talk. Or drive around with the radio turned up too loud. Or whatever you'd like.

Will shrugged. I don't know what I'd like.

A white extended-cab Chevy blared by, too fast, its ear-splitting pipes blatting louder than half a dozen industrial machines running full-bore. Will waved. Somebody's arm snaked out the window and gave them the finger. Will laughed.

Maybe you like duallys, Raymond said.

Will took out his phone and played with it. Naw. Not really.

Well, what do you do these days? Last we spent much time together, you was catchin up on *Harry Potter* and *Star Wars*.

I watch a lot of Longhorns ball games. Momma keeps askin me who I'm datin. I keep tellin her nobody. She don't believe me.

Mommas are born suspicious. It's what keeps us alive long enough to grow up.

The boy laughed again. Sweat trickled from his hairline. He wiped it away. Soon the breeze would grow cooler. The leaves would turn brown and fall, covering yards all over America. The grass would die. The air would turn bitter and sharp, and rains would freeze into sleet or snow, and the world would turn and turn.

Well, anyway, Will said.

Raymond pushed himself off the truck and kicked a rock. Look. When your aunt Marie died, I was a mess. You wouldn't have wanted to hang out with me.

Will brushed a lock of hair from his eye. And now?

I'm still a mess. But a little less so, I hope.

Seems like you made a couple new friends. Maybe between them and Darrell you'll make it.

That's the plan. And when you're ready, I'd like to catch up. Come over here and go fishin, like we used to.

Or I could come see you. I ain't been to New Orleans in years, and I'm almost old enough to do all the fun stuff.

Raymond smiled. I'd like that. If you're serious.

The boy looked at the ground. Maybe. After graduation, though. If you're still okay.

I'll make up the spare room.

They stood for a while, each looking toward nothing in particular. More traffic on the road. A faint siren. Birdsong, and the buzzing of some insect. Soon Raymond would have to get back in his rental and drive out to the Thornapple place, right into the teeth of Red's grief and all that quiet. For now, though, he stood beside his nephew, who was almost a man, and listened to life's score swelling and ebbing, swelling and ebbing. The days were still warm, the sun bright, and so much seemed possible.

CHAPTER THIRTY-ONE

September 21, 2016—Dallas, Texas

Twenty-four hours later, they waited for takeoff on their Delta flight, the rental cars returned, their luggage checked. Raymond and Frost sat together on the right, LeBlanc and McDowell on the left—she at the window seat, he on the aisle. Frost was already asleep, head against the window. Raymond bought them all earbuds, even though the flight to New Orleans would take less than an hour. Tireder than ever, hand throbbing, he wanted a drink. Vodka or bourbon or whiskey, something strong. Instead, a Percocet would have to do once they reached cruising altitude. And in New Orleans, he would hand the pills to LeBlanc or McDowell. From now on, he would look life in the eye, no matter how much it hurt.

His broken wedding band lay ensconced in his suitcase. Unwearable, unless he followed McDowell's advice and melted it down, recast it, transformed it. But what could it ever really be, if not itself?

The plane taxied and trundled down the runway and lifted into the air, Raymond's balls shrinking even as his stomach flip-flopped as it always did during takeoffs and landings. McDowell had taken LeBlanc's hand again. She looked straight ahead and yawned. As if it were contagious, Raymond yawned, too. Soon the plane would land in

New Orleans. His bed would still be half empty, the other pillow still cool, Marie's side of the closet as bare as an oak in winter. But maybe he could stand the silence now. Perhaps he would tell Marie about Bob Bradley and Joyce Johnstone or the ones who had lived. Perhaps one day soon, he could bring himself to speak with God.

He plugged in his earbuds and put them on and waited. When they reached cruising altitude, he would turn on a radio station, jazz if he could find it, and syncopate all the way home.

ACKNOWLEDGMENTS

No book is written alone. I'd like to thank my wife, Kalene Westmoreland, for her love, her unwavering support, her reading every draft of this book and making helpful suggestions, and her ability to put up with me, even when I'm at my worst. I truly do not deserve her.

Thanks to my children—Shauna, Brendan, Maya, and John—for never making me feel guilty when I lock myself in my office and write.

Thanks to our fur-babies—Cookie, Tora, Nilla—for soothing my soul in its darkest night.

To my friends and colleagues, thank you for believing in me.

To Vicki Adang, my editor on this project--thanks for both indulging my eccentricities and pushing me to make this book better.

To Megan Edwards and Mark Sedenquist of Imbrifex Books, thank you for believing in this story. Your passion and professionalism are models to which the publishing world should aspire.

Finally, to every single person who reads this book, thank you. I'm honored you chose to make my story a part of your life. I hope you liked it.